Suburban Hustler

Suburban Hustler

Stories of a Hi-Tech Callboy

Aaron Lawrence

Published by Late Night Press, P.O. Box 4001, Warren, NJ 07059.

Author Website: http://www.aaronlawrence.com
Author E-mail: njescort@aol.com

Cover model: Aaron Lawrence

Cover photos by David J. Martin

Cover design by Mirage Studios, Inc.
http://www.miragestudios.com

ISBN 0-9667691-0-4
Library of Congress Catalog Card Number 98-96656

For Jeff
Patient beyond words

About the Author

Aaron Lawrence has worked as an escort since May 1995. When not entertaining clients, he is pursuing a career as a porn star as well as producing his own line of amateur tapes. A longtime exhibitionist, Aaron can be seen on a number of adult websites and in the September '98 issue of *Freshmen*. He is the webmaster of www.aaronlawrence.com, the most popular escort homepage on the Internet. Aaron lives with his lover in suburban New Jersey. This is his first book.

Stories

Preface

During my third year of college, I was finally able to prove what I had long suspected. I didn't want to be anything when I grew up.

I have Psychology 401 to thank for my evidence. An assignment required our class take the Strong-Campbell Interest Inventory, a tool used to assist career choices. My results from the inventory revealed a low to low-average interest in every major career field. The only jobs the inventory remotely suggested were travel agent and farmer. The former presumably because I like to travel, while the latter derived from my future interest in growing a flower garden.

In retrospect, I realize neither Strong nor Campbell gave any attention to the sex industry as a career option. Had they included questions on casual sex, the inventory would almost certainly have suggested I pursue a career as an escort, porn star, or politician.

Of course, these questions were not included in the inventory. No career revelations occurred to me that day, nor in the months that followed. It was years later on my knees in the back of an adult bookstore when everything finally fell into place… but you'll be reading about that soon enough. Before you reach that point, I want to get a little business out of the way.

First and most importantly, the work of a professional escort is and always should be confidential. With the exception of my boyfriend, myself, and a few other minor characters, all names, both real and on the Internet, have

been changed. Other specific details have been altered for the same reason. Outside of these changes, essentially everything in this book occurred as written.

Second, I want to thank everyone whose curiosity has brought about this book. Since the day I started escorting on the 'net, hundreds of people have asked me questions about my work. How long have you been an escort? How does your boyfriend handle it? How do you deal with ugly clients? Have you ever been attacked?

Eventually someone asked me the logical question. Have I ever considered writing a book about my experiences? The thought had occurred to me, but I dismissed it as unrealistic. I considered myself an escort, not a writer. Obviously, I learned. You hold in your hand the final result.

Finally, thank you for allowing me to share my stories with you. I have learned over time that life is far more enjoyable when I can share my experiences. You will find these stories are sometimes erotic and sometimes disturbing, but always insightful and revealing. I hope reading these pages will allow you to take a few steps along the path I have chosen in life. I suspect it will be a familiar experience for many of you because I am constantly amazed how many people have bought or sold sex at least once in their life.

As you read the book, consider how you would act if you were experiencing these stories. You will undoubtedly disagree with the way I handle situations at times, and may even on occasion call my ethics into question. Still, I think you will find I bring a strong dose of reality to a career that demands illusionary perfection. Just don't say I didn't warn you that escorting, like myself, is not all it appears to be.

Enough talk. You've paid good money for this book, and it's time for you to get to the good stuff.

--Aaron Lawrence

First Trick

December 22, 1993

As long as I live, I will never understand why I make such stupid decisions. I am on my way to have sex with a total stranger in exchange for money. I'm probably going to wind up dead in a ditch somewhere.

It really is Citibank's fault. Had it not been for their high interest credit cards, I might have my finances under control. I owe three thousand dollars on my Visa card, and can barely keep up with the minimum payments. Managing finances on a student's income is a serious bitch.

Deep inside, I know my blame is misplaced. When I first e-mailed Gary two months ago, I knew exactly what I was getting into. The meaning in his online advertisement was obvious. The idea of making a quick buck was simply too appealing to pass by.

Attractive 43-year-old executive wants to explore the body of a young, smooth white male. Will be very generou$ in return. E-mail me if interested.

Gary

Reading his message for the first time was like a dream come true. I knew I would have no problem having sex with an older man for money. Especially if it meant making my card payments for several months. Having my dick sucked was an added bonus. It was a win-win situation beyond anything I could have hoped for.

My first e-mail to Gary was a basic description of myself. "Dear Gary," it read. "I saw your posting and wanted

to respond. I am 22, 5'5", 130 lbs., and I have dark blond hair and blue eyes. I am very boyish looking and look about 16. I would like to talk to you more about getting together. Let me know if you are interested." I signed the note "Aaron" because I didn't want him to know my real name.

To my delight, Gary was interested in meeting me. He wrote back explaining he was a virgin with men and wanted to try sex with a young man. According to his message, his fantasy was for me to lie back and enjoy myself while he touched and licked me all over. He promised he would stop if I became nervous or scared.

Our messages continued for another two months as we debated what would be a fair price. I had no idea what to ask for and Gary was equally confused what to offer. We finally settled on one hundred dollars, enough money to pay off Citibank for another two months. All I have to do is spend two hours with him at a local motel. It would be both easy and fun.

At least I thought it was going to be easy. Now that I am driving to our meeting place outside a suburban New Jersey diner, I find myself struggling to relax. I know I have no need to be nervous. Gary seems very friendly and I am sure we will get along well. I need the money in any case. Nerves have no place in a business transaction like today's.

In spite of my anxiety, I find what I am doing today to be very erotic. I have been out of the closet for seven years. In that time, I have been to bed with well over one hundred men. One of the reasons I am so promiscuous is because the idea of having sex with vast numbers of men excites me. I once read about a former porn star and escort who claimed he slept with over 5,000 men. The idea simultaneously amazed, shocked, disturbed, disgusted, and aroused me.

Thinking about his exploits, I realize I will die of old age before I sleep with even a quarter of his total. I'll never become an escort or porn star, either. That sort of lifestyle

is reserved for muscular men. Certainly not for scrawny, nerdy, and young looking guys like me.

I suppose it's just as well. I'm a college student with career aspirations. I also have a new boyfriend who would be hurt if he knew I was playing around behind his back. I care a lot about Jeff, and I want nothing more than to see our relationship continue for years to come.

I pull into the diner and spot Gary's Lexus. My stomach tightens within me. I'm feeling very nervous again. I pull up next to him and wave my hand in greeting. I open my door and prepare to meet my destiny.

Stepping out of my car, I am pleasantly surprised to find he is a tall, good-looking man. His face sports a friendly smile below a pair of twinkling eyes. Although I normally do not care for men with facial hair, his neatly trimmed auburn beard does nothing to diminish his looks.

"Hello," he greets me with his smile through an unrolled window. "Would you like to ride in my car over to the motel?"

"Sure," I reply nervously, accepting his offer. I open the passenger door and sit down next to him.

There is an awkward moment of silence that is broken as Gary speaks. "I guess I'm not sure what to say. I've never done this before."

"Well," I reply slowly, "do you still want to do this?"

"Very much so. You're a lot younger looking than I expected, not that that's a bad thing or anything," he reassures me. "I like young guys, I just don't have any experience with them."

His compliments begin arousing me, helping to control my anxiety. I reach out and take his hand. "Well, I like older guys most of the time. And I'm also looking forward to this."

To my surprise, I realize that I really am looking forward to this. I was afraid I would find him unattractive, but now I know that isn't a problem. A wave of arousal hits me as I anticipate the feeling of his beard rubbing the flesh between my legs.

He pulls out of the lot and begins driving toward the motel. "What made you decide to post that message?" I ask.

He appears somewhat embarrassed. "For the past ten years I've had a fantasy of being with a guy in his teens. Nothing illegal," he stresses. "Just someone who has a smooth chest and body."

"And you've never done anything with a guy before?" I ask, hoping to learn more about him.

"There was one guy I met at a business conference. We masturbated together but we didn't do anything else. It wasn't a very enjoyable experience. So, I posted the message. You're the only one who replied to it that was serious."

The conversation continues until we arrive at the Greenbrook motel, the sleaziest establishment for miles around. Seeing the rundown buildings brings back memories. "I lost my virginity here," I admit.

"Really?" Gary asks in a surprised voice. "It's not that nice of a place to do that sort of thing in."

"Yeah. I was fifteen and was really excited to try it."

Gary appears startled at my confession, but recovers quickly. "Fifteen? Wow. I wish I had been there!" We both have a good laugh, and then Gary goes into the motel lobby to rent a room for the afternoon.

Moments later Gary returns with a key. "They never even asked me for my name on the room card."

"They never do at these places. This is hardly the Marriott." We laugh again.

We enter a sparsely finished room lit by a single light bulb. A low dresser sits against the far wall with a single remaining drawer scratched full of graffiti. The television is bolted to the top of the dresser, and the faucet in the bathroom drips into a tub surrounded with cracked and missing tiles. Sadly, the room is exactly as I remember it being seven years ago.

I notice Gary pause as he takes in the sleaze of the atmosphere. "It's okay, Gary, don't worry about the room.

We're not here for the ambiance, we're here to see each other." He nods agreement but still appears uncomfortable with the surroundings.

"We don't have to come back here in the future," I point out. He brightens up a bit at the thought.

We sit down on the edge of the bed next to one another. Gary appears unsure what to do next, so I begin removing my shoes. Dropping them off the side of the bed, I lean back against him. "Mind if I remove my pants?" I ask.

He almost chokes at my forward approach but nods his head. I pull my jeans down and rest my legs across his lap. He slowly strokes my legs as he becomes comfortable with the idea of touching another man. My legs are surprisingly hairy for such a boyish looking person, but he doesn't seem to mind. He appears quite content exploring my body little by little.

"It's all right," I encourage him with a smile. "You're welcome to reach as high as you'd like." He begins sliding his hands up my thighs until he reaches my underwear. I spread my legs slightly, opening them to the warmth of his touch. He is happy to answer my invitation as he slides his hands inside my underwear. He brushes up against the stiffness carefully tucked within.

"I'm sorry," he apologizes, pulling back his hand.

I begin laughing. "Don't apologize, you're welcome to touch all you'd like."

Gary blushes for a moment then continues to touch me. I lean over to kiss him, wrapping my arms around his body. He pulls me on top of him, and lies back as our lips meet. I push my tongue into his mouth. He resists for a moment before he gives in to his desire. His arms hug me tight as he frees his gay sexual urges for the first time.

We continue to passionately embrace, pausing only for the occasional breath. His tongue explores my face while the soft bristles of his beard rub against my cheeks. The scratching and tickling feeling is new to me. I am not sure if I like it, but it is certainly different. I vaguely wonder what it will be like as he goes down on me. Will I feel his

beard slide up and down my balls as he sucks on me, or will I feel it more on my cock itself? I am excited to find out.

After a few more moments, Gary pulls back. He pulls my T-shirt over my head and tosses it gently onto a nearby chair. I slide my hands inside the cotton of his dress shirt and touch the hair on his chest. Unlike my body, there is nothing boyish about his. His body is not solid, but is not soft either. He finishes removing his shirt and tie then tosses them onto the chair as well.

Leaning over, I begin to lick his nipples. He arches his back and presses his chest against my face. I must have hit a sensitive spot. I put an arm around him and pull him closer. Slowly I move upwards as I lavish attention on him. I soak his chest hair with saliva from my tongue, then proceed onto his neck. Nuzzling the soft flesh below his ears drives him wild. Finally, I slide my tongue into his mouth again. His arms encircle me entirely and pull me on top of him. We roll around the bed together with our tongues and bodies intertwined.

Finally, it is time for Gary to experience the hardcore part of gay sex. I unbutton his pants and reach my hand inside them. His breathing is heavy as I touch the wet spot on the front of his underwear. I lick my damp fingers, tasting the essence of his precum. The sweet taste is intoxicating.

To my surprise, Gary stops me. "I want you to lean back and enjoy yourself," he tells me. "Remember what I said in my posting? I want to explore the body of a young man. So lie back and let me do the work."

Always eager to please, I roll over and lie on my back. His gentle hands touch my body, lightly caressing my soft skin. I close my eyes and lose myself in his touch, feeling his fingers across my face, my chest, my legs, and finally on top of my underwear. He strokes the fabric above my erect cock causing me to moan softly.

He pauses for a moment to undress me completely. Moments later, I am totally nude as his hands continue to

explore my body. He reaches my erect cock and begins stroking. Another soft moan escapes my lips.

The feeling of his warm breath on my erect cock is maddening as he begins licking the head. Slowly at first, but with increasing speed and confidence, he acquaints himself with my manhood. Finally, he slides his mouth over the hardness as much as he can. A relaxing warm and wet feeling surrounds my shaft.

As Gary begins enjoying the delights of giving oral sex, I relax and enjoy the feeling. "Can I tell you something?" I ask him.

"Anything," he murmurs, never taking my dick out of his mouth.

"I have never been able to have an orgasm from oral sex, although I love what you are doing."

Gary pauses from his sucking for a moment and looks at me with surprise on his face. "Really?"

I shake my head. "Never."

In fact, I am lying. I have been able to cum from a blowjob, but only through gloryholes in the walls between booths in adult bookstores. Even then, I have only been able to do so a handful of times. I have never fully understood why. I'm embarrassed to admit my "condition", but want to make sure Gary understands my limitation.

I am unsure why I have such a difficulty reaching orgasm, but I rarely regret that fact. What my dick lacks in sensitivity is more than made up for by my balls. Touching or licking them can put me in total heaven. My favorite way to cum is to jack myself off while someone plays with my balls.

It does not take Gary long to discover all of this. When he pauses to lick the small sack, I involuntarily arch my back and moan in delight. The feeling of his beard combined with his hot tongue is unbelievable. When he sees my enjoyment he completely abandons any sort of restraint and begins lapping my balls excitedly.

"I want to see you cum," Gary whispers as I begin stroking my cock. I surrender any pretense of wanting to

hold back and begin pumping myself furiously. The sight of the bearded man devouring my balls in his mouth excites me tremendously.

My arousal does not allow me to hold back long. Within seconds I am shooting hot loads of cum all over myself. Gary pulls back to watch but I beg him to continue. His licking increases the intensity of my orgasm. Slowly the ecstasy fades, leaving behind a hot and sticky mess and a set of wet balls.

From what little I can see, Gary is wide-eyed from his experience. I have collapsed back on the bed and can barely lift my head from the pillow.

"Thank you," I whisper between gasps of air.

He fetches a towel from the other room and returns to wipe the cum off my stomach. He lies down beside me. "This is so exciting!" he exclaims with an almost childlike enthusiasm.

His innocence makes me laugh. "Our meeting is only half over. As soon as I regain my strength, we'll switch places. Oh, and Gary?"

"Yes?" he asks.

"Men give much better head than women do."

He looks surprised at my statement but nods his head. "I guess I can see why. Gay men would not be as intimidated by oral sex as women might be."

"That's right," I agree with a mischievous grin on my face. "So be prepared for the best blowjob of your life." His eyes light up at the thought.

I am certain that I can provide what I am offering. Being sexually experienced with multiple partners has its advantages, such as being an expert cocksucker. I lay Gary back on the bed and slowly lower my mouth onto his extended rod. I begin the oral delights as I take his entire shaft in my mouth.

I increase the speed of my sucking to inflict the maximum amount of pleasure. Within minutes his breathing becomes heavy as he slowly starts bucking his hips. "Slow

down, I'm going to cum," he warns me, his face filled with pleasure.

I ignore him and continue sucking.

"I mean it, I'm going to cum. Stop now or I'm going to shoot in your mouth!"

That is exactly what I want. I speed up even more, plunging my face down into the hair at the base of his dick. Sucking the entire length, I milk his dick for everything it's worth.

Seconds later my efforts are rewarded as he gushes several large loads of cream. I don't even pause as I suck every drop. When he finally stops pouring fluid into my mouth, I begin slurping on the hypersensitive end of his shaft. He begins whimpering for me to stop.

I have a grin on my face as I wipe the cum off my chin. I want him to know how much I enjoyed sucking him. From the look in his eyes, he has never experienced an orgasm this intense.

After ten minutes of affectionate cuddling and a shower together, Gary is driving me back to my car at the diner. We hold hands as he drives. Although he talks a great deal, he does not say very much. He repeats what a wonderful time he had and how he is looking forward to seeing me next time I'm on break.

We arrive at the diner where Gary pays me the money we agreed on. I give him a hug then walk back to my car.

I drive home thinking about my sexual adventure, never once realizing the afternoon is a snapshot of my future.

Cruising

May 30, 1995

As he unzips his pants and pulls out his dick, I can't help but to feel depressed. There is nothing arousing about this situation.

Precisely why I am on my knees in the back of this dingy adult bookstore is confusing to me. I don't feel horny and I'm not in the mood for sex. My day has been boring but I'm not cruising out of boredom. Perhaps I am here out of depression. I certainly have a lot to be depressed about. Pleasuring a man often pulls me out of a bad mood. I purposely avoid considering whether or not I may be a sex addict.

This is my fourth trip to an adult bookstore since I completed my master's degree two weeks ago. So far this year I have had no job offers and almost fifty rejections. This infuriates me, since I graduated with an almost perfect grade point average from one of the top college and university administration programs in the country. I attended Michigan State precisely so I would find a job when I graduated.

In addition to my career troubles, my boyfriend of three years is a thousand miles away. Jeff is living with his parents in Iowa while I search for a job as a college residence hall director. A job, I am growing to fear, that will never come.

The man standing in front of me knows nothing of this. Having his semi-hard dick sucked is his only concern. I am nothing more than a piece of meat to him, an attractive young man giving him the cheap thrill he desires. I have no

particular desire to give him that thrill but wrap my mouth around his rapidly expanding dick anyway.

Having sex in an adult bookstore is an involved experience for me. I much prefer to have my own dick sucked, particularly through a gloryhole. Something about pushing my crotch up against the wall of the booth while a mouth slides down my hard cock drives me wild.

My experiences in adult bookstores without gloryholes are entirely different. Strange men follow me throughout the bookstore in the hopes of joining me in an available booth. Once we are alone they begin whispering commands like "suck it," "lick this," or "kneel down." More often than not, the encounters focus around their needs rather than my own.

I ponder all this and more as he pulls the back of my head deeper into his crotch. He begins softly moaning, seemingly unaware the people in the next booth can hear him. I reach up and start massaging his balls to increase his pleasure. He spreads his legs pushing his balls down into my hand.

I continue sucking so I can watch the inevitable result. Forcing men to cum never ceases to interest me. I love doing things to increase their pleasure, my own sexual skills growing with every man I touch. My growing skills in turn can be used to produce increasingly spectacular orgasms. Making men cum is a drug that can never make me too high.

I lost count many years ago how many men I have had sex with. I know it's more than one hundred, but have I reached twice that number yet? I've spent dozens of evenings in bathhouses, bookstores, and sex clubs. Most of my experiences have been exhilarating and wonderful. Many of these encounters have even become some of my favorite memories, such as gentle lovemaking with a newfound friend or the time I had my ass passed back and forth by three attractive strangers. I prefer not to dwell on the more depressing encounters.

Some people find it disturbing I have been with so many men. Yet to me it is not only natural, it is a good idea. How can a person develop his sexual skills if he is not engaging in sex with a variety of partners?

I am jolted back to my surroundings as I feel the stranger's balls tightening against his body. I know from experience his body is preparing to shoot its load all over me. Understanding how to receive verbal and nonverbal messages from a sexual partner is skill that constantly improves with experience. The tightening of the balls is an easy one. There are hundreds more to be learned.

I pull my mouth off his cock and begin rapidly stroking him. The stranger turns his body to the side as his cum spurts inches from my face. I am grateful for his thoughtfulness. Having his load all over my face might excite me, but would prove very difficult to clean off in the present surroundings. I would prefer not to exit the booth with my hair plastered against my head.

The man reaches down and pulls up his pants. He is embarrassed, but not enough to prevent him from a brief moment of affection. He leans down and gives me a quick kiss on my forehead. "Thank you," he whispers. He unlatches the door and disappears into the hallway.

I am surprised. I hadn't expected his sudden burst of affection. People often thank me but rarely show affection. I stand up and lock the door. I need a moment to clear my head.

I realize I am rock hard as I sit down on the bench. I hadn't noticed that I became erect as I blew the stranger. I feel less depressed now and even feel excited to some extent. Fucking around in adult bookstores usually cheers me up, even if for a little while.

The memory of his kiss still has me wondering. What emotion was I bringing out in him? Was it a paternal instinct of some sort? Did he see the encounter as being more meaningful than an anonymous fling with a young stranger?

I unlock the door and exit from the booth. Standing outside in the hallway are three men, all hoping to have a

dose of what the now departed stranger enjoyed. It really is too bad there aren't any gloryholes in here. They would line up at the chance to suck me off.

It must be my youth. I can't believe they are attracted to me for my body. At 161 pounds, I am at the top of the "average weight - large build" column for my height on the weight charts. Unfortunately, I don't have a large build. I packed on the pounds in grad school, and now need to lose thirty, preferably forty pounds. I'm chubby and I know it, but I'm not motivated enough to change. It's easier to suck cock than to diet.

I know I shouldn't be so hard on myself. I do have beautiful blue eyes, and my honesty, intelligence, and warmth always warm men up to me. All I have to do is start talking and people gravitate to me. I have the looks of a seventeen year-old, the mind of a thirty year-old, and the waistline of a fifty year-old. Still, those who love chicken love me.

Having a big dick is the clincher. When I first started having sex with men, I was surprised to learn that I was bigger than most everyone. I startled most of my sexual partners with my erection. For years I hated having a bigger dick because no one could suck or be fucked by the entire length. Only when I began frequenting bathhouses did I find anyone who could. My anonymous sexual experiences taught me to orgasm from a blowjob, to cum while fucking someone, and even how to be jacked off.

Back in the hallway, the cruisers continue to stare at me. I quietly walk around the corner into another hallway of booths. Steps echo through the bare corridors as my entourage follows my every move.

A bookstore is like a hunting ground for most cruisers. Everyone sets their eyes on their prey and then maneuver around the halls in an effort to catch them. My own strategy is a bit different. I wait to see who is my most aggressive pursuer. As long as he is remotely my type, I usually fuck around with him. I have learned over time that the

people who pursue me the hardest are the ones who want me the most.

Catching up with me, the cruisers take up positions at varying places in the hallway. They all stare, trying desperately to look normal in an abnormal situation. A display case featuring this week's movies suddenly becomes worthy of intense scrutiny. The looks of concentration on their faces almost make me laugh.

I lean back against the corner of the last booth. Facing my audience, I slide my hand into my pants. I close my eyes and slowly will myself an erection. Moments later I remove my hand, revealing a large bulge in my pants. The display case loses its interest as all eyes turn on me.

It's time for action. I enter the booth behind me. I slowly close the door, leaving it open a crack in the universal symbol of invitation. Reaching down, I undo the top of my jeans and pull out my stiff cock. I want whoever follows me into this room to instantly feel welcome.

I have spent enough time on the other side of the door in this situation to know what is going through the minds of the cruisers. They all feel a sexual interest and want to enter my booth. Yet they are afraid that despite my signals, they may have misunderstood my intentions. More importantly, they are embarrassed to enter the booth in front of the other men. They already know everyone else is interested, but they somehow hope the other two will leave so they may enter discreetly. I know from experience that someone will eventually gather the courage to enter.

Moments later footsteps approach the booth. A hand hesitantly opens the door, revealing a nervous middle-aged gentleman. He is dressed in nice yet casual clothes. Spreading my legs slightly, I smile and give my dick an extra stroke. He smiles in return and enters the booth. He locks the door behind him then turns toward me.

"Hello," he whispers as he reaches for my cock. He touches it slowly at first, but after a moment of consideration he wraps his hand around it and begins stroking.

"You have a nice dick," he admires. "Do you do this a lot?"

"On occasion," I admit. "I usually do this when I'm bored or horny."

He nods his head in understanding. "I'm the same way," he explains trailing off into silence. He appears more interested in my cock than talking. I close my eyes and let myself experience the sensation of his touch.

I hear his clothes rustling as he kneels down. A sensation of heat surrounds my cock as I feel his mouth envelop my stiffness. He licks me from tip to base, then lowers his mouth over it again.

I lean back against the wall of the booth as he uses my body for his enjoyment. It is nice to be serviced because I am usually the one doing the servicing. He is quite skilled at oral sex, managing to even take the entire length into his mouth. I am most definitely not used to that feeling. I am usually too big for men to deep throat.

He moves his hand from the base of my shaft down onto my balls. I stifle a moan because I am embarrassed someone outside the booth might hear me. I like it when the men I am blowing can't help moaning aloud, but I don't want anyone to know I am enjoying myself. Deep down inside I feel ashamed a total stranger in the back of a sleazy adult bookstore is blowing me.

A wave of irritation washes over me instantly sweeping away my guilt. Why shouldn't I be here? I'm a consenting adult and I want to enjoy myself. There is absolutely nothing wrong with what I am doing.

I am here because I want a stranger to have sex with me. I want to be valued for my looks, youth, and willingness to have sex. I may not be a prize when I'm out dancing or when I'm meeting guys my own age, but in the back of an adult bookstore I'm considered to be very hot. I can compete with anyone else and emerge on top.

The precise value of being the king stud of an adult bookstore is simple. No one harasses me about my high school acne. No one points out I am overweight for my

height. No one snickers at my choice of clothing. On my knees in a darkened booth, I'm the most popular guy around. This is precisely why I value cruising. Nowhere else in my life do I feel so popular and appreciated.

I am filled with feelings of sexuality and power. Dropping to my knees, I gesture for the stranger to stand up. I reach toward his buckle, and within seconds his belt is undone. Pulling his pants down, I begin servicing his engorged cock with tremendous energy. Ravishing him with my tongue and mouth, I send wave after wave of pleasure through his body.

I continue to suck his dick with an almost aggressive style. I'm no longer sucking cock with the same detachment I felt in the other booth. I'm sucking because I am very good at it and because it makes people want to be around me.

Regardless of the reason I am on my knees, the stranger braces himself to keep from falling over. Despite my domineering style of oral sex, he is enjoying himself immensely. His moans are soft at first, but they quickly increase in volume and intensity. Footsteps in the hallway cease as the cruisers stop to listen to the audio show. The man I am sucking either fails to notice or is beyond caring. He doesn't even move as I continue sucking him for all he is worth.

Moaning even louder now, he reaches out and puts his hands in my hair. He starts pulling my head into his crotch. The thrill of being desired fills me again and I double the speed of my oral labors.

Before I realize his orgasm has even begun, I feel a blast of his sweet, sticky cum shooting into my mouth. I push my face deep into his crotch as his cum pours straight down my throat. His hands cease pulling me toward him and begin trying to push me away. The sensations must be too much for him. Unfortunately for him, I do not intend to stop now. He can scream if he needs to, but I am not going to stop.

Wad after wad of cum shoots into my throat. I swallow every drop without letting up, pausing only to slide my mouth toward the tip to increase his already overwhelming sensations. His knees buckle beneath him but my mouth and hands keep him pinned to the door.

Moments later his orgasm ends. I suck the final drops from his body then release him. For a moment I think he is going to fall, but he opens his eyes and stares at me. "Good God," he whispers. "Where did you learn to do that?"

"I like sex," I reply by way of answer.

"I can see that. I'm surprised you're not being paid to do that. You could make a lot of money with your skill and your boyish look."

Money? The thought had never occurred to me before. I did hustle once since my experience with Gary. A guy in Michigan paid $150 to fuck me. I always thought they were chance encounters, the inevitable propositions young men receive. Not indications that I could make a career out of this. Perhaps there is something to what the stranger is saying.

Lost in my thoughts, I scarcely notice the stranger is becoming self-conscious and embarrassed. Pulling up his pants, he instructs me to wait in the booth for a few moments after he leaves. I barely hear him as I nod my head dumbly. He unlocks the door and leaves. I lock it behind him and drop two tokens into the slot. I need a minute to sit and think.

Ignoring the movie on the screen, I pull up my own pants and sit down on the chair. Could I really charge money for sex? I hardly have the body for it, although I am very boyish looking. I do have the sexual skill for it, I realize, as well as the ability to perform with all types of guys. I have done some ugly looking men in these booths. I could certainly do so again if business required.

Sitting in the flickering light of two naked bodies on the screen, I wonder if I really could work as an escort. I suppose I could investigate if there is a market for it on the Internet. I am approached for sex by a lot of guys on

America Online, but turn most of them down. Although I dislike dealing with those men for more than sex, I would be willing to get to know them for money.

My time in the video booth runs out and the screen clicks off. I stand up and unlock the door to the booth. The cruisers in the hallway outside are gone. Perhaps they realized there would be no more sex from me today.

As I leave the bookstore, I understand I have already made my decision. My mind is filled with questions at the thought. How will I find my clients? Can I keep my family from finding out? How much will I charge? Do I really have what it takes to be an escort? Will I wind up rich and retired, or will I destroy my health and wind up in jail?

The whirlwind of questions in my head continues as the door to the bookstore closes behind me forever.

Lessons

June 4, 1995

It is a warm summer afternoon and I am happily sitting at my desk wearing only yesterday's underwear and a t-shirt. Boyishly soft whiskers sprout from my unshaven and unwashed face. My head is buried deep in a Stephen King novel as I munch on a late breakfast of cookies and milk. I lean back in my chair while my feet are propped up next to a whirring computer. No one in a million years would believe I am prostituting myself.

Despite my misleading appearance, that is exactly what I am doing. I have been parked next to my computer for the past four days endeavoring to learn as much about hi-tech hustling as I can.

The decision to escort online was a simple one. I know absolutely nothing about hustling. Even if I knew where hustlers hung out, I wouldn't know how to act like one. I know there are escort agencies here in New Jersey, but I strongly suspect they prefer a more built and muscular applicant. My decision was almost made for me from the beginning. If I wanted to find clients, I would have to do so on the Internet.

Being a bit of a computer nerd does have its advantages. I have been using a modem since I was fourteen, and consider myself highly familiar with online services. Logging on and getting started on America Online was a simple matter.

My first step toward becoming a hi-tech callboy was to create a screen name. My first several tries were all taken.

NJcallboy, Callboy, and NJBoy4Hire. Just how many escorts were on AOL, anyway? I finally settled on NJEscort.

After creating my new handle, the next step was to create a profile. Once I had a profile, anyone searching the member directory for escorts in New Jersey would find me. After a few minutes, my profile was complete.

NJEscort

Your Name:	Aaron
City, State, Country:	Bridgewater Area, NJ
Birthday:	I'm 24!
Sex:	Male
Hobbies:	Computers, Reading, Eating Cookies, and Gay Sex.
Computers Used:	Gateway 2000 386 machine.
Occupation:	Callboy / Escort for Men. I'm for real. IM me!
Personal Quote:	I'm 24, 5'5", 150, blond hair, and blue eyes. Very boyish and very cute. No pic to send, sorry.

The profile was almost true. I weighed ten pounds more than I was admitting and my hair had become more auburn than blond, but the rest was accurate. I hoped by lowering my weight and asking people to send me an instant message, I would receive more inquiries.

The day after I created my profile and began cruising the chat rooms, I met BlkStudNJ. I glanced at his profile and was surprised to find his profile said he was an escort. I immediately sent him an e-mail introducing myself. He replied saying his name was Jamal.

I spoke to Jamal over an hour that day. I learned he worked four to six times every week at $150 per hour. He had a day job, but escorted at night for extra money.

He gave me a number of ideas about how to run my business. He suggested I charge $125 per hour, but I wanted to encourage people to hire me for more than one

hour. To encourage additional hours, I set my rate at $125 for the first hour, but only $50 per additional hour.

After I returned from my first client, Jamal eagerly listened to me talk about my first real escorting experience. I described how I had sex in the back office of a catering business with the married owner. I found the entire situation quite amusing. Between congratulations, Jamal said I would undoubtedly have stranger experiences if I stayed in the business for long.

Outside of the advice I was receiving, my first lesson was that escorting is far slower than I had imagined. Whether someone stands on a street corner, works his local hustler bar, waits for his telephone to ring, or searches the Internet for business, prostitution takes time. Every hour I spend with a client requires eight more behind the scenes. My lack of experience may have something to do with it, but somehow I don't think the time involved is going to significantly change.

The computerized chime of an instant message wakes me from my daydreaming. Brushing cookie crumbs off my lap, I reach for the keyboard. I tap a few keys and the incoming message is displayed.

Ted03423: hello.

"Hi," I type back. "How are you?" The screen flashes again.

Ted03423: i am fine. i saw you in your profile. you sound good looking. u are an escort???

I hate it when people type in all lowercase and use poor grammar, but I put aside my pet peeves for the sake of business. "Before I answer that," I begin typing, "are you a member or volunteer of any local, state, or federal law enforcement agency?" I press return and wait for his response.

Ted03423: no i am not. u are an escort?

I reach over and grab another cookie before I type my reply. "Yes, I am a male callboy for men. Are you thinking about hiring one?"

Ted03423: i might be.

"Well, I am $125 for the first hour, and $50 per additional hour. And if I have to drive over an hour to get to you, I charge a two hour minimum."

Ted03423: i am in par-troy. it is near parsippany.

Par-Troy is an easy half-hour drive from me. "I can drive there. Would you be interested in setting something up?"

Ted03423: u have sex with me? u act str8?

Of course I don't act straight! I have sex with men. How straight is that? Absently munching on the cookie, I reply, "Yes, I will do whatever you would like. Safely, that is. And yes, I am very masculine in a boyish way. Where shall we meet, and when?"

Ted03423: meet tomorrow at 3:00 before my wife get home. we meet at cost cutters on rt. 46 in par-troy. i am asian, and drive blue nissan sentra. I am ted.

"Okay, I will be meet you outside Cost Cutters on Rt. 46 in Par-Troy at 3:00. You will be driving a blue Nissan Sentra, and I will be driving a red Honda Civic," I confirm. "If you cannot make it, please write me an e-mail by tomorrow early afternoon."

Ted03423: okay, see you there.

I am elated. I write the information on a piece of paper so I won't lose it before tomorrow. Clicking a button on the screen, I cause a blank e-mail message to pop up. I quickly begin typing the good news to Jamal. He's probably been through this a hundred times, but I am excited. I made less than $125 in a week in graduate school. This is $125 for an hour and is tax-free.

The following day finds me sitting in my car in the Cost Cutters parking lot. There is no sign of a blue Nissan Sentra anywhere in the lot. I strongly suspect I am being stood up.

The minutes continue to pass. The more I think about it, the more I wonder if my information is correct. Was he actually supposed to be driving a blue car? Were we supposed to meet outside or inside the store? I need to buy a

small bag to carry my condoms and lube anyway, so I might as well look inside the store. Perhaps I will find the elusive Ted.

Inside the store, I find a black book bag that will serve my purposes perfectly. I also think I have found Ted. More accurately, I think Ted has found me. I notice a strange Asian man in his early thirties following me around the store. Every time I look up he looks away and hides around a corner. Whenever I return to my shopping, I feel his eyes staring at me.

Finally, my curiosity gets the better of me. I walk up to him. "Ted?" I inquire.

"Aaron," he replies as he holds out his hand.

I shake his hand in suspicious silence. My intuition is telling me there is something wrong about him. My suspicions are soon confirmed when he says, "I thought you would look very different. More mature. You aren't really my type."

I am surprised at his forwardness but am more annoyed than anything else. He is obviously wasting my time with odd mind games. "I'm sorry if I'm not your type," I reply in an irritated tone, "but I am exactly like the stats in my profile. If you expected someone older looking, you shouldn't have hired me. My profile said I was boyish looking."

"You're not ugly or anything, you're just not my type. I would still pay for you, but not as much. I'll pay you sixty bucks for an hour."

I am astonished at his rudeness. "Absolutely not."

Ted stares at me with an almost identical look. He apparently cannot comprehend why I am not accepting his offer. "Why won't you do it for sixty? Some money is better than none."

"We had a deal," I explain in an angry tone. "That's why I'm not bargaining. If you didn't like the price, you should have said something to me then. If you don't want to pay, I'll leave."

"I'm saying something to you now. You're simply not worth it. But I'll still pay you sixty bucks."

I set the black bag down and turn to leave. This asshole has wasted my time.

I hear footsteps behind me as I exit the store. Ted calls to me, so I slow down. He catches up with me to make another unacceptable offer. "I'll give you eighty bucks."

I stare at him incredulously. Who does this moron think he is? I do not even bother to reply. I turn and continue walking toward my car.

Reaching my car, I pull my keys out of my pocket and jam the correct one into the lock. Ted is walking toward me again. He catches up and makes another offer. "Would you accept $100?"

I am having urges to punch him in the face. "No," I tell him coldly as I open the door to my car.

"How big is your dick?" Ted asks me. The question takes me off guard.

"I'm about eight inches long."

"Are you really?" he challenges me. I stare at him in angry silence.

"I'll make you a deal," Ted finally gives in. "Let's go back to my place near here. If you are as big as you say, I'll pay it all."

Greedy for his money, I accept the offer. It never occurs to me to ask for the money up front. He tells me to follow his car back to his place. As he walks back across the lot, I notice him unlock a car that is not a blue Nissan Sentra. A flash of understanding hits me. By not driving a Sentra, he planned to check me out from a distance. If I was not his type, he would have left without saying anything to me. What a bastard!

I follow Ted to a condominium development. Before I have a chance to open my door, he is standing next to my car. I exit and follow him inside. He appears nervous to be seen with me in front of where he lives. He leads me to a small but comfortable one-bedroom apartment. It is heavily furnished with momentos and souvenirs.

I barely have time to take in the apartment before he grabs at my clothing. He unbuttons my pants and pulls them down around my knees. I lean back against the wall to maintain my balance as he scrambles to pull down my underwear.

Although I am not hard, what he sees is enough to capture his interest. He reaches out and touches my soft prick, running his hand up and down its smooth surface. He kneels and takes it into his mouth, sliding his tongue across the head. I feel myself beginning to swell inside him. He may be a serious jerk but he isn't all that bad looking.

I feel myself continue to stiffen. I run my hands through his hair, pulling him toward me. He gags slightly on my dick and is forced to pull back. Deep throating is definitely not his specialty.

Abruptly he stands up and moves toward the couch. He pulls off the pillows revealing a foldout bed. He pulls the bed out of the couch and slowly unfolds it. Since the bed already has sheets, I remove my pants the rest of the way and lie down. He lies down next to me, and within moments we are having sex again.

He is as bad at kissing as he is at deep throating. We manage adequately, more due to my ability to adapt than any skill on his part. I dart my tongue in and out of his mouth as my hands begin untucking his shirt from his pants. Reaching beneath the fabric, I run my hand across his stomach to his left nipple. He begins trembling with delight at my touch.

I unbutton the top three buttons of his shirt revealing his smooth chest. I lean toward him and lick each of his nipples once. His trembling increases. I lick them again then slide my tongue back and forth between them. I unbutton the rest of his shirt and pull it apart. Now his entire chest is open to my tongue bath.

He enjoys my licking a great deal. I am unsure if he has a highly sensitive body or if he is simply horny. Either way, I undo his pants and reveal a sizable bulge in his underwear. As I slide them down, his stiff prick springs to

attention. It is only four or five inches long, but is hard as is humanly possible. I adjust the area of my tongue's attention to my new toy.

Despite the sex and my own physical arousal, I am not enjoying myself at all. I did not like the way he treated me before and I do not find him at all appealing any longer. His physical attractiveness is overshadowed by the ugliness within.

I spend the next fifteen minutes giving him the best blowjob of his life. I lick, suck, touch, stroke, and worship his cock. I doubt his wife has ever done this for him, certainly not with anything approaching my skill. He is most appreciative of my efforts, moaning softly as he rocks back and forth on the bed. Twice I have to slow down to keep him from cumming.

He finally looks me in the eye. "I want to fuck you."

Having anticipated he may want to, I brought plenty of condoms and lube with me. I remove my shirt and toss it on the floor. I reach for my pants to grab a rubber and tube of KY out of the pocket.

Once he is ready, I pop open the top of the KY. Squeezing the tube, I pour a healthy dose into my hand. I mechanically smear the cold gel onto Ted's sheathed dick and my own ass. What little eroticism I felt has gone out of this encounter. Not that there was much to begin with.

Ted moves aside and motions for me to lie on my back. As I do so, he lifts my legs in the air. Kneeling on the edge of the bed, he slides his dick into me. It is painful but Ted doesn't seem to notice or care. I force myself to relax as Ted begins pumping me. After a few minutes it does feel slightly pleasurable, although nothing near what I am faking. He wants a show so I am giving him one. He cares nothing about how I really feel.

Ted continues pumping my ass with a look of rapture on his face. "Are you going to cum soon?" he asks me with glazed eyes. A slight trail of drool oozes down his chin.

I am not anywhere near cumming, so I close my eyes and begin stroking my cock. I try to forget about the idiot fucking me as I fantasize about my boyfriend.

I experience a pang of guilt when I think about Jeff. I feel awful that I am cheating on him, but this is what I need to do right now. Since I'm going to be screwing around anyway I might as well be paid for it. I silently promise that I will find a job soon so we can live together again. The rejections can't happen forever. Eventually I'll have a lucky break.

I switch my fantasies to something a bit easier on my conscience. I concentrate on a night I spent in a hot Canadian bathhouse. I screwed around quite a bit that evening. I still remember the way one man played with my balls. It's too bad that Ted doesn't know I like that. He never expressed the slightest interest in pleasuring me.

Thinking of Ted makes me open my eyes. His pumping is faster now as he nears his climax. My stroking has made me close enough so I can shoot as well. I surrender myself to the feeling and begin shooting a load across my stomach. Despite the fake moans, my orgasm leaves me feeling empty and cold.

I feel Ted let loose within me. He moans several times as he pumps deeply and fills the condom with his juices. He pulls out of me and instantly appears regretful of what he has done. He rushes from the room toward the bathroom, removing the condom as he runs. Normally I would talk to him and help him become more comfortable with his gay self, but Ted is such a jerk I don't care. I begin looking around for my clothing.

By the time I button my shirt, Ted is standing in the doorway. An odd expression has appeared on his face making me nervous. He hands me a wad of bills.

I stop and count them. To my surprise the money is not all there.

"What is this?" I ask in irritation. "It's short forty-five bucks."

"You enjoyed it so I thought it would be okay," he says lamely as he glances at the clock.

"No, it's not okay. We agreed on the money and I need it. It's what I need to pay my bills." The anger in my voice is obvious.

"But I need it too," he justifies in a whining voice. "I have a lot of bills to pay too and I have a wife. You're not even married."

I argue with him briefly but I realize I have already lost. I have no doubt I can get the money out of him. I can threaten him with physical violence or I can bluff that I am going to tell his wife what we did. Judging by the way he glances at the clock, she will be home soon.

Sighing inwardly, I put on the remainder of my clothes and gather my belongings. The money isn't worth fighting for. More importantly, he has taught me a lesson in trust. The next time someone attempts to renegotiate, they are paying up front and paying extra for wasting my time.

I walk out his front door and spit on it.

He follows me out to my car and awkwardly approaches me. I roll down the window.

"Can I see you again?" he asks.

I stare at him in astonishment. I cannot even begin to imagine how he has the nerve to ask such a question.

"Fuck off," I snarl.

I start my car and back out of the parking space. I accept he is a jerk. I even understand why he tried to cheat me. But I will never comprehend why he followed me out to the car. Did he honestly think I would say yes?

Still angry from my bitter lesson, I peal out of the lot hoping never to see him again.

Reality

June 23, 1995

Ever since I was seventeen, I have equated callboys with tuxedos.

My association began one winter night when I snuck out of my parents' house to dance at a local gay club called the Yacht Club. The bar was unusually friendly to gay youth and allowed me to enter as long as I promised not to drink. I never broke my word, either. I was going there to be picked up for sex, not to get drunk.

I remember the club that night as being packed from wall-to-wall. The DJ had completed a song and the crowds were clearing the dance floor. Throngs of panting and sweaty customers eagerly moved toward the bar while my friends and I, not being able to drink, walked toward the railing near the side wall.

A man in a tuxedo stood near the end of the railing. He appeared to be about thirty years old, although he was trying to look younger. His blond hair looked like it was held in place by an entire can of hairspray. I nudged a friend of mine and asked him who the stranger was. I do not recall his answer, but I remember my friend telling me he was well known around the bar as a callboy.

A callboy in New Jersey! The thought was surprising to me. I imagined the life he must live, wealthy men buying him expensive gifts and flying him around the country. I wondered what it would be like to travel first class, eating in the finest restaurants, and driving fancy sports cars.

Recalling this memory now, it is all I can do to stifle a disappointed laugh. My views were quite naïve, especially

considering my current situation. For the past fifteen minutes I have been lying nude across the lap of Mike, an Asian man in his early thirties. He is enjoying himself as he fingers me and pushes the crotch of his jeans into me in an unusual act of frottage.

When I arrived at the motel half an hour earlier, Mike explained he had a cold. He didn't want to take off his clothes and did not want to kiss me because he was afraid he would pass it on to me. I thanked him for his concern although I thought he looked fine to me. Still, he is the client and I'm the escort. It's his decision what we do.

Instead of foreplay, Mike requested I pull my pants down around my knees and lay across his lap. He adjusted my position to make himself more comfortable then reached for the KY. He has been happily fingering my ass since.

This is not the fantasy I dreamt about in my youth. There are no sports cars and no trips around the country. There are no wealthy benefactors with tickets to the Met or reservations for a late candlelight dinner. I understand now the reality of an escort is clients and cash. Middle-class clients and a constant influx of cash. It may not be as enjoyable as the fantasy, but it does have its advantages. I have enough money that I can buy my own first class ticket or my own expensive wardrobe.

I find it hard to believe how much money there is to be made by escorting. Chubby little me, living with my parents and escorting on the Internet, made $2,000 in just over three weeks. I would have made more except I can't have clients call me at my parents' home. Without a telephone, the business is much more difficult.

The fact that I was interviewing in New England for four days didn't help either. I attended two placement conferences for entry-level positions in college administration. Between the two conferences, I interviewed for sixteen residence hall director positions. Many of the interviewers seemed genuinely interested in me. Driving home, I was almost sad that my escorting would soon end. I was making far more than I would make at any college or university.

Just as importantly, I would miss how much I enjoy escorting. Even my bad experiences, like being paddled by a German businessman and being cheated by Ted, taught me interesting lessons about sexuality and sex work.

Apart from my few bad experiences, most of my clients are enjoyable. They want to kiss, cuddle, suck and be sucked, and fuck and be fucked. They often have preferences of what they like best, but all seem to enjoy our time together.

My clients are very typical in appearance. When I began escorting, I was worried all my clients would be ugly, extremely overweight, or very old. To my surprise, none of those predictions came true. My clientele does have a definite leaning on the older, heavier, and homelier side, but not overwhelmingly so. Some of my clients are even quite attractive.

Perhaps the one factor that almost all of my clients have in common is a low self-image regarding their looks. My clients often view themselves as being "over the hill," overweight, or ugly, even when that is not the case. Some of them are, I admit, but most are unnecessarily hard on themselves.

This lack of self-esteem is only one reason why my clients hire me. They hire me for convenience, to save time finding someone on their own. They hire me for discretion, because they fear their families or neighbors will learn of their same-sex interests. They hire me out of simplicity, because they do not want to expend the effort to find someone on their own. They also hire me because I am willing to do what they want, how they want, wherever they want, whatever time they want, in whatever positions they want. Some men find that opportunity too attractive to pass up.

Mike begins to hump faster beneath me. His finger slides in and out of my ass as he inhales a series of shallow breaths. He reaches his other hand toward me and rubs the cheeks of my ass. Pulling my buns apart, he rams his finger one final time into my ass. He thrusts his crotch upward

and lets loose a stream of cum. To my amazement, Mike has just orgasmed through his pants.

He collapses back onto the bed. He opens his eyes and gives me an embarrassed look. "I needed that," he admits. "Is it okay that I came?"

"Yes," I reassure him. "It felt great and was very exciting. You don't realize how sexy it is that you were able to hump me through your pants."

Mike says nothing but motions for me to climb off. I do so and he vanishes into the bathroom. When he returns a minute later, I am pulling on my shorts.

"What are you doing? We still have another half an hour left," he reprimands me.

I quickly apologize. "I'm sorry, I had thought we were done. I would be glad to stay. What would you like to do now?"

He gives me a simple request. "I want to lie on the bed with you next to me."

It's a reasonable request. Unfortunately, it is also a boring one. Because of his cold, Mike makes no effort to either kiss or cuddle. He seems content to lie on the bed with his eyes closed while I lie next to him. I am anxious to go home to prepare for my next client, but Mike wants me to stay for every minute he has paid for. Still, he is the client and I am here on his time, so I close my eyes and let my mind wander.

My thoughts eventually settle on one of my favorite subjects: money. I had done some calculations a few days before. If I found a job as a college residence hall director, at best I would earn $25,000 per year, or $480 per week including room and board. In the first three weeks of working the chat rooms, I averaged over $650 per week. At my current rate, I would earn almost $35,000 per year.

I know I can even make a lot more money than that. Right now, I am escorting with several severe handicaps. I am escorting without a picture of myself to send to potential clients. I am not advertising with any sort of print ads. I do not have a phone line where clients can call me. I also

know I would gain more business if I lost a bit more weight. Properly run, I estimate my business could earn more than $50,000 per year, perhaps as much as $75,000.

Even though it is possible, I do not have any grand ambitions to raise my business to that level. These days I am concentrating on meeting a goal of a $1,000 per week. Finding a job in my field will mean my business will end before I reach that level for any extended period of time.

Thinking about my job situation is depressing. I am not any closer to finding a job than I was a month ago. My room at home is littered with rejection letters. I have now received over sixty of them. Fortunately, I am still in consideration for a position with at least thirty more schools, and have about twenty more to apply to beyond that. I am confident I will find something.

Living with Jeff in a college dormitory as part of the staff will be very exciting for me. Admitted, I won't be having as much sex as I am having now. Unless Jeff decides once per day isn't enough. The thought does have certain advantages.

I wonder what Jeff would think if he knew that I was escorting. He would probably feel hurt, betrayed, and deeply saddened that I did this to him. The act of prostitution itself would not bother him. He is too far beyond conventional morality for that. He would probably be upset because I did something that was clearly outside the rules of our relationship. Although I want an open relationship, Jeff has not agreed to one so far.

I wish I knew if Jeff would stay or leave if he knew. He has forgiven my lapses in the past. He even allowed me to spend an evening in a bathhouse once. He is a remarkable person, and I feel guilty that I am doing this to him. Perhaps it would be better if he did leave me. That way I would no longer be able to hurt him.

Waking myself slightly, I look at the resting form of Mike. His eyes are closed and his breathing is even. I wonder if he is asleep.

I wish I could do the same. I don't sleep at night as much as I used to because I am up late searching chat rooms for clients.

I force myself to close my eyes again. In another five minutes I will wake Mike and tell him it is time for us to leave. I have another appointment early this evening, so I want to go home and take a shower.

I can't say I would not trade my career for the world, because I plan to trade it for much less. If all works out, I will be trading my lifestyle for my boyfriend, a cramped dorm room, and a heart full of regret that I will never learn if I could have made it as an escort.

Do callboys wear tuxedos and drive sports cars? Hardly. They wear jeans and bend over for anyone with a wad of twenties. But it is a living, and it's the one I am choosing to enjoy for now.

Photography

June 28, 1995

"Move a little to the left. Slide that arm down. Spread those legs. Perfect! Hold that pose." The room fills with the flashing, clicking, and whirring of the camera as my image is captured on film.

His words remind me of the stereotypical sleazy porno director. He certainly looks the part, his excess weight oozing over the top of his pants underneath a face flushed with sweat.

I am sitting on the photographer's bed in his South Brunswick home. My clothes are scattered across the room, evidence of our rush to begin the evening's activities. Our agenda has two items: photography and sex, not necessarily in that order.

The photographer, Mark, approached me online several days earlier. After chatting for a few minutes, he was surprised to learn I did not have an online picture of myself. "I think you could earn a lot more money if you have a good picture to send people." Listening to him, I had to agree. I have a list of almost forty prospective clients who will consider hiring me once I have a picture. If even a tenth hire me, I stand to make well over $500. It is more than enough money to make it worth my while.

Unfortunately, the process of sending a picture is easier said than done. Not only do I need to find someone to take revealing pictures of me, I also have to find someone to scan them onto disk. It would hardly be appropriate to have

my local copy shop scan my nude pictures.

"If you would like," Mark had continued typing, "You can come over to my place sometime. We can take a few rolls of pictures and I can scan them in at work. I'll even pay for the film and developing."

His offer was attractive. The money from the prospective clients is very tempting, to say nothing for additional business in the future. Of course, Mark was not making the offer for free. The unspoken terms were perfectly clear. I wanted the pictures. He wanted my body. I agreed, and the evening's agenda was set.

Back on the bed in Mark's apartment, I turn over to let him snap a picture of my ass. Although I am wearing a g-string, it does nothing to cover me from behind. Flash, click, whirr. I hear the sound of the camera.

Mark pauses. I feel hands touch my asscheeks and pull them apart. Moments later I feel a probing tongue licking between them. I tremble with delight. He may not be my type, but his touch and skill feel great.

I kneel down even farther, pressing my chest and face against the bed. He continues to ream my ass, burying his face into the depths. A momentary pang of worry hits me, I hope my ass is clean.

If Mark has any problem with my ass, he doesn't show it. He continues licking the hole, sliding his wet tongue up and down the crack. I shiver with ecstasy. The sensations he is sending through my body are incredible. I wish all my clients would make me feel this good. Then again, if they did, Jeff might be history as I switched professions permanently.

Bracing his hands on the bed, Mark stands back up. "Enough play. We still have a roll and a half to go," he says. "Change into those slinky black shorts and we'll take a few photographs of those."

"All right," I agree, wishing he would eat out my ass for the next several hours instead. He really is good at it. "Toss me my shorts, would you?"

After a moment of thought, I decide I'm glad he stopped. I am enjoying the sex, but I am here to have pictures taken. If I have sex with him now, he may lose interest in the photography. I'm also aware that my cock is rock hard from his attention. As long as he keeps up these momentary interludes of sexual attention, I will be as stiff as a board for the camera.

I pull the white mesh g-string off me and playfully throw it at his retreating figure. He chuckles softly as he bends over to pick up and tosses my shorts to me. "How do you plan to put them on with such a woody?"

I grin evilly. "I'll make you blow me until I cream, then I'll put them on."

"That can be arranged, you know."

I pull the shorts up to my waist. I stand up and walk to the mirror. I may not be able to do much about my body, but I can make my hair look presentable.

Looking in the mirror I feel despair at my reflection. My stomach hangs over the front of my shorts. I am not severely overweight or even moderately, but I do need to lose at least twenty pounds. More like forty if I want to escort for a living. I would work on losing the weight, but a residence life job offer will come along any day now. I won't need to worry about my figure once I am happily living with Jeff again. Sighing slightly, I turn back to Mark.

"You look great, Aaron," he reassures me. "Your hair is fine and I think you look totally sexy."

"It's not that," I tell him, "it's just that I need to lose some weight."

"You think you need to lose some weight? Look at me! I'm the one that should be chained to an exercise machine."

"You're also the one who isn't an escort," I point out.

"That's true," he admits. "Come lie down on the bed. I want to get some pictures of that adorable smile of yours while you're lying down. You'll look like an innocent kid."

"Perfect! Just the look I want. So you dirty old men can molest my virginal body."

Mark takes a playful swipe at me. "Shut up and lie on the bed, boy. Let the photographer do his work."

I laugh and climb on the bed. I turn around and lie on my stomach with my feet in the air. I look up into the camera and give him my innocent smile.

Flash, click, whirr. "Great, Aaron. Don't move!" Flash, click, whirr. "Now sit up," he instructs me.

I sit up rubbing my eyes from the blinding effect of the flash. Mark climbs onto the edge of the bed and aims the camera down at me. I look up and hold my pose. The flash blinds me again.

Needing a break, I crawl toward Mark. I reach up and pull on the top of his shorts. He is not wearing any underwear, and his dick springs out completely at attention. It isn't very big, perhaps four or five inches. Fortunately, it doesn't have to be big for me to distract him.

He is so excited he starts moaning before my mouth touches him. I begin sucking him in slow, steady strokes. Wetting the entire surface, I pay careful attention to the tip of his cock. I roll my tongue in circles around him as another soft moan escapes his lips.

Perhaps a minute later I stop sucking and sit down on the bed. Mark has a dismayed look on his face. "You are a cruel boy, Aaron."

"I know, Mr. Photographer. Shall we continue? Oh, and I wouldn't have done that except for how quickly you stopped after you started licking my ass."

He laughs. "Okay, I guess I deserved that. Shall we continue?"

Over the next few minutes, I pose in several different positions as he snaps picture after picture. Several of them prominently feature the large bulge in my pants. Although we do not stop to screw around again, Mark does find several excuses to reach out and grope me. Sexual harassment is not only tolerated in this photographic session, it is encouraged. The sexually charged atmosphere keeps me hard.

Eventually the roll is complete. "Move the lighting into the stairwell," he instructs me. "I'm going to change the film."

"Sure thing, stud," I reply as I stand up.

"Put on that rainbow g-string of yours, too. I think we should see how revealing we can get these pictures on the stairs."

It is not easy to set up the lighting in the stairwell, but I manage. I am worried Mark will knock over one of his lamps with his girth, so I am careful to place them at the ends of the L-shaped stairs. The lighting isn't perfect but the bright overhead light in the stairwell should help illuminate everything.

As I change from my shorts into the g-string Mark plays with his camera. "These pictures will be so hot," he says. "I can't wait until I get a chance to develop them. I think I'll want to keep a roll for myself."

"You're welcome to keep one, you know," I tell him. "I want to make sure they're not nude. I don't mind having revealing pictures out there, but I do not want nude pictures floating around. Someone might recognize them and send them to my parents." This is doubtful, but is as good of an excuse as any not to let Mark take nude pictures of me. I want to avoid telling Mark I don't trust him.

"I know, I know. We talked about that already. I won't take any nude pictures. Just really sexy revealing ones."

"Thanks," I reply. Pulling on the g-string, I am ready for the next set of pictures. My erection has gone down slightly, allowing the g-string to fit better. Normally the length of my shaft pulls the material of the g-string off my balls. It looks strange when it does that, but as long as my erection is slightly down the g-string fits.

Mark stands in the middle of the stairs as I pose provocatively at the top. The camera is perfectly level with the top of the stairs, forcing me to lean back slightly to fit into the picture. Leaning back is actually a good pose, as it al-

lows me to stretch out and make myself look thinner. Sucking in my stomach, I ready myself for the camera.

Flash, click, whirr. The sound has become familiar to me. I smile and spread my legs. Flash, click, whirr. A few moments later boredom begins to set in. I need a bit of excitement.

"Mark," I say, "put down the camera and come here. I think you should fluff for me."

"Fluff?" he asks. "What do you mean by--" he cuts off as I pull down my g-string and motion for him to come closer. "Oh! I understand."

He puts the camera down and walks up the stairs toward me. He smiles and wipes the sweat from his forehead. Noticing the horny expression on his face, I spread my legs even further in invitation. Any apprehension he had vanishes as he leans toward me. He buries his face in my crotch as he starts sucking my prick.

I lie on my back at the top of the stairs with my legs spread apart. The flexibility of the base of my dick to bend at almost any angle comes in handy as Mark bends it almost parallel with my legs. He lies on the staircase on his stomach while sucking me. It is a surprisingly comfortable position for both of us.

I gasp in surprise as he begins to deep throat me. I grab his head and pull him into my crotch. My dick grinds in the back of his throat causing him to gag. I loosen the pressure on his head, but he doesn't budge. He overcomes his gag reflex and pushes his head farther into my crotch.

"Oh, Mark!" I cry out in ecstasy. "That's incredible! Please keep sucking me."

He bobs his head up and down instead of answering me. His style of oral sex is exciting. He is sucking me very tightly on the up motions, but he opens his mouth wide as he descends. The end effect is to create a sensation of pulling on my dick. It almost feels like I am being masturbated with his mouth.

Knowing I rarely cum from a blowjob, I feel no pressure to cum for him. I simply relax and let him suck my

cock for all he is worth. The feeling is incredible. The warmth and wetness consumes my consciousness.

I am aware we are being distracted from the rest of the photographs, but I don't mind. It's exciting to consider how fun this distraction can be. Who says you shouldn't mix business with pleasure? I do it almost daily now. I have had twenty-five clients since I began escorting almost a month ago.

I contemplate the look on Mark's face. It is almost euphoric, as if he is an addict having a badly needed fix. His eyes are slightly open but do not appear to see anything. He is sucking out of instinctive need, his face a contorted mask of pleasure.

I realize I had better stop this before it goes on too much longer. I put my hands out in warning. "Whoa, boy! You're getting me too excited. We need to finish the shoot."

For a moment I think Mark is going to ignore me, but slowly he stops. "Do I have to?" he asks.

I start laughing. "It's not so bad. We'll be done with the shoot in a few minutes. I think you should do some ass shots, what do you think?"

He playfully grabs my thighs. "I'm not complaining about any of this. This is so hot. You are really sexy, you know."

I blush in my boyishly innocent way. "Thanks." I deliberately pause, acting unsure what to do next. I want Mark to see me as a lost little boy in need of guidance. It's an image I like to portray. Judging by the number of times I have been picked up, men respond to it well.

"Just turn around and look cute," he responds. "I'll take care of the pictures from here."

I remember a scene in a porno tape when Kevin Williams was auditioning for his first movie. He was kneeling on a bed and twisting his torso around. It was very sexy to watch. Thinking of the scene, I try to copy his pose. Kevin had a lot better body than I have, but I try my best anyway. Mark appears sufficiently impressed.

He begins taking pictures rapidly as I pose provocatively. Soon there are only two pictures remaining.

"Wait, Mark, I want to get into an extra special position for this," I tell him. In truth I am certain we have enough pictures already, but since we are about to have sex I want to begin it with a bit of special excitement.

I turn around and kneel on top of the stairs. I lean forward pushing my face and chest against the floor so my ass sticks into the air. Mark whistles in approval.

Moments later the final pictures are completed. "Hey, Mark," I request, "how would you like to pull down my g-string in this position?"

Mark doesn't even bother to reply. He knows what is going to happen now as much as I do. He climbs the stairs toward my ass and touches me. I feel his hands wrap under the elastic strings and slowly pull them down. He cannot remove it in this position, but he can pull it down from the crack of my ass.

"Ooooh," he marvels. "Your ass is so hot." He puts his hands on my buns and begins to rub them. Stroking my ass in a circular motion, he slowly and gently moves his hands across the surface. Every few moments he slides his hand toward the center and dips his thumbs into the crack to rub the sensitive flesh within. I softly moan every time he does so.

He leans down toward my ass and begins tonguing me again. His hands pull my buns apart exposing even more of my flesh to his probing mouth. I push my ass up in the air toward him. He is reaming out my ass like he did on the bed, only now I am even more excited. This time I can have him pleasure me until I cream.

He continues to eat out my ass. He pushes his tongue as far into me as he can, then rests himself by taking long strokes from the base of my balls to the top of my ass. He even slides a finger into me using his saliva as lubrication. I am totally hot for his touch and want him to get me off so badly.

"Mark, pull out of me for a second," I instruct him. "I want to turn over."

He leans back giving me room to maneuver. My cock sticks a full eight inches in the air. It usually doesn't get this erect, but then again I am rarely this turned on. I reach down and begin stroking myself. "Play with my balls with your hands. My favorite way to cum is to jack off while someone rubs them."

The moment his hands touch my balls I moan loudly. I vaguely wonder if he has any neighbors that can hear us, but I can't bring myself to care. The feelings are too intense. I continue to masturbate while he plays with me.

His touch is surprisingly sensual. When we first met, I had not expected him to be anywhere near this fun in bed. His weight and receding hairline are hardly signs of sexual virility. Obviously appearances can be deceiving. This guy is a stud when it comes to arousing my body.

He gently lifts one ball while he pulls on the other. His fingertips massage the tender surface of my testicles through the skin. I lose track of everything else as the feelings become even more intense. I struggle to focus my mind as I beat myself off to his touch

It is difficult not to cum too fast. I am used to taking a long time to orgasm with my partners, but today's foreplay has me extremely aroused. I have been turned on since the moment I arrived. I pump my cock through my hand and howl with delight. I cannot keep my feelings to myself. I need to shout them to the world.

Moments later my orgasm erupts with a scream. Streams of cum fly out of my dick and land all over me. Wave after wave of pleasure racks my body as I lose control of my voice and sob in ecstasy. Everything around me ceases to have any meaning. I collapse in total exhaustion, trails of cum running down my body.

Although my eyes are closed, I hear Mark pulling his pants down. He sounds as if he is leaning over me while he jacks himself off. I know I should do something to help

him out, but I can't move. I have no strength left in my body.

Fortunately, Mark is doing fine without me. His breathing quickens as he nears his peak. It does not take long before he is blasting wads of cum all over me. Hot, juicy, and wet streams of cum land all over my own in a series of puddles across my body.

His orgasm sounds nothing like mine, but it doesn't have to. We have both fulfilled our ends of the bargain. I won't be seeing any more clients today. I know I am too exhausted to achieve the weakest of erections. All that remains now for me is to gather my strength, clean up, and head home for the night.

As I lie across the top of the stairs, I feel my mind drifting. I shouldn't fall asleep here on his staircase. It is a useless struggle to open my eyes. As sexually-induced exhaustion overtakes me, I close them and drift off into the darkness.

Troubles

August 26, 1995

Whiners are a bit like black holes. They sit around absorbing attention from everyone around them without giving anything in return. No matter how much attention they receive, it is never enough.

Today's client is one such person. I am growing to hate him, mostly because his troubles are nowhere near as great as mine. Thomas, of course, has no idea of this. He is thoroughly enjoying having me as his captive audience.

"You feel very hurt by his actions," I reflect aloud. "How do you plan to resolve the issues in your relationship with Eric?" Inwardly I wonder why he is bothering to talk about this. His boyfriend is an alcoholic bum but for some indecipherable reason, Thomas won't throw him out.

I wish he could look at things from my perspective. If he is going to keep the boyfriend around, couldn't he at least have the decency to stop talking about him? I can't solve their problems. Judging from the number of years they have been together, no one else can either.

Nestled in the comfort of my naked body, Thomas is feeling loved, safe, and warm. Having my captured ear is too good of an opportunity for him to pass up. "If I can show him how much I love him," he continues unendingly, "he will have to change his ways. He really does love me, I can tell." Thomas looks at me almost pleadingly. He wants me to reassure him.

Silencing my inner thoughts, I force myself to smile. "Of course he loves you. He just sometimes forgets that fact." I would tell what I really think, but I have already

tried that. Thomas simply disagreed with me and continued his complaining. Now I understand that he has no interest in my opinion. He only wants to dump his troubles on me.

My thoughts grow angrier as he continues the conversation. His troubles are nothing compared to mine. I can't find a job with any of the smallest, most insignificant colleges in the country. I have over a hundred rejection letters. I could turn them into wallpaper and decorate my room. Wouldn't that be trendy? It would be a motif based on failure.

Unfortunately, there is more to my depression and anger than my career difficulties. Last night I tore Jeff's heart out when I told him I have become an escort. After several hours on the phone, he even began to cry.

"So what do you think?" Thomas asks.

I think I want to strangle him. "What I think isn't important," I reply in a neutral tone. "It's what you think that matters."

Thomas nods his head in agreement and begins babbling again. I promptly tune him out. I can't believe we finished having sex in the first thirty minutes of our two-hour appointment. Now I have to listen to him for the rest of the session.

I normally do not mind listening to my clients. They often share their most intimate secrets with me. However, I dislike listening to clients who fail to use even a slight amount of common sense to solve their problems.

Meanwhile I am upset about my own problems. I want hot sex to take my mind off my troubles, not Thomas's incessant whining. I mentally sigh to myself. At least I am being paid for this.

The thought makes me curious. I start doing the math in my head. One seventy-five for two hours is about $1.50 per minute. That's about two and a half cents per second. Somehow it doesn't seem nearly enough. Although time passes quickly, every minute seems like an hour when I listen to Thomas.

I know ignoring him is not the proper attitude for a successful callboy, but I am also aware perceptions are more important than reality. As long as Thomas doesn't realize I am ignoring him, he will think I am captivated by his every word. For all my irritation, I am too skilled to let him catch me ignoring him.

Snuggling back into the soft bed, I consider how I reached this point. For months during the summer, my parents watched me lose interest in my job search. They assumed my loss of motivation was from all the rejection letters I received. What they did not take into consideration was my overwhelming success in my newfound job as an escort.

The new pictures I had acquired were a great boost to my business. I was now routinely earning my goal of $1000 per week. In one week, I made almost $1,500. I was losing interest in college administration because I no longer wanted to leave escorting and take a fifty-percent pay cut.

Knowing none of this, my parents believed only that I was no longer seriously searching for a job. They fretted over the situation until two weeks ago. In a surprise move, they invited Jeff to move in with us. They hoped Jeff's arrival would bring me out of what they thought was my depression. After talking it over, Jeff and I decided he would move in after his sister's wedding in mid-September.

Jeff's impending move put me in a crisis. I wanted to live with him again, but I didn't want to give up escorting. I enjoyed my work far more than anything I had ever done before. At the same time, I knew Jeff would never approve of my new career. Telling him what I had done would make him feel hurt, betrayed, and disappointed in me. He would undoubtedly force me to choose between him and my new career. Life without Jeff was unimaginable. Unfortunately, the idea of returning to a "normal" job was becoming increasingly unappealing. Assuming I could even find one. My job search was still in ruins.

For weeks after my parents' offer, I clung to the hope that a small college would come to my rescue. Although

the idea of working as a hall director no longer appealed to me, I was growing desperate. I may be able to give up escorting for a residence hall job, but Jeff or no Jeff, I would never give escorting up to wait tables or work behind a cash register.

My hopes grew dimmer with each passing day as rejection letters continued to arrive. Two days ago I finally accepted that my job search had failed. There would be no job offer, no small college, and no happy ending to my summer in New Jersey. It was time to be honest about what I had been doing and wanted to do in the future.

So last night I spent three hours on the phone with Jeff. I came out to him as an escort. At least that was how I wanted to view it. In fact, the conversation was more like a confession. I admitted I had cheated on him and prostituted myself while we were living apart. Furthermore, I had lied to him numerous times to cover it up.

He was devastated. Although he had suspected I might be doing something along those lines, he had chosen to accept my word as the truth rather than question my integrity. It tore my heart to know I had irreparably damaged his trust in me. Yet I had made the decision to escort, so there was no one to blame for my lies except myself.

Jeff cried several times during the talk. He still loved me and wanted to be with me, but not at the expense of having a boyfriend that moonlighted as a callboy. In the end he gave me the expected ultimatum: the relationship or the career.

I chose the relationship. I promised I would not see any more clients, although I knew it was a promise I had no intention of keeping. I felt awful inside to know I was going to damage his trust in me yet again, but I saw no other way to keep both my career and my love life. I ended the phone call wondering if this is how the living damned feel.

Returning my thoughts to the present, I realize Thomas is looking at me. He must have asked me a question. "Sorry, Thomas, what did you say?" I recover smoothly. "I was thinking about what you said a minute ago."

"I asked if you'd ever been in a relationship with someone as confused as Eric," he repeats, oblivious to my lack of interest.

"No, I can't say that I have." I decide to give Thomas a piece of my mind. "I've never dated someone like that because I would never allow someone to treat me that badly."

Thomas raises his voice as he half-heartedly denies my accusation. "He doesn't treat me badly. He just doesn't take my needs into account sometimes."

"Oh, don't give me that. It's a lot more than that and we both know it. He ignores you constantly because he wants to go out drinking. He only calls you when he needs money to pay his bills. At least I'm up front about having sex with you for money. He is prostituting himself to you but neither of you will admit it." My eyes blaze with anger and irritation.

Thomas is silent. I realize I have struck a nerve. Maybe now he will do something about Eric

He recovers his composure and looks at me. "He doesn't prostitute himself to me. He just needs some help with his finances, and I can afford to help him out. It's my choice to do so."

I shrug my shoulders. "Okay, if you choose to stay with him, then you have to live with the consequences. There isn't anything I can do."

I realize my irritation with Thomas's whining is causing me to be unprofessional. It's not my place to tell him how to run his life. I have been hired to be nonjudgmental; to sit here, suck dick, and to stay out of his personal business. "Except be here for you if you need me to listen," I force myself to add. Irritating or not, his money is as good as anyone else's. I have a personal stake in keeping him happy. I fervently hope he will never need me to listen to his problems again. One can only take so much whining.

"Oh, you're so sweet," Thomas replies. "I appreciate knowing I can count on you when I need someone to talk to."

I smile as I begin ignoring him again. Predictably, he continues droning on.

Out of the corner of my eye, I glance at the clock. 4:17. Forty-three minutes to go.

Shifting my thoughts back to Jeff, I wonder if I can ever reconcile him with my escorting career.

Even if I can, what price will he pay? Is it fair for me to put Jeff through such pain? Early in our relationship, I had several brief affairs. After telling Jeff about them, I said he would be better off with someone who could be sexually monogamous. The roads I need to travel in life may be painful for him. Yet he chose to stay. Does that give me the right to hurt him now?

In the back of my mind, I realize I have already made my decision. I will escort for the remaining three weeks and then stop when Jeff moves in. Perhaps I can convince him to let me escort again. If not, I may sneak behind his back to do it. My work as an escort is too rewarding for me to give up easily.

I glance up at the clock. 4:22. Thirty-eight minutes left in the session. Then I begin the real countdown. Three weeks until the end of it all.

I close my eyes and try to drown out Thomas's never-ending dialogue of dependency.

Three weeks to go. God only knows what will become of me then.

Hell

June 4, 1996

Climbing into a dumpster while wearing my best suit was not exactly what I had in mind when I accepted this job. Yet here I am, filth caked all over my clothing, wading through the refuse in search of a two bottles of medication. Believe it or not, this is work. For the past six months I have been supervising a group home for retarded adults.

Reaching inside the dumpster, I shove a particularly odorous bag of garbage to the side. I spot what I am looking for, a pair of small bottles. One of my residents had thrown them out in a fit of anger. Jumping back down onto the ground, I control my irritation at the resident. I'm not allowed to become angry in my job. I have to control my emotions at all costs.

Finding the medication is just the beginning of my afternoon. The next several hours will be filled with damage control. There are phone calls to be made to assorted pharmacists, nurses, and doctors. Incident reports need to be filled out, medication routine logs need to be updated, and all staff members must be alerted. My world has come to a halt because a single resident felt I wasn't paying her enough attention. In the necessary process of solving her tantrums, I am letting the needs of eleven other residents slide.

Thinking about my day makes me bitter. The job described to me when I accepted this position was totally different than what I am doing now. I was told I would be supervising a staff of nine for a program with twelve residents. They were to be mildly retarded adults employed

in simple jobs or attending day programs. I would work afternoons and evenings to make sure everything flows perfectly.

Shortly after arriving at the Essex County Apartment Program, I realized the truth. Only six of the nine staff positions were actually filled. The program was in violation of dozens of state licensing standards. The system of keeping track of medical appointments had fallen apart resulting in the overmedication of a resident on tranquilizers for eight months. I even learned that five of the twelve residents had behavioral or psychiatric issues requiring constant attention and observation.

I spend my days at work putting out fires instead of making progress. Besides climbing into a dumpster, I also spent two hours today convincing a depressed resident to visit her psychiatrist. When that was through, I spent another hour assembling furniture for a room in violation of licensing codes. I would have delegated these tasks to my staff, but I had them working on even more important projects. In my program there are always crises.

After six months, I have grown to hate my job. I work twenty hours of unpaid overtime each week in an effort to bring the program up to code. I deal with neurotic residents, angry neighbors, families stealing welfare money from their retarded children, frustrated day program staff, and my own supervisors paradoxically telling me to work less and accomplish more. My job is highly difficult, extremely frustrating, and totally impossible.

Walking away from the dumpster, I choke back my emotions. I am far too busy to even consider becoming angry right now. I have ten hours worth of work to cram into four hours before I have to leave for a formal event. An event I may wind up attending covered with filth if I don't do something soon.

Struggling to maintain my composure, I enter the building with a forced smile on my face.

Three hours later I am slumped behind my desk with

telephone in hand. I am ready to collapse from exhaustion, but my day is far from over. I still have an hour of paperwork before it's time for one of the residents and I to leave for a choral concert.

Sitting across from me at my desk is Jeff. He drove here after work to join me for the event. We had planned on going out to dinner first, but there is no time for that now. We'll be lucky if we arrive on time.

Ignoring him for a moment, I continue talking with my supervisor. I am explaining the story of the medications and the dumpster so she will understand the paperwork when I fax it to the main office. Finishing my story, I hang up.

"You actually climbed in a dumpster?" Jeff asks in astonishment. "Why?"

"What choice did I have?" I snap back in irritation. "It would have taken even more time to replace the medications. What else was I supposed to do?"

An awkward silence falls between us. "I don't know how you can stand it," he finally admits. "I couldn't deal with it for more than a day."

"Well, unless you're prepared to let me return to my old job there is nothing I can do. We need the money."

It's an old fight and we both know it. I want to return to escorting. He doesn't like the idea. So I continue in this miserable job, hating it more with each passing day. For all my frustrations, I know I shouldn't be taking them out on Jeff. No one forced me to choose the relationship over escorting.

"I'm sorry," I apologize in a quiet tone. "I don't mean to make you feel guilty. I don't know how much longer I can go on like this. I'm working sixty hours per week. I received a poor evaluation for not accomplishing enough. My supervisors are even asking me to forge paperwork missing from before I arrived. This isn't working out the way it was supposed to."

Jeff pauses as he chooses his words carefully. "The museum called me this morning."

"That job you applied for?"

"Yes. They want me to join their education department. But there's a catch."

"That's wonderful!" I congratulate him. At least one of us may find a job we like. "What is the problem?"

"It's only part time. The job is only mornings, and isn't always five days a week."

There is a silence between us. We both understand we can't afford for Jeff to take the job. Our finances are tight enough as it is. A pay cut is out of the question.

I've been waiting for this opportunity. Perhaps I can use this to my advantage. "I think its time I'm honest with you about something," I slowly begin. "You know I love you very much and you know that you mean everything to me. We have been together almost four years and I want to spend the rest of my life with you, but you know we can't go on like this. I'm burning myself out. My hatred of my job is rapidly overcoming my love for you. If something doesn't change soon I'm going to wind up breaking up with you over this. I'll stay at ECAP if you want me to, but I'll be honest. I don't think I can do it for more than a couple of months. This is total hell, and ECAP isn't going to get any better."

Jeff takes on a serious expression as he considers my words. I realize I have backed him into a corner. He either accepts that I go back to escorting, or makes his stand and risks losing me.

"Come here, pookie," I say softly. Jeff obliges and cuddles next to me. "I don't want to sound mean about this. It can be a lot better living for us. We'll probably make more money, and you'll be able to go work at the museum. I know you don't like it at the bookstore. You'll be able to quit. I'll be able to leave ECAP and we'll have a lot more time to spend together."

Jeff looks at me and I see tears in his eyes. I know this decision is hurting him a great deal, but it is a necessary step. My life cannot continue like this.

With a sigh, Jeff nods his head in surrender. Although his answer is noncommittal, I already know what he has decided. "Let me think about it for the next day or two. If I agree to this there are going to be certain rules. You will not break those rules. Understand?"

I nod my head. Although the final negotiations remain ahead of us, the outcome is no longer in doubt. I will be leaving this hell and will go back to what I have longed to do.

The prospect frightens me. Escorting last summer was fun, but I wasn't doing it to earn a living. Now I'm talking about quitting my job and risking my financial survival on an illegal career as a male prostitute. The stakes are suddenly a lot higher.

Regardless of what happens, I am excited at the opportunity. From here on Jeff and I are making our own rules in life. The rewards and consequences are ours for the taking.

Only one question remains: how far can I go? I have no answer, but am glad Jeff and I will learn it together.

The Worst Ever

November 23, 1996

Jeff's rules are simple:

1 - No clients under twenty-five years of age.
2 - No overnight visits.
3 - Jeff is to have a way to contact me at all times.
4 - No having sex with anyone for free.
5 - No becoming emotionally involved with my clients.
6 - Our families are not to learn I am an escort.

I could add a seventh tonight. No enjoying the sex. Maybe even an eighth, no client under 5'7" may weigh less than 290 pounds.

My evening client lies on his back in the center of the bed while I straddle his chest. While this is normally a simple position for me, Jim provides an interesting challenge to my routine. His bulk is too great for me to kneel over. Instead, I have to kneel on one leg while standing on the other. Every few minutes I lose my balance and pitch forward into the head of the bed.

Unfortunately, my predicament is even more difficult. My client and I are having sex in the upstairs of a small house. Instead of the usual cubical shaped room, the slope of the roof of the house makes the room trapezoidal. Leaning against the sloped wall is difficult at best because an ornamental handkerchief hangs down into my face. Even worse, the wall has several nails sticking out of it. It is extremely difficult to avoid the nails and hold the cloth out of

my face while straddling Jim's chest. It is all I can do to manage half an erection in this position.

Although I am fully aware my lack of an erection is not my fault, I am still embarrassed. I try to stroke my cock into an erection, but Jim stops me with a muffled "mmmph." Apparently, my slightly erect dick is more than enough for him. He pulls my body close to his head knocking me against the wall again.

Suddenly $200 for two and a half hours doesn't seem like very much. I quickly do a bit of math in my head. $1.33 per minute or 2.2 cents per second. Somehow knowing that makes it seem like even less.

I glance at the clock. 7:33. Just under two hours to go. It will be an eternity in this position. I can hardly believe I have only been here for half an hour. It seems like so much longer.

Jim had asked me several days ago if I had a problem with overweight clients. "Of course not," I responded truthfully. After all, why would I? The money of a fat man is just as good as the money of a thin one. I know from experience that friendly, overweight clients are far preferable to rude, good looking ones.

I also find a twinge of excitement at my overweight clients. Not excitement at their bodies, I am not a "chubby chaser" in the slightest. I know, however, they are more likely to view my own body as being in better shape. A man who is one hundred pounds overweight will probably overlook my own love handles.

What I had not anticipated was how short Jim would be. Two hundred and ninety pounds is not necessarily bad on a man who is six feet tall, but on a 5'6" frame the bulk is amazing. I'm not sure he is only 290, either. At least he's only thirty years old. I don't think I'd be able to continue if he were also seventy. Even an escort who can sleep with "anyone" has his limits.

Outside of his weight, Jim isn't actually bad looking. He even has a cute look to him that is able to shine through.

As he sucks on my limp dick, I try to concentrate on his face instead of the nearby bald spot.

I glance at the clock again. 7:36. Another four bucks since I looked last time. I encourage myself to keep hanging in there. It isn't easy. Not only is the position uncomfortable, it's also boring. I am not very sensitive to oral sex under the best of circumstances. In this position I can barely feel anything.

Suddenly my leg cramps. Squatting in place has finally taken its toll. I adjust my position so my right leg stands while my left leg kneels on the bed. Jim opens his eyes to look, keeping me inside his mouth the entire time. I finish adjusting and begin massaging the cramp in my legs. A few moments later the tension vanishes.

A thought occurs to me. If I get Jim excited enough, perhaps he will have a heart attack. I almost giggle at the thought. No, that's a bad idea. I haven't had a client die on me yet. I'd better keep it that way. Dead clients are bad for business.

7:38. Time feels as though it is slowing down. That's an unexpected lesson I have learned. Escorting can be quite boring at times. A day like this is doubly difficult because I have to concentrate on not falling over. If I was lying on my back, I could at least think about something interesting.

With this thought in mind, I look at Jim's face between my legs. For the moment he has stopped sucking me and is stroking my cock with his hand. He seems unaware that I am not hard.

I spend the next half an hour in the same position. My mind grows increasingly bored and irritated as my legs become exhausted. As near as I can tell, he has no idea how uncomfortable this position is for me. At least I'm being paid to suffer like this.

Resigned to my current situation, my mind drifts back to how my life has changed since my discussion with Jeff. Two days after my day of hell, I turned in my resignation. I cut back on my hours and began letting tasks slide. As my

workload decreased so did my stress. I was even able to work part time as an escort during the remainder the month.

By the end of June, I had made over $2,000. July grossed almost double that, and my income increased slightly in both August and September. In October, I earned $5,610, almost three months salary at ECAP.

To my surprise, success brought a number of problems. My own sex life with Jeff diminished rapidly as I conserved sexual energy for my work. My business had also acquired a number of clients other escorts would not work for. I also discovered my rates were low enough to undercut several other escorts in the area. As a result, I now find myself working in large volumes for annoying clients for comparatively low pay.

Making money by working in bulk isn't so bad, but irritating clients are. Like Jim, many of my clients contort me into uncomfortable positions. Others pay no attention to my pleasure until the last instant when they demand I cum all over them. It isn't easy when they do this, but somehow I always manage. I masturbate furiously to produce a weak orgasm on demand. I exaggerate the intensity of the orgasm by moaning and telling them how wonderful they are in bed.

When I returned to escorting I was surprised to discover how convincing I can be. I make clients believe I am having a wonderful time with them. Doing so is often easy because I really do enjoy most of the sex. Even when I do not enjoy their efforts, I still act convincingly. I always try to remember they are paying me to make them feel good. That includes mentally as well as physically.

I enjoy sex with numerous different men. I enjoy experiencing their different styles of sex and lovemaking. Perhaps it is the psychologist in me, but I find the differences in the way they act and think to be fascinating. Even the bad clients are interesting in that regard.

I try to keep in mind that when I am with an irritating client, there is often a reason for his behavior. In Jim's case, I feel sorry for his weight. While some heavy people

are active, Jim finds it difficult to manage most sexual positions. Lying on his back and sucking my dick is about all he can do.

I look at the clock again. 8:12. One hour and eighteen minutes to go. It's time for a break.

"Hey stud. My legs are killing me. I have to take a break. Is that okay?"

Jim opens his eyes and looks at me. Spitting my limp dick out of his mouth, he replies "Okay, go ahead and sit down. You can blow me for a while."

I am not pleased with his idea of a break, but at least it will give me a moment to rest my legs. They are really hurting me.

I hop down from the bed and walk around to Jim's left side. Sitting down on the edge of the mattress, I begin to play with him. His cock is about four and a half inches, an easy size to go down on. I stroke his dick until he becomes fully erect.

Bending over I take the shaft fully in my mouth. I begin sucking it immediately. Moments later I grimace as I smell something wafting upwards. Jim's crotch and ass have an odor of sweat and other things that best remain nameless.

I turn my head so he cannot see the expression on my face. Every time I descend to the base, I get a whiff of something awful. It's not as bad as what I have smelled on other clients, but it is bad enough that I lose what little interest I have in sex. I wish he would have done what most of my clients do, and bathed thoroughly before I arrived.

I continue sucking Jim for the next few minutes. He seems oddly uninterested in what I am doing. A thought occurs to me and I stop. "Jim, have you ever cum from a blowjob before? You almost seem bored with this."

Jim stops and thinks for a moment. "No, I guess I haven't. I can't feel very much from it."

"It's all right. We don't have to do that right now. Is there something else you would like to do? Except straddle

you again. I need to give my legs a few more minutes to recover."

An odd expression comes over Jim's face. "You could fuck me. I've never done that before."

I am turned off at the idea. I am unaroused as it is. I can't imagine actually fucking him. The idea repulses me quite a bit.

I command myself to take control of my emotions. I'm a callboy, not a two-bit whore. I will overcome my distaste and give Jim a good time. I've been hired to be a stud, not to give him excuses.

"Sounds fun! I'd love to slide myself in your ass," I lie. "I just need to get myself hard. Why don't you grab the condoms and lube from my little bag?" We had left the bag downstairs. I hope a few moments alone will allow me to grow some sort of erection.

Jim grunts in agreement then sits up. As he lifts his bulk off the bed, the mattress springs noticeably upward. He takes several steps out of the room and vanishes around the corner. Footsteps slowly disappear down the stairs.

Grabbing my own dick, I begin pumping myself. I have only a few moments to get hard. Once he arrives back, he will undoubtedly do something to make it more difficult for me.

At first my body does not respond. A wave of panic hits me. What will I do if I can't get it hard? I force myself to relax. After a few moments of intense concentration, my stiffness begins to spring back to attention. The comfortable feeling of my own hand is all the help I need.

By the time Jim returns to the room, my erection is almost complete. He hands the bag to me. I unzip the top and reach inside to grab a condom and my tube of KY.

"Put this on yourself," I instruct Jim as I hand him the KY. I could have lubed him myself, but would prefer to touch his ass as little as possible.

I pull out a condom. Slipping it on, I notice my cock has begun to wilt. I rapidly stroke myself up and down.

Although it is more difficult with Jim watching me, the dwindling erection returns in full force.

"Hand me the lube and lay down on your stomach," I order him. I know the tone of my instructions is almost rude, but my ability to stay hard is limited. If I don't hurry, I won't be able to fuck him at all.

Jim complies with my instructions, handing me the lube and lying down on the bed. I squeeze a glob of KY out of the tip, then smear it up and down my latex-enclosed shaft. I lift myself up and prepare to straddle Jim's ass. It looks huge and imposing.

Holding my dick at the base, I begin sinking into him. I'm not exactly sure where the hole is but I probe as best I can. Fortunately, there is no need to probe for long. My dick finds the entrance to his ass and slowly penetrates the surface. Jim continues to lie there, seemingly unaware of my actions. He must be feeling this but he isn't responding at all.

"Are you okay? Does this feel all right?"

"Yeah," he replies, "just take it slowly. It feels like I have to go to the bathroom or something."

It occurs to me that Jim might not be aware that bottoms should always "empty themselves" an hour before they have sex. I hope he doesn't really have to go, or this may be my worst sexual experience ever. It's already pretty close.

The penetrating continues until my thighs reach the surface of his ass. His butt is simply too big to push in any farther. I am barely in him, perhaps only three or four inches of my length, but it's the best I can manage. The rest of my cock is needed to reach through the layers of flesh.

I begin bouncing up and down on his ass, sliding in and out of him rapidly. Between the condom, Jim's wide ass, and the lack of any sensation in my own dick, it is all I can do to maintain half of my erection. I begin recalling my hottest sexual experiences in an effort to excite me.

I remember the time I had a four-way in a bathhouse in Indianapolis. I fantasize about the two lovers I met in

Boston who passed my ass back and forth for hours. I even recall in vivid detail the way my college roommate would fuck me on the couch in our living room. Nothing seems to help.

Eventually I stop worrying about staying hard. If I can't help losing my erection, there is no sense in stressing myself over it.

I continue to fuck Jim with my half-hard dick for the next few minutes. Eventually the inevitable happens and I slide out. Having a sudden inspiration, I ask Jim, "would you like to fuck me?"

He considers the question for a moment before he replies, "okay."

Jim turns over and lies on his back while I pull the condom off my dick and fling it onto the floor. Jim can clean it up later. I grab another packet out of my black bag and rip the top off it. I unroll it on Jim's cock until it touches the base. I squeeze another glob of KY out of the tube. I slide the lube up and down until it coats the entire surface of the rubber. I smear the remaining lubricant on my hand across the center of my ass.

Standing over Jim's crotch, I slowly lower myself onto his awaiting manhood. I realize I will have the same problem in this position as I had on his chest, he is simply too large for me to kneel over. I'll have to manage as best I can. I squat down on one knee as I feel him slide into me.

I begin moving myself up and down. It works for a moment, but suddenly I feel Jim slide out of my ass. I reach down and grab his dick so I can slide down, but I realize he is losing his erection as well. That's the danger of small dicks and condoms, if they lose their erections they become too small to stay inside someone's ass. This appears to be the fate Jim is headed for tonight.

I delay the end as long as I can by taking him back within my ass. By using shorter strokes, I hold him within me for another two minutes before he slides out a second time. This time he is not hard enough to even try again.

Jim looks up at me with dim comprehension on his face. "I think I've gone down a little bit. Get it hard and put it back in."

I stare at Jim in mute surprise. Doesn't he realize that I can't magically give him an erection. Telling me to "get it up" is not a solution.

"Why don't you stroke it with your hand?" I suggest in a patient tone. "You know your body better than I do, so you'll be able to get extra hard." I feel proud at the way I handled the situation. Now it's his responsibility to manage an erection. If he can't get it up, he can't blame it on me.

Sure enough, he isn't able to. "I guess I can't do it with the condom on, sorry." He is very embarrassed, as if his masculinity has been wounded.

"Don't worry, I have the same problem sometimes," I comfort him. "It's hard to do it in this position, and the condoms don't help. It's not your fault."

My words appear to reassure him somewhat. "Come up here," he instructs me. He indicates he wants me to straddle his chest again.

I scoot up on the bed and squat down over his upper chest. I feel the mild sensation of warmth around my dick as we return to our familiar uncomfortable position.

I glance at the clock. 8:34. Fifty-six minutes to go.

Jim looks happier now that he is sucking my cock again. He really does prefer sucking to anything else we do. I wouldn't mind too badly, but the damn handkerchief is still in my face and I keep scratching my arms on the nails in the wall. Still, Jim is the customer. I always give the customer what he wants.

I become increasingly irritated over the next thirty minutes. The position does nothing for me except strain my legs. I lose my erection frequently, only managing to bring it back up halfway with the few strokes Jim allows me to take before he grabs it back. Wave after wave of irritation crosses me.

There has to be a better way. Dealing with clients like this is simply not worth it. I am working almost every

day now. There must be a way I can weed out the clients who aren't worth the money.

Sudden inspiration fills my mind. I could raise my rates for new clients. Instead of charging $125 for the first hour, $50 for every hour after that, I could charge more. Like $150 for the first hour and $75 for every hour after that. On a night like tonight I wouldn't be going home with $200, I would be going home with over $250. That would make this evening far more bearable. This is a good time to raise rates in any case, because I'm about to expand into print advertisements.

I feel content for the first time all evening. I am still contorted in an awkward position while Jim sucks my limp dick, but I no longer feel the pain in my legs. I am excited at the prospect of expanding my business.

I glance at the clock. 9:02. The evening is beginning to end. In a few minutes I will make Jim let us both have our orgasms. I can't wait until I get home and tell Jeff about my idea.

This evening has been the worst sex I have ever had in my life, but in the end it turned out for the best. With a bit of luck, Jim will soon be paying me enough to make him worth my while. It's my first price hike, and I am excited at the thought. Like when I decided to resign from ECAP, I wonder how far my career will go.

Working Vacation

March 23, 1997

I don't recall his name if he ever told it to me.

I am sitting on a barstool in the back of the 825, a popular hustler bar in Fort Lauderdale. Go-go dancers strip to the rhythm of the music while hustlers work the bar in search of their evening tricks. There is little else to do. All that matters here is buying and selling. I am selling and the nameless stranger is buying.

"So what brings you here tonight?" he asks.

"I'm on vacation." In an effort to be obvious of my intentions, I continue, "I do this back home in Jersey, although not in bars."

"You're an escort?" he asks with some surprise.

"Yes. I started after I graduated from college. I do it for a living now."

"Oh really! That's very interesting," he says surprised. "How do you meet your clients? If not from bars, do you find them from ads or do you work for an agency?"

"I've never worked for an agency. Agencies take too much money. I find some of my clients through print ads. The rest I find on the Internet."

"You mean over the computer?" he questions in an astonished tone. "I don't know anything about computers and modems and all that stuff."

"That's okay, I do. So what bring you out tonight?"

He pauses before he answers in an embarrassed tone. "I have a lover of many years. I love him a lot but we don't have as much sex as we used to. So, I come out here to look at the dancing boys. I never touch them, I swear."

"It's quite all right, you don't have to justify yourself to me," I reassure him. "It doesn't affect your relationship with your lover if you come here and meet with the occasional dancer or hustler. You still love him either way."

He appears relieved at my understanding. "I did hire one guy once, but I didn't have a very good time. He was very beautiful but wasn't very smart. He acted like he only wanted to get my money and leave. I don't know what ever happened to him."

"You're probably right," I agree. "He most likely only wanted your money. Most of the guys around here look like they are in search of a quick buck. That's why I do so well back home. I'm not like that. I care about my clients so they treat me well in return."

He pauses again. "How much would you, umm, charge?" he asks.

I have no idea what to say. If I answer too little, I risk giving my services away. If I ask too much, I could lose the sale. I decide to be evasive. "What are you looking for?"

Before he has the chance to speak, I notice a well-muscled man playing pool while looking at me. He is quite attractive so I smile at him. I make a mental note to introduce myself later.

I return my gaze to my companion, but he is already speaking. "...Want to blow you and maybe have you do me. I know a place we can drive to that isn't far. My truck is parked outside."

"What is the going rate around here?"

"I think it is about $75 or $80. You could charge more like $100 or $125. I'll be honest though, I only have $80 with me."

I look the man up and down. I had wanted more than $80, but I was here more for fun than money. Not to mention he isn't bad looking. He is a tall and slender man in his early forties. He is clean-shaven and has interesting brown eyes. Most importantly, he has the look of intelligence in his eyes that I like. I make my decision. "Okay, $80 is fine. Shall we go?"

"In a moment, let me go to the bathroom first. I'll be back in a second." He walks away while I wait at the bar.

I sip my drink and look around the bar. Nothing has changed. The hustlers are still hustling while the dancers show their stuff.

A hand taps me on the shoulder. "Are you busy?" the attractive man from the pool table asks.

"Actually, umm, yeah," I regretfully pause. "I have to leave in a minute. But I'll be back in an hour or so."

He appears disappointed. "Well, come and find me when you get back. I'd like to talk to you about something mutually beneficial for both of us."

"You bet," I grin. "I'll find you as soon as I return. Oh, and don't worry, I'll be ready for you."

"Great! See you then." He turns and walks back to the pool table.

Moments later my companion returns. "Shall we go?"

He escorts me out to his truck. I almost laugh when I see it. It's one of those butch trucks that rides way up off the ground. The metal gleams and shines, while the tinted windows dimly reflect the parking lot. We can fuck all night inside this truck and no one will know what we're doing.

A chilling thought occurs to me. He could also murder me and no one would see a thing. I push the thought from my mind as I open the side door.

"Sorry I can't take you to my place," my companion apologizes as he starts driving. "My lover is home. I'd take you to a motel but I don't want to have to pay for the room. I'd rather spend the money on you. So I'm going to take you to a nice secluded place."

I say nothing as he talks. I already know where this is going. He's going to need to talk about himself and his life. I've heard his story many times before.

My mind drifts as we drive toward our destination. It's amazing how I arrived here this evening. Just three days ago Jeff and I were ready to kill each other.

We have been vacationing in Florida for the past six days. Moments after our arrival, we began fighting about sex. I wanted to make this a wild vacation for the two of us to "sow our wild oats" together. Jeff wanted a peaceful monogamous vacation without any sexual pressure from outside. As a result, we had been fighting nonstop and making each other miserable.

We tried to negotiate a compromise, but every time I found someone attractive to join us in a three-way, Jeff rejected the person on some trivial issue. It wasn't long before we stopped trying.

We finally made up earlier today. Jeff agreed to stay back in our hotel room while I went out to the 825. In return, I'd only stay for an hour or two then spend the rest of the vacation peacefully with him.

So here I am. I haven't cum in six days and I am extremely horny.

I almost laugh when my companion pulls into his secluded area. It is the middle of a parking lot of a large apartment building. He explains to me that by parking in a lot full of cars our presence will go unnoticed, whereas parking on an empty street might attract unwanted attention. I am not sure I agree with his logic, but it's not worth arguing over.

My thoughts scatter as I feel the nameless stranger run his hands all over me. He has unbuckled his seat belt and reached across the front seat of the truck. Grabbing the top of my pants, he unbuttons them with an almost animal insistence.

I reach my own hands down to assist him in his efforts. Within moments my shorts are around my knees and my shirt is on the floor. He touches my chest, my legs, my dick, and my balls. I am flushed with the forbidden excitement of sex in such a public place. Dimly I wonder where the hustlers hang out in New York City. I may have to try this more often.

He leans over and lowers his face into my crotch. The feeling is incredible. Although being sucked off usu-

ally bores me, tonight I am surprisingly into it. Six days of abstinence have left my body hypersensitive and hormonal.

I enjoy the sucking, but I realize there is still no way I will be able to cum from it. He senses a bit of hesitation on my part and looks at me quizzically. "Sorry," I reply, "I love this but I know I won't be able to cum from it."

He slips one hand underneath my balls and cups them as he begins jacking me off. Instantly a moan escapes my lips. He continues to jack me, slowly speeding up the pace of his strokes. The sounds escaping my lips increase in volume as I feel the tension build in my balls. I want to yell with pleasure, but I am afraid the sound will travel.

The fire in my balls reaches a peak. I arch my back as I feel cum begin rushing from me. Instantly his mouth descends on my shaft. He sucks the gooey warmth from my cock before it can land on the seat of his truck. I giggle slightly as I realize the practicality of his action.

I barely have time to lean back in my seat before he speaks. "Would you suck me off?"

"Sure!" I reply with more enthusiasm than I feel. Now that my excitement is dwindling, I am remembering the money again. Eighty bucks is far less than I should be getting paid, but I might as well get it over with.

The steering wheel is partially in the way so I unbutton his pants and slide them down while aiming his body off to the side. I have time for ten, perhaps twenty strokes before he loses his control and fills my mouth with gushing cum. I swallow it all, conscious of the mess it would make in his truck.

Finished, I lean back and look at the expression on his face. I see embarrassment, but no guilt. I am glad. I hate it when my clients feel guilty.

He pulls his pants back on and immediately begins driving me back to the bar. "Thank you," he tells me. I expect him to continue talking but he falls silent. I am unsure what to say in return so we continue the drive back in silence.

He stops his truck halfway down the block from the bar. Pulling out his wallet, he is embarrassed to discover he only has $77. "I'm so sorry," he apologizes. "I forgot I bought a drink. I didn't mean to cheat you."

"It's okay," I reassure him. I was hustling more for fun than the money. He is grateful I do not make an issue of the missing money.

"Do you mind if I drop you off here? That way no one will know you were with me. They'll all know otherwise."

"Sure, its okay." He gives me a kiss before I exit the truck. I watch his brake lights flash once before he turns the corner. He vanishes from sight and is gone.

As I walk back to the bar, I notice three hustlers in their late twenties sitting on the curb. "Oh, honey, you're walking the walk of shame!" one calls out. "Don't we know it well!" another yells. They laugh drunkenly as I pass them by.

I laugh with them until a thought occurs to me. Will I end up like them? Will I drink myself into oblivion as I watch younger and prettier boys pass me by?

I shudder for a moment then continue my walk back into the bar.

High Society

March 18, 1997

A few months ago my friend Jason called me. We have been friends since we were children and over the years I have come to rely on his advice and insight. Although he is straight and doesn't understand all the specifics of the gay community, he has a sharp mind that often challenges me to increase the effectiveness of my own business.

"I've been thinking," Jason began. "Many of the most successful businesses sell cheaply to many, but in your business you can't do that to any great extent. Therefore, it would seem advantageous to cater to a more upscale clientele. By increasing the income level of your clientele, you should be able to make more money by working less."

Although I was not certain Jason's approach was the right one for me, I agreed that catering to an upscale market was worth a bit of research. Unfortunately, I was unsure how to enter this sort of market. I am intelligent and educated, but I am also aware of my limited ability to interact in formal circles. I can't bring myself to spend money on anything but the most basic clothing styles, much less expensive colognes and fine wines. Words like Armani, Cartier, or Versace scarcely exist in my vocabulary, and certainly do not exist in my wardrobe. I am as impressed by a thousand-dollar suit as by a cheap one.

It is an interesting statement of my values. I earn hundreds of dollars in a single night, but drive miles out of my way to avoid a thirty-five cent toll on the way home. My thriftiness can be seen in my small apartment, J.C. Penny wardrobe, and non-existent wine rack.

With all of this in the back of my mind, I stand on the steps of the Townhouse, New York's most upscale gay bar. Do I have what it takes to dabble in high society? I fully intend to find out.

The inside is unlike any gay bar I have ever seen. Decorative vases sit on end tables next to expensive couches. Chairs rest on a floor covered with expensive carpeting. Music that might have been popular two decades ago flows through the speakers, almost masking the sound of a piano in another room. The sound of gay men singing showtunes echoes from the back.

The clientele of the Townhouse is equally different, consisting mostly of upscale professionals of varying ages. Here and there in the crowd I spot a younger man, many of them obviously plying the same trade as myself. By the looks of the patrons, they come here to socialize, sing, drink, forget, and cruise for new meat. Heads turn as I walk into the room. I realize I am that new meat.

Lounging seductively near the bar are several other young men. A dark-haired, European boy in his early twenties wears a leather jacket. Another young man flirts outrageously with an older gentleman. Still another leans against a doorway with his hand suggestively close to his crotch. This is hustler territory. It wouldn't be any more obvious if there were neon signs.

I make my first enemy within five minutes - the boy with his hand on his crotch. The young hustler had been checking out an older gentleman in a maroon sweater on the other side of the bar. The gentleman appeared to be interested in him, but changed his mind when he noticed me. The gentleman stares at me for a moment before politely introducing himself.

"I'm George. Can I buy you a drink?" he asks.

"Sure," I reply. "I'll have a Sprite." I immediately regret my order. I should have ordered a glass of wine so I would look upscale.

Then again, what would I have asked for? I have had perhaps two glasses of wine in my life and know literally

nothing about ordering them. I would have hated making a fool of myself by ordering something in appropriate.

George begins talking about himself. I pretend to listen to him while I take in more of the atmosphere. Out of the corner of my eye, I notice the young hustler glaring at me. I hope I didn't step on his toes too badly. I am hustling in unfamiliar territory. I have no idea how things are done here.

The drinks arrive as George and I continue to chat. I force myself to listen attentively although he is quite boring. I learn he is a professional of some sort on vacation in New York to attend the theater. He talks while I politely nod, answer his questions, and touch his arm flirtatiously. I want him to know my interest in being here, but not so obviously I look like a cheap whore.

Soon the conversation shifts to what I do for a living. I pause for a moment, considering how to explain myself. "I, ahhh, entertain people for a living," I finally answer. He appears confused for a moment then grins in understanding.

"How much do you charge? Not that I'm looking to hire you, I'm just… curious," he says.

I decide to tell him the truth. "To be honest I'm new to the Townhouse. I don't know the going rate here."

"Hmmm," he says looking me over. "I would think you could ask $120."

"That would be acceptable," I answer. I silently berate myself for making such an obvious mistake. I should never have accepted his initial offer. Had I negotiated, I would have almost certainly made more.

We chat for a few more minutes before George puts his arm around me. "Would you like to go for a walk?" he asks.

"Sure. It's stuffy in here," I reply.

We walk downstairs so George can retrieve his jacket from the coatroom. As we walk out the door from the Townhouse, George suggests we walk to his hotel. I wonder which one he is staying in. The Plaza? The Four Seasons? Perhaps even the Waldorf. Would he be in a luxury

suite or a penthouse room? I am filled with excitement as we walk together.

As we arrive at his hotel, I feel my dreams of high society crash around me. His hotel is scarcely a step above a sleazy by-the-hour joint. There are no luxury suites, no waiters with bottles of champagne, and no romantic hot tubs for two. There is only a dumpy businessman, a naïve hustler, and a hotel in dire need of repairs.

The room is one of the smallest I have ever seen in a hotel. It is barely the size of my bedroom. The bed takes up most of what little space there is. I vainly try to control my dismay as I survey the room. It's not a lot different from the room in which I was first paid for sex, but somehow this seems a lot worse. As George slides his arms around me and begins kissing my neck, I feel an intense wave of disgust. For the first time since I began escorting, I feel cheap, dirty, and used.

I find the sex between us to be unrewarding and unenjoyable. It is difficult to enjoy George's touch knowing I am making less money than I would have made at home. The money situation is even worse when I add in parking and tolls. I hope I can find enough business back at the Townhouse to prevent the evening from being a total disaster.

Knowing none of my thoughts and feelings, George enjoys our time together immensely. Even in my lowest moments, I am too professional to give poor quality service. I whisper to George how wonderful he makes me feel. In the beginning I find it difficult to lie, but it becomes easier as time goes on. I want to get it over with and leave.

I wipe the cum off me as soon as we are finished. Standing up, I begin reaching for my clothes. George stops me and gives me a big hug. "You are so wonderful," he whispers in my ear. "I can't tell you how much I am looking forward to the rest of our night together."

My jaw drops in shock and horror. He's out of his mind if he thinks I'm going to spend the rest of the night

with him. I should have clarified our length of time together. I feel like smacking myself for my stupidity.

"Ummm, George," I begin, "I'm not spending the rest of the night here. At least not for what we agreed on."

George is confused. "What do you mean? Where do you have to go?"

"Back to the bar. Our time is up."

"But I don't understand. You said you would spend the night with me--"

"No, I said I would come back here with you. We never agreed how long we would be together," I pause for a moment. "Do you know what I charge normally?"

He looks at me sadly. "No, what?"

"These days, I charge $160 for the first hour, and $100 for every hour after that. For overnight visits, I charge $500. I used to charge less, but my business has grown enough I've raised my rates twice."

He whistles in amazement. "That's a lot."

"It's nothing compared to what I plan to charge someday. Anyway, I'm sorry we had this misunderstanding. You really are a very sweet person. But this is how I make my living."

George nods his head in understanding. "You're right, I'm sorry. I guess we didn't understand each other. I'll pay you the money."

I feel like I've kicked him in the face. I hope I haven't ruined his evening. Of course he has unintentionally ruined mine. I was hoping for something exotic, not this dump.

I reach for my clothes again and begin dressing myself. This time George does not stop me. Still looking sad, he hands me a wad of bills. I shove them in my pocket. "If it's any consolation, it was still worth it," he tells me. "You are really sexy."

I silently agree with him. I'm down to 132 pounds. I haven't looked this good in years.

As we walk back to the Townhouse, I realize George wanted the illusion where a young hustler was so enthralled

with him that he would stay the entire night. I console myself knowing George would be far less happy if he knew how most escorts would have treated him. I was much nicer to him than most would have been. Still, it was a sad encounter. Neither of us achieved our dreams.

I rejoin the fun back at the Townhouse. During the next two hours, I meet several interesting people. Keith is a college professor who says he would love to take me home. After I politely explain I'm a callboy, he declares angrily, "I should have known," and walks off in a huff.

Eric is a cute Italian graduate student from Philadelphia in town for the weekend. He invites back to his hotel, but I gently turn him down. I'd rather not be cheating on Jeff on my first night at the Townhouse. He's not thrilled I am here in the first place, and I don't want to make it any worse.

I briefly hope the third person might be interested in hiring me. Jack is an attractive man in his late thirties who tells me repeatedly how attractive I am. Everything seems to be perfect. Until we broach the subject of money. He hesitantly offers me $50 to come back with him. When I make a counteroffer of $125, he chokes and turns me down in a flash.

I never learn the name of the fourth person. He's drunk and asks me if I'm looking to be picked up. When I admit I am hoping for that, he grabs me and lifts up off the floor. He shakes me in the air and asks me if I'm having a good time. When he sets me back on the ground, I disappear into the crowd as fast as I can.

Escaping from the drunken idiot, I need a moment to think. I find the men's room and park myself in a stall. I close my eyes and try to relax. Two hours of hustling and not a single lead. This isn't like the 825 where the men were practically fighting over me. I have seen several hustlers around the bar, so there must be a market here. My problem is that I don't know how to tap into it.

After thinking for another moment, an idea occurs to me. I'll stop talking to anyone who doesn't look like a rich

"daddy" type. Perhaps that will be a more effective way of finding clients.

My new plan does have some merit. I need to increase the efficiency of screening potential clients. On the Internet, I can even conduct five or six conversations with potential clients at once. Compared to that, hustling in a bar is highly inefficient, especially when I spend precious time talking to people that are not interested in paying for sex.

Convinced my idea has merit, I return to the bar to try again. A few minutes later a well-dressed man in his early sixties strikes up a conversation with me.

"I'm Curtis," he introduces himself warmly.

"I'm Aaron," I reply shaking his hand.

After a few minutes of pleasantries, he begins talking about me. "You are very cute. I noticed you earlier this evening. You seemed to be having some trouble with a rather drunk admirer."

I giggle boyishly. "He was a bit literal in the way he tried to pick me up. I prefer it when men are figurative in their approach," I reply humorously.

"So tell me, Aaron. What brings you out this evening?" he inquires.

After thinking for a moment, I decide to claim I'm a college student. "A Friday evening in the city was too appealing of an idea to spend studying, so I came in here to the city to see what was going on. To be honest, I sometimes come to the Townhouse when I have overdue bills. The people here are often very generous when it comes to helping out with my education."

Curtis's eyes sparkle in comprehension. "I understand exactly what you mean. There are a number of young men who come here for the same reason. Of all of them, you were the only one who interested me. You have a very natural and refreshing look about you."

I blush slightly, keeping in line with the boyish image I have created for myself. I pause innocently, as if unsure what to say.

"I have a house up in Saratoga Springs," Curtis continues, "that I would love for you to come see. When I come to New York City I stay with friends, otherwise I would invite you back with me tonight."

I am not particularly interested in traveling to his home, so I decide to stop his invitation before he takes the idea too seriously. "Oh, I couldn't travel there because I'm still in school. On breaks I go home to my parents' house."

"Certainly you could come visit me. I would take very good care of you and make it worth your while. Did you know I helped my last lover become a Calvin Klein model?" Curtis continues on, telling me a story about his former lover and a photo shoot on the beaches of Italy.

I am not sure what to make of Curtis. I can tell from his appearance that he has money, but I have no idea if his stories are true or not. I know I tend to trust people and can easily be fooled by a good storyteller.

As I begin to sort out my thoughts, I realize Curtis has continued on to another subject.

"...Working for Governor Pataki of New York on several of his state committees. I am one of the premier psychiatrists in the state, you know."

"I hadn't known that. You must really be important!" I reply in mock astonishment.

A few moments later the conversation takes a turn for the worse. "If you came and lived with me in Saratoga Springs, I would love to expose you to cultural experiences like the ballet, the opera, art, and the theater. I am sure you would come to love all those things."

I try to keep myself from gagging on his overbearing personality. I can't stand most traditional cultural experiences. Spending an afternoon at a museum is not my idea of a good time.

"I would love to take you shopping, too. You are wearing nice clothes, but they are nothing compared to what I could buy for you in Paris. Have you ever been there? We could fly first class."

"No," I am forced to admit. "I've never been to Europe. I've always wanted to go but have never had the money." I hope he notices my hint and makes me an offer. I'd be willing to deal with the opera if it meant making thousands of dollars in the process.

"You would be so adorable in Paris," he continues. "If you are serious about wanting to go to Europe, then perhaps we should talk about you moving in with me. You can always transfer to a school in New York State."

I recoil in horror. This is not what I want out of him. It is time to terminate our conversation. "Curtis," I begin. "I have to tell you something and you're not going to like it."

"What is it, my dear boy?" he asks in a concerned tone.

Holding back an urge to throttle the overbearing fool, I begin explaining the truth. "My name isn't Aaron, and I'm not a twenty-two year-old college student hustling his way through college. I'm twenty-six and I have my graduate degree. I'm a professional callboy and have had a boyfriend for over four years."

Curtis stares at me in muted shock.

"Aaron is simply the professional persona I assume while I am working," I continue. "Essentially everyone in the sex industry uses a fake name and identity to protect their privacy and safety. In using a persona, I often leave much of my own personality behind. I adapt to the needs of those around me. You have fallen for me because I instinctively responded to your own needs. I apologize for leading you on, but it would be inappropriate for me to continue this charade."

The expression on Curtis's face turns from shock to anger. "I would be negligent if I did not point out a few things to you," he begins warning me. "What you are doing is psychologically extremely dangerous. Your double-life is inherently damaging and will in the end bring you to the point of self-destruction."

He continues lecturing me for several minutes, pausing only to belittle the lifestyle I have chosen. "You could be so much to someone like me. I would have taken you places and given you experiences you cannot even begin to appreciate right now. Of course, I cannot do it now. You already have your little boyfriend. You disappoint me, Aaron or whoever you are. You could have been so much more than a worthless prostitute."

His final insult makes me snap. "Curtis, I really have no interest in listening to you judge my behavior, my life, and my values. I think you badly underestimate how little I care about your opinion.

"Besides," I add, "right now you are upset and angry because I rejected you. Your allegedly professional opinion is open to extreme personal bias, wouldn't you say?"

Curtis' eyes flash with anger. "I am fully able to make a professional judgement about the way you are living your life. You cannot imagine what you are doing to yourself. The danger you are putting--"

I never hear him finish. I walk away, leaving him spluttering and fuming to himself. Curtis is a perfect example of why I call myself Aaron. I meet too many unstable people to consider doing otherwise.

I walk up the stairs from the lounge to the main bar. Hailing a passing waiter, I order myself another Sprite.

Someone bumps into me from behind. "Watch it!" I snarl in irritation.

"Sorry!" a surprised voice apologizes.

I turn around and locate the speaker. He is somewhat different from the rest of the people at the Townhouse. His jeans and t-shirt do not belong in this semi-formal atmosphere. A slightly unkempt beard emerges from a smiling face.

"I'm Tony," he introduces himself while offering his hand.

"I'm Aaron." I take his hand and shake it firmly. "Sorry about snapping at you. Someone pissed me off a few minutes ago. I didn't mean to take it out on you."

"Never get mad in a bar. It's not worth it," he advises me.

I nod my head in agreement. "Sound advice."

"What did he do to make you so mad?" my new friend inquires.

I think for a moment and decide to tell the truth. "I'm a callboy. I was talking to some rich guy downstairs who looked like he might hire me. Instead of hiring me, he goes on and on about how much he wants to take me to the opera to 'culture' me. When he asked me to move in with him, I thought it was time to explain a few facts of life to him. He didn't appreciate me doing so, and said some things that irritated me."

Tony begins to grin. "Sounds like you should have let him finish his tirade, then given him a bill for your time," he jokes. We both start laughing.

It feels good to laugh. It makes me realize another mistake for the evening. Never let anyone upset me. Tony is right, it's not worth it.

The waiter returns with the drink I ordered. Tony immediately pays for it. "I'm only a college librarian, so I don't have enough money to hire a cute boy like yourself, but at least I can buy you a drink."

His candor makes me smile. "So why were you talking to the jerk in the first place?" he continues. "He hardly seems like the type of person you should be associating with."

I briefly describe my telephone conversation with my friend Jason. "I'm trying to cater to an upscale clientele instead of my usual hi-tech hustling. It's certainly different than what I am used to."

"With all due respect," Tony cautions me. "Your friend gave you an incorrect strategy. You should not be trying to market yourself to an upper-class crowd of people like Curtis. You are a middle-class person with middle-class values. Your business would be best served by catering to people with the same values and interests as yourself.

Middle-class people are the ones who will hire you repeatedly.

"Making a few hundred bucks in a single night here at the Townhouse will be nice, but is nothing when you compare it to a middle-class client who may spend thousands of dollars on you over the course of a year or two. By not hustling, you will save considerable time as well as lessen your legal and safety risks."

I realize that much of what Tony says is correct. Although leaving the Townhouse with a small fortune would have been nice, the benefits of developing a steady clientele far outweigh the occasional rich daddy. If I'm going to play at the Townhouse, I should do it for fun, not for profit.

Driving home an hour later, I have much to think about. By the time I arrive home, my mind has cleared enough to look at the evening in perspective. I only made $120, but I learned several new lessons along the way. Not bad for an evening's work.

Hitting the Jackpot

April 11, 1997

I gently place my hand on Keith's arm. He is exactly the type of client I like: charming, witty, handsome, wealthy, and horny. I am not about to let him get away. This time I have hit the jackpot.

I'm in the Townhouse yet again. Now that I've stopped worrying about money, I'm having a lot more fun. I've even met several attractive men in search of young male companions like myself. The one I'm talking to now is definitely a real prize.

"Would you like to go to dinner, Aaron? There's a great restaurant down the block."

I am tempted to accept immediately, but doing so may be a mistake. If I agree to join him without determining a price, I risk returning home with a fraction of what I may earn elsewhere. On the other hand, I don't want to appear ungrateful at his offer. "I'm interested, but I was expecting to meet a friend here this evening who was going to… give me some money he owes me," I explain. "If I go out to dinner with you, I may miss him. Otherwise I would love to join you." I hope I have addressed the issue tactfully.

"How much does your… friend owe you?" he inquires with a smile.

"If I stayed here I would probably go home with $500," I reply. "I would gladly go with you for the evening if I thought I could somehow go home with that much." I have never made that much in an evening at the Townhouse, although I did go home the week before with $400. I

don't always make a lot of money here, but I return because hustling is a welcome change from the normal routine of waiting for my phone to ring.

"I'm certain it will be worth your while to join me."

"In which case I would be glad to join you for dinner. Shall we gather our coats?" I ask while giving his arm a flirtatious squeeze.

A moment later we depart the bar. The doorman bids the two of us good-bye while giving me a quick wink. He knows perfectly well what transaction has occurred.

Keith and I walk to the restaurant he has picked out. I notice it is also called the Townhouse. The same people must own it. "The food is excellent here," he explains. "I eat here whenever I am in the city."

"I've never been here before, but I've always wanted to try it," I lie pleasantly. I hadn't known the restaurant existed until we arrived.

I find the atmosphere of the restaurant refreshing. It is like most other nice restaurants in the city, except the clientele and wait staff are male and gay. I feel very much at home here.

The maitre d' seats us in a dimly lit corner in the back. Pulling out a box of matches, he lights a candle in the center of the table. Keith orders a glass of wine for himself. I almost order a glass as well, but decide to maintain my youthful image. I order a Sprite and smile innocently. Keith seems pleased.

After we order dinner, Keith begins asking me about myself. I decide to be creative with my answers to prevent him from guessing I'm a full-time callboy. "I'm a student at Rutgers. I do this to support my education because I don't receive very much support from home."

"Interesting," Keith says. "Do you work very often at this?"

"Oh, a few times a week," I reply vaguely. "It's what I have to do to pay for school. Since a lot of guys like a boyish kid like me, I do well."

"I can see why," Keith says with a smile. Reaching across the table he takes my hand. "I can certainly see why."

We talk about a variety of subjects over dinner. I am careful to lead the conversation away from my escorting. I do not want to accidentally slip and reveal the truth.

As dinner comes to a close, Keith excuses himself for a moment. Curiously, I pick up the check. Scanning down the receipt, I notice the dinner cost him over $80. Maybe there is something to this high society thing. I cringe every time I spend over $30 for dinner.

Keith returns to the table. "Shall we go?" he asks.

"After you," I respond deferentially, and follow him from the restaurant.

As we walk down the block, Keith speaks up. "With your permission I would like to take a little excursion before we go back to the hotel."

"I'm not in a hurry. Where to?"

"It's a surprise. Come on, I'll hail a cab. It's not far, but I'd rather not walk."

I feel excited as I follow Keith. Is he taking me shopping? A few of my clients have given me gifts before, usually sexy underwear to wear for them. One gave me a few books he thought I might enjoy reading. None of them have ever taken me shopping. A thrill passes through me. How much would he spend?

A cab pulls up next to me and we step inside. Sitting on the plastic seat, I wait to hear Keith's instructions. "Central Park South," he says to the driver. A wave of disappointment passes through me. He's not taking me shopping. We're only going for a carriage ride.

Once I console myself to the fact I am not going shopping, I begin to wonder why he chose a carriage ride. The night air is quite chilly. A carriage ride would be one of the last activities I would want if I had an attractive young man with me. Perhaps he has something else on his mind, like wanting to add a bit of romance to our evening together.

The cab begins to slow down. As I suspected he would, Keith requests the driver drop us off next to the carriage stand.

Taking my hand, Keith assists me into the lead carriage. "The long ride," he instructs the driver while handing him a wad of bills. He climbs into the carriage and pulls a blanket across us.

I find the carriage ride pleasant if a bit cold. I nestle into the curve of Keith's body to stay warm. He wraps his arms around me and holds me close. We ride together in silence enjoying the moment together.

Eventually my curiosity gets the better of me. "Where are you staying?"

"Oh, the Waldorf-Astoria. I always stay there."

I am elated at his answer. I was at the Waldorf once for afternoon dessert during a family gathering. I remember being stunned that they charged twelve dollars for a small pot of hot chocolate. If Keith can afford to stay in that hotel, he must be quite well off.

"When is the last time you were with someone intimately?" I inquire as the carriage rounds a curve in the road.

Keith pauses awkwardly before responding. "About eight hours ago."

I stare at him in shock. "You're kidding, right?"

The expression on Keith's face becomes one of embarrassment. "Nope, I'm serious."

"Who?" I ask before I can stop myself. "I mean not that it's any of my business, but I've asked that question before and never received an answer like that."

"To be honest, I was at a bar in the Village earlier today when a hustler approached me. I found him quite attractive and he managed to intrigue me, so I bought him lunch. We talked for a while and then I offered to take him back to my hotel. I guess I did it because I wanted to see the expression on his face when I told him what I was willing to pay him. I offered him a few hundred dollars for an hour."

Several hundred dollars for an hour! I am elated. "That's a lot of money."

"I know."

In my mind I find it difficult to get past the issue of money. If he paid that much to a street hustler, he is certain to pay me well.

The carriage ride slowly continues through the park. Eventually we approach the end of the ride. Keith hops out of the chair, and in his usual gentlemanly fashion extends his hand to me. I climb down with his assistance. He holds my hand as we walk toward a nearby taxi. "To the Waldorf," he says, and we are off.

Moments later we arrive. Keith leads me through an opulently furnished hallway to a small elevator. Once inside, he inserts a key in the panel and presses the button for the executive level. "I stay in a suite," he says with a grin.

The elevator opens into a short hallway. Several doors line the hallway, all presumably leading to suites. Keith unlocks one and extravagantly gestures for me to enter.

"You're such a gentleman. Aren't you going to carry me across the threshold?" I joke.

"Just get in there, you young prince," he laughs.

Stepping inside the room, I discover myself in an entryway. Across from me is a closet. To my left and right are entrances to the bedroom and living rooms. I turn and look into both rooms. Both are smaller than I had expected, but are furnished exquisitely.

I race into the bedroom and throw myself on the bed. "Oh, Keith," I exclaim. "I love the room! I've never been in anything like it."

I am telling the truth. Most of my hotel calls have been to rooms ranging from sleazy to nice, but never luxurious. "How much does a room like this cost for a night?" Instantly I regret my question. I already know the answer. A lot.

He appears amused at my question. "It's about $500 a night."

I recoil at his answer. I feel guilty if I spend fifty bucks for a night at a Super 8 Motel.

Keith laughs at the expression on my face. He walks toward the bed and sits down next to me. He leans toward me and prepares to kiss me.

As his lips descend on mine, I think about the entire evening. It has turned into an almost magical encounter. A charming stranger, a candlelight dinner, the carriage ride in Central Park. All it would take is an hour or two of love-making to make this a grand memory of my escorting days. I have always struggled to reach high society. Perhaps this is it. I may have just arrived.

Keith begins to undress me with a gentleness and sensuality usually found in the closest of lovers. He pulls me down on the bed and lays next to me. He kisses me once, twice, three times. Lifting his head, he looks me in the eye. For one brief, perfect moment our souls almost merge. The entire evening has been leading up to this moment.

"Aaron," he says, breaking the silence. "I want you to do something for me."

"Anything, Keith. You've been so good to me. I want to make you happy."

He takes a deep breath. "I want you to tell me what you would do if you were a teen S&M master and I was your slave."

I am dumbfounded. He has to be kidding!

Unfortunately, he is not. "I want to masturbate while you describe what you would do to me if I was tied up," Keith continues. "I want to hear you tell me how you would subject me to the most sexually exquisite tortures."

Slowly my mind begins to operate. "Okay," I pause. "I can do that." I do not know what else to say beyond this. The entire mood for the evening has been shattered and I need a moment to recover. "Is there anything else you want me to do?"

"No, just what I described. You don't even have to get off if you don't want to. I love hearing young guys tell me S&M stories."

"All right then," I begin. I take a deep breath. "Picture this. You are lying here in bed. Four bedposts stand up about 18 inches above each corner of the bed. Holding your legs and arms apart are a set of leather restraints. Not the cheap kind, mind you, but the expensive ones that bite into your flesh when I pull on them..."

I continue the storytelling as best I can. S&M has never been my strong point even under the best of circumstances, and I am certainly unprepared to ad lib an extensive story. Although I do the best job I can, I know my storytelling is forced and unoriginal. Twenty minutes later Keith shoots his load all over his stomach.

"I'm sorry that I wasn't very good at storytelling," I apologize. "I hadn't been expecting it this suddenly."

"It's all right," he acknowledges. "The sex was only one part of what I wanted this evening. I have enjoyed your company and your affection a great deal. You are one of the most warm and friendly people I have ever met. Those are especially difficult traits to find in an escort."

As I dress myself, Keith fishes several bills out of his wallet. Handing them to me, I immediately tuck them in my pocket. At his request I write my number on a piece of paper, but I know he will never call. Our evening has not ended on a high enough note to keep him as a client. All that remains is to move on.

Back in the hallway, the elevator doors open before me. Stepping inside, I pull the bills out of my pocket. One, two, three, four, five, six, seven. Seven hundred dollars! I have never made that much in one session. If all my clients were like this, I would be living in a mansion.

Walking out of the hotel, I realize it is only half past eleven and the night is still young. I hail a taxi and instruct the driver to take me back to the Townhouse.

As the taxi whips up 3rd Avenue, I think back on the evening. I consider my own greed, Keith's romantic interlude, and finally S&M storytelling in the hotel room. I lean back my head and begin to laugh.

I'll be laughing all the way to the bank.

The Party

April 13, 1997

I lie on my couch enjoying the warm spring air blowing through the window. Business has been crazy ever since I started running print ads. It's my first day off in over a week.

I am startled by the sudden ringing of my telephone. Sitting up, I glance at the caller ID hoping it isn't one of my irritating clients. I'm in luck. It's a phone number and name I don't recognize. Always in search of new work, I enter callboy mode and reach for the phone.

"Hi. Is Aaron there?" a nervous voice asks.

"This is Aaron. What can I do for you?"

"My name is Daniel. I saw your ad in the *Advocate Classifieds*. I was wondering if you might be available later today."

"Yes, I don't have anything scheduled for either this afternoon or this evening. What can I tell you?"

"Well, do you do parties?"

I chuckle for a moment. "Do you mean do I work as the centerpiece of a giant orgy?"

"Oh, no," the voice laughs. "I meant would you mind being given as a gift at a party. It's a small dinner gathering for a friend of mine. He likes young men, and we were wondering if you would mind being given as a gift."

My dick springs to life inside my shorts. I have never been given as a gift before and the idea is quite exciting. "I'd be glad to do it. We'll have fun."

Daniel and I negotiate the rest of the details for the evening before we hang up. Turning around, I find Jeff staring at me with a frown on his face.

"What was that all about?" he asks suspiciously. Jeff is tolerant of my work but is always wary I am having a bit too much fun.

"I'm being given as a gift for someone's fiftieth birthday party," I explain as I lie back down on the couch. "It's not going to be a wild orgy, and I'm being well paid for it. You can relax, it's not that different from my usual work."

"What did they tell you about the guy and the party?"

"Not much. It's a dinner party. There will only be four of us there; the birthday boy, his lover, Daniel the host, and his friend Tony. I didn't understand all the details. Daniel is hosting the party but Tony is the one that lives there. I'll find out more on that tonight.

"Anyway, I'm supposed to be there at 8:30. They want me to sneak in the back and put on a g-string. They'll have a cake ready for me to carry out. I'll be having sex with the birthday boy but not with anyone else."

Jeff is still unhappy but elects not to make an issue of the party. Although I have been escorting for close to a year now, he is still uncomfortable with unusual requests.

Fortunately, he is patient with my work because of the amount of money I am making. Ever since I began advertising in *HX*, *Next*, and the *Advocate Classifieds*, my business has doubled. My earnings in January jumped over $3,000 to just under $8,000. February was even higher, coming in at almost $10,000. March was slower at $5,000 because I took two vacations and was sick for a week. Now April is progressing steadily, and it looks like I have a good shot at breaking $10,000. In three and a half months time, I have made over a year's salary at ECAP.

I have been pleasantly surprised during this time at how well Jeff is dealing with my escorting. He no longer worries about my safety every time I visit a client. He has even met several of my clients. Although he is hesitant to

befriend them, he has at least stopped putting them down every time we are alone. I think that is because he finally realized I am not going to leave him for any of my clients.

Jeff has even become inspired by my business and is starting one of his own. Although he still won't give escorting a try, he has turned to what he loves most - his art. When not working at the museum, he is beginning his own freelance illustration business. It's slow in developing, but over the course of the next few years it will grow into a booming business.

At 8:30 sharp I pull into the driveway of what has to be one of the most poorly numbered houses in the state of New Jersey. It is a large residence in the upscale community of Short Hills. Like most of its neighbors, the house has a three-car garage, a pool, and a professionally landscaped lawn. I am in the presence of obvious wealth.

As I walk up the path to the back door, a bearded figure unlocks it to admit me. "Hi," he whispers. "I'm Daniel. Come inside."

I step into the house and find myself inside the kitchen. Several balloons are tied to a weight next to a cake in the middle of the room. Leaning against the counter is a second person, presumably Tony. "Nice to meet you," he whispers as he extends his hand.

I give him a good look as I take his hand. He is an attractive man in his late thirties. Short brown hair is neatly combed above slightly squinting eyes. Daniel indicates for us to follow him and then disappears through another door. He guides me into a large laundry and storage room. "You can get changed here," he offers. "I brought a few porno magazines in here so you can get hard."

"Thanks, just set them down." I start stripping off my clothes down to the rainbow g-string I am wearing. Out of the corner of my eye, I notice Tony eyeing me closely. I make a mental note of his interest then return to the task at hand.

Once I am down to just my g-string and a matching woven rainbow bracelet, I look up at Daniel for directions.

"Tony is going to go back to the party. We'll wait about one minute, then I'll hold the door open as you carry the cake into the dining room."

Tony walks back into the kitchen. Seconds later we hear the door to the dining room open and close. Daniel and I go into the kitchen and start readying the cake.

As Daniel lights the candles, I tie the balloon strings to my g-string. Once the cake is ready, I pick it up plate and walk toward the swinging door to the dining room. Daniel opens up the door announcing, "Bill, I have a present for you!"

Seconds later, I emerge into the dining room. A very surprised man in a blue shirt sits at the head of the table, while his lover, also surprised, sits across from him. I set the cake down on the table, lean down, and give Bill a kiss on his cheek. Standing back up I maneuver my crotch into his face. "Make a wish and blow!" I teasingly command.

Bill blushes furiously while everyone laughs at his embarrassment. Startled to the point of not thinking clearly, he keeps repeating "I can't believe you guys did this!"

"Believe it, Bill, because they did," I tell him. "Pull back your chair so I can sit on your lap."

Bill is clearly surprised at my request but instantly complies. Smiling, I sit down on his lap and pull his arms around me. In a few moments he will start wondering what the limitations are. When that thought occurs to him, I want his hands in a convenient place. I set his hands on my thighs as I turn back to the laughing faces of his friends.

Everyone begins reciting their impressions of what happened when I entered the room. "You should have seen the look on his face!" Tony says. "When Aaron came in the room, Bill sat there totally shitfaced!" he bursts out laughing again.

"What about Jon?" Bill says, laughing at his lover. "Once Aaron sat on my lap you know that Jon was wishing he had a guy on his lap, too!"

"Yeah, right!" Bill's lover exclaims sarcastically. "Like you were looking at me. You couldn't take your eyes off Aaron's body!" Everyone laughs.

The conversation continues like this for several minutes before Jon asks, "Who came up with this idea, anyway?"

Tony speaks up. "Daniel was showing me the *Advocate Classifieds* earlier today. I was curious to see what escorts were here in New Jersey. When I saw Aaron's ad, I realized he might be Bill's type. I called him and he said he was very boyish looking. I thought he was perfect for it." Something tells me there is more to the story than what Tony is saying. I have my own suspicions as to why he wants me here.

Beneath me, Bill is becoming rock hard in his pants. He rubs his stiffness through his jeans into my bare buns. I purposely grind my ass into his crotch. As if sensing the sudden sexual tension, the others excuse themselves and leave Bill and I alone.

I turn around and face Bill. I slowly begin kissing and licking his neck and ears. I feel him stirring beneath me as he pushes up against me. He reaches into my g-string and pulls out my very erect cock. Excited, embarrassed, and wary at the same time, he pauses. "Just how far are you willing to go?"

"All the way," I respond nuzzling his neck with my lips. "They hired me to do whatever you'd like."

Within moments Bill's hormones get the best of him. Still in the dining room, he stands up and leans me back against the table. He pulls my g-string down and tosses it on the floor. He slowly begins sucking my cock.

Suddenly, Tony walks through the room and into the kitchen. Although I find an audience highly arousing, Bill is very embarrassed and immediately pulls me down again on his lap.

Almost as sudden, he stands me up again and takes my hand. He leads me through several rooms into a spare

bedroom. I turn him around, lay him back on the bed, and begin undoing his clothes.

I quickly pull his pants and underwear down around his knees and lower my lips onto his hard shaft. I suck him repeatedly, and within two minutes he begins to moan as he creams into my mouth. Sharing his intensity, I suck every drop out of him. I continue to suck even as he returns to his flaccid state.

He opens his eyes and apologizes. "I'm sorry for cumming so quickly."

I shrug my shoulders. "You came because you were excited." I touch his body to soothe and relax him. If he is anything like my other clients, he will soon begin pouring out his heart to me.

He does not disappoint my prediction. Hesitantly at first, he begins to confide in me. "I have been together with Jon for almost twenty years. We don't have sex as much as we used to, so this is really nice." He pauses as if contemplating some internal struggle. "For the past few years I have been looking at young men more and more. I'm just not as attracted to him. I love him, but I find young men so much more attractive."

I sense he has not told me the entire truth. Nodding my head, I urge him to continue. "What else is on your mind?"

"Jon tested HIV-positive three years ago. So now we really don't have sex much anymore." Seeing the look on my face, he quickly adds, "Oh, don't worry, I'm negative. We have always had a somewhat open relationship. That's how he contracted it."

I nod my head in sympathy. "I understand what you are saying. Any couple who is together for that long has a lot less sex than when they were first seeing each other. It's perfectly normal. You're not the first person to discover he likes young men," I remind him. "In the past I have been hired by couples to help spice up their sex life. HIV status doesn't turn me off because I can make even ultra-safe sex into a highly exciting encounter."

Although Bill does not realize it, I am trying to manipulate him into hiring me again. Marketing myself like this is an important part of my business. From the look in my eye, I can see he has taken the bait. He will ask me for my number before I leave.

I notice a figure in the doorway. Looking up I see it is Jon. "May I join you? Or are you busy?" he asks.

"Come in," Bill invites him.

"I don't mean to interrupt you," Jon says as he sits on the edge of the bed. "I wanted to come in and check on you guys."

I sit up and start massaging Jon's back. I'm done with my sales pitch for Bill, but getting on Jon's good side can't hurt.

Jon and Bill begin talking for a minute. I ignore them while I continue massaging Jon. Kissing his neck, I notice his body is responding to me. When he finally turns to kiss me, he does so in a shallow fashion while keeping his tongue and saliva to himself.

The entire issue of AIDS strongly concerns me. My profession places me at high risk for contracting the virus. To keep myself HIV-negative, I have adopted a strict policy of using condoms for anal sex. No slips are permitted under any circumstance. Although I do not require condoms for oral sex, I do not work if I have any sort of cut or sore in my mouth. Almost humorously, I have discovered that dentist visits always mean several days off work as a mini-vacation.

A few moments later Jon stands up. "I'm going back in with Tony and Daniel. Have fun!" He walks out of the room before either us can ask him to stay.

Bill looks after him, then stands and begins to dress himself. Following his lead, I walk into the dining room to find my g-string. Moments later we both hold hands as we enter the living room where the others are seated. Bill leads me to a mostly empty couch, so I lean against him with my legs across Jon's lap. Jon shyly rubs my legs as Bill touches my chest. I enjoy being the center of attention, so I

continue to stay and talk to the four friends although it is now beyond the agreed-upon time limit.

As the party winds down, I find myself sitting on Tony's lap. He surprises me with the speed of his physical response. His hands touch me all over. "I love young men as much as Bill does, if not more. Does that surprise you?" he asks me.

"No," I honestly reply. "I know you've been looking at me all evening."

He chuckles. "Would you be willing to stay after the party with me? I would enjoy your company a great deal for an hour or two."

I quickly agree. "I would love to," I honestly tell him. It is flattering to be hired again like this. I feel like some sort of sex symbol.

Before Bill and Jon depart, I offer them my number. With a slightly embarrassed look on his face, Bill admits Tony already gave it to him. A pair of good-byes later, they depart. Daniel quickly excuses himself from the kitchen leaving the two of us alone.

"Would you like to go upstairs?" Tony asks. I accept and he leads me by the hand into another part of the house.

Minutes later I find myself lying in bed with an affectionate and gentle Tony. He prefers talking to sex, so we lay in each other's arms discussing our respective backgrounds. Slowly the talk turns into passionate kissing, which quickly evolves into hardcore cocksucking.

Tony is only semi-hard, a fact that bothers him greatly. "It's not your fault," he assures me. "It's mine. I drank half a bottle of wine at dinner. I shouldn't have had that much, but I was nervous about what would happen when you arrived. I knew even before you got here that I wanted you."

Switching from hardcore mode into a more sensitive one, I brush aside his concerns. "Whether you are rock hard or not isn't important to me. I stayed because you wanted me to be with you, not because you wanted a quick fuck.

Whether you cum or not isn't important. I'll cuddle with you either way."

Tony appears greatly relieved. Feeling less pressure, he prepares to help me jack off. His hands drop to my balls and he begins rubbing them up and down.

I stroke myself for several minutes while he plays with me. He pleasures my balls with his hands, with his tongue, and finally with both at once. In the end, the pleasure is more than I can bear. I moan loudly as streams of cum shoot across my stomach. Tony grins as he licks every drop from my body.

We talk a bit more, but we both know it is time for me to go. We dress again and walk back downstairs. Escorting me to my car, Tony gives me a gentle kiss.

"I'll call you again, Aaron. I promise you."

"I know you will. I'll come back when you ask me to."

He leans over and kisses me once again before he returns to the house. I absently wonder how long until his birthday arrives. I already know what he wants.

Roughly

April 16, 1997

I drive for what seems like an eternity before I reach the end of the driveway. It terminates in the middle of a heavily wooded area, perhaps half a mile from the nearest neighbor. I cannot help but to recall the words of an old movie poster, "In space no one can hear you scream." I hope that doesn't also include secluded houses.

I was sitting comfortably in my apartment an hour ago when the phone rang. "Describe yourself for me," the voice on the line demanded.

I was taken aback by his tone, but continued to answer politely. "I'm twenty-four, five-feet, five-inches, one hundred and thirty pounds, dark blond hair, and blue eyes. I'm very boyish looking and look about eighteen or nineteen. I have a smooth chest and I'm pretty well hung. What else can I tell you?"

"How much do you charge?"

"I charge $150 per hour in northern New Jersey. Are you in south Jersey or New York City? I charge a two hour minimum to travel there." I am pleased at being able to charge this rate. My business has been so successful I've raised my rates yet again.

"I'm in Bedminster," he responded, naming a town about twenty minutes away. "Can you be here in an hour?" I agreed, and the evening was set. I learned his name was Brett as he gave me directions.

Parking my car outside his house, I cannot shake the feeling that his house is too isolated. I look around hoping to see an obvious sign of danger. Nothing appears out of

the ordinary. I am looking at an unremarkable house in the middle of a darkened wood. I wonder what exactly I was hoping to see.

As I step out of the car, a side door to the house opens. In the doorway is an attractive man in his early thirties. A very large attractive man, I notice. He is much bigger than most of my clients, standing at a few inches over six feet and well over 200 pounds of bulk and muscle.

"I'm Brett," he says curtly, extending his hand to me.

I shake his hand. "I'm Aaron."

"Follow me inside." He turns and walks through the door leaving me standing alone in the darkness. I guess he is a man of few words.

We walk through several rooms before we reach a large living room. A large L-shaped couch sits under two bay windows.

"Sit down," he commands.

He grabs me before I am able to comply. Pulling me toward him, he forcefully kisses my lips. His tongue pushes its way into my mouth probing the wetness within.

Although startled by his forcefulness, I respond quickly to the sudden change in mood. Arching my back and pressing my chest against him, I let him take control of my body. I have fantasized for years about men gently but firmly using my body for their own pleasure. I think about how exciting it is to be dominated by an attractive stranger.

There is no way Brett can know my fantasy but he acts as if he does. He pushes me back on the couch and climbs on me. I revel as his body lies on top of me. It comforts me, holds me, and surrounds me. He kisses me passionately again and again.

After several minutes of making out, his weight begins to crush me. When he finally rolls off I am grateful. I quickly scramble into another position.

Wanting to avoid any more uncomfortable positions, I try to engage him in conversation. "Wow. You are hot at that," I begin. "Where did you learn to do that?"

"Just natural, I guess," he grins. He reaches for me.

I move back from him slightly. His dominance has me alarmed. "I'm curious to know a bit more about you."

"What do you want to know? Come sit by me and I'll tell you," he invites as he continues reaching for me.

I slide back a second time. "Oh, there are lots of things. Like what do you do for a living?"

"I'm a pro-hockey player. Can't you tell?" He gestures at several hockey trophies on a shelf. Suddenly Brett lunges for me. He grabs my wrist before I can jump back. Pulling me toward him, he begins touching my body all over.

Although I am afraid he is going to be rough with me, his touch is reassuringly gentle. He slowly unbuttons my shirt. Removing it, he begins rubbing my chest and tweaking my nipples. He runs his hands down my stomach to my pants and begins to remove them. Pulling the rest of my clothes off, he casually tosses them on the floor behind him.

Almost dramatically, he stands up and begins stripping off his own clothes. He is an impressive figure, his muscular chest covered by a short layer of dark hair. He is a very sexy man. I involuntarily gasp when he drops his pants. He is at least eight inches and very thick. I rarely see such size in my work.

He drops to his knees in front of the couch and begins playing with my body. He rubs my chest, strokes my erect shaft, and plays with my balls. I am enjoying his attention. Despite my earlier discomfort, I am highly aroused again.

Soon his touch becomes more insistent and aggressive. Pulling becomes yanking, rubbing becomes pinching, and touching becomes grabbing. He looks me in the eye as I flinch from his touch. "You know you love it, boy."

A sudden feeling of fear crosses over me. He actually believes what he's saying. For the first time in the history of my escorting, I am afraid for my safety.

Clients have hurt me before, but usually because they are lousy in bed. Once I teach them what they are doing wrong, they usually become better lovers. I realize in an instant that Brett is different. He is convinced that his part-

ners enjoy his aggressive style. He may believe they enjoy it even when they say no.

Another realization follows the first. This man attacking me!

Brett grabs me, pulling my hair as he forces me to go down on him. I suck him as best I can, but his eight thick inches are too big for me to handle. I begin choking and gagging as he slams his dick into the back of my throat. I try to breathe but he doesn't let go.

He begins moaning loudly. "You have such a hot mouth, boy. Keep sucking my big cock. You don't know how lucky you are that I'm giving it to you."

His date rape style of sex is alien to me. I have always adhered to a sexual code of courtesy and respect. Brett does not seem to feel constrained to follow any sort of sexual courtesy. I realize I have two options. I can confront him and leave, or I can submit and stay.

I am worried Brett will become abusive if I attempt to leave. I don't want to give him any more excuse to hurt me than he already has created for himself. I am also afraid he might rape me. Hospitals and crisis centers are poorly equipped to handle male-to-male rape. If I have to go to an emergency room, they will contact the police. It is very possible I could be arrested for prostitution.

Even if I manage to press charges and avoid arrest, there isn't a court in the land that would believe a prostitute over a sports hero. Brett would be let off as a hero while I would be considered a social degenerate.

So I take the second option, to submit and stay. I lie on my back with my head off the side of the couch. Brett jams his dick into my throat. I gag with every plunge as my jaw sends pain through my head.

Just when I think I can't take it any longer, he pulls out of my throat. "I'm going to fuck you good, boy. But first I want to tell you something."

I gasp for air. He can tell me anything he wants as long as I can breathe.

"There's this boy who works at the local 7-11. He's real cute like you. I think he's nineteen or twenty. Anyway, one day I picked him up and brought him back here. I fucked him on this couch the same way I'm going to fuck you. He wasn't able to take it up his ass very well, but I'm sure you can."

For the first time in my life, I am glad someone is going to anally hurt me. At least I will be able to breathe. Being fucked is also something I can handle, even when the top is hurting me. I have dealt with discomfort and pain in order to pleasure my partners. This will be nothing new.

I am also aware that no top can completely dominate a bottom without his assistance. He can spank me, hurt me, and do all sorts of unpleasant things to me, but unless I submit he will find it difficult to possess me completely.

I look up in time to see Brett grabbing my black bag. He roots through it in search of my tube of KY. Finding it, he sets it on the table. He ventures back into the bag and I am relieved that he is at least going to use a condom.

Finding one, Brett opens the tube of KY. He squeezes a glob of the clear jelly onto his fingers. Reaching down to my ass, I feel him begin to finger me. It is not a pleasurable sensation, his digits pushing themselves inside me without any regard for my comfort. He is lubricating me out of basic practicality rather than for pleasure.

"Put the rubber on me," he commands. I reach over and take the condom from him. I slowly rip the packet open, trying to delay the inevitable every second I can. Glancing at the clock, I see I have thirty-five minutes to go. I am not sure Brett will adhere to any sort of time constraints, but I will have a much better chance of making my stand at the end of the hour. I believe he is more likely to let me leave then rather than if I try to leave now.

I finish unrolling the condom. He grabs his dick with his hand and slathers lube all over it. "Lie on your back," he demands gruffly. I lean back as he holds my legs in the air. I feel something begin to press up against my ass.

Suddenly he shoves his entire dick into me. I cover my mouth to stifle a scream. The pain is excruciating but I am glad he is fucking me. The struggle to contain the pain is far preferable to choking on his dick.

He begins his act of conquest by pulling his dick out and slamming it back in. Each stroke is a nightmare of agony that brings tears to my eyes. I take long breaths of air as I try to control my body's natural urge to tense up.

It is not easy to control myself. His thrusts are deep and push into parts of my body that were not meant to be touched. I struggle to relax one muscle, one cramp, and one inch at a time. Concentrating on my violated hole, I focus my thoughts until pain lapses into extreme discomfort.

I fight Brett as best I can. I cease any indications I enjoy his actions and stop supporting my own weight. If Brett wants my body he can have it, but he will not find me a willing partner. Although he is a strong person, I hope the effort of lifting my lower body off the couch will tire him.

Like a mantra, Brett keeps repeating himself. "Boy, take it! Yeah, get fucked, boy! Get fucked! You know you love it." He rides me like an animal as he slaps my ass with his bare hands. My skin stings and turns red at his touch.

The muscles inside my ass have now loosened and are actually able to draw some pleasure from the experience. They do not experience the sort of sensations I willingly endure, but rather a natural feeling in response to any sexual stimulation. I loathe to embrace the sensations. The encounter would be easier to endure if I submitted, but I cannot bring myself to do so. Somehow that feels like it would be letting Brett win. I want it to hurt rather than to feel good, because Brett's touch should feel like rape, not lovemaking.

Brett shifts positions as he continues to fuck me. He fucks me on my back, on my hands and knees, lying helplessly on my stomach, and while I sit on his dick. He even fucks me while the weight of my entire body painfully rests on my shoulder blades. A quick look at the clock shows fifteen minutes to go.

He pulls out of me not a minute too soon. My ass hurts like hell but I don't think he has torn anything. I hope I am not bleeding, but if I am I hope I stain the couch.

Brett throws the condom aside. "Suck on me again, boy," he demands. I despise the man and feel like vomiting on him. I keep telling myself to maintain control, my time is almost at an end. Returning to the position on my knees, I begin sucking him. His hands reach up and begin pulling my hair. My eyes water in pain as he fucks my face again and again.

Two minutes later I feel him getting close. He starts forcing me to suck on the tip of his shaft. I feel his balls tightening as they prepare to shoot.

In the last instant before he orgasms, I pull my head off his dick and half-heartedly jack him off. As the streams of cum shoot all over my chest, I revel in knowing he wanted to cream in my mouth. I hope I have spoiled his orgasm.

Brett appears angry but says nothing. He walks into another room, stopping only to throw a towel at me. Moments later I hear the sound of running water.

I wipe the cum from me. In a small act of defiance, I rub the towel on the couch. I hope next time he has company they notice it. I consider hiding my underwear under the couch in case he has a wife, but I decide against it. I put on my underwear instead and continue dressing.

Brett returns and hands me a wad of cash. I stuff it into my pocket uncounted. Moments later I am dressed and ready to leave.

As I drive away from his house, I see the convenience store Brett mentioned. I briefly consider stopping in and seeing if the young man is working. Did he do to him what he did to me?

I do not stop. I am hurt, I am afraid, and I want to go home.

Busy Day

April 19, 1997

Morning has arrived. I feel rays of warm sunlight shine across my face. A shadow falls across me as I feel hands caress my body. They touch my face and gently trace the lines of my body. Arms encircle me and pull me close. I wish I could remember where I am and who is holding me.

I open my eyes. He is not bad looking as far as my clients go. He is in his mid-thirties and is balding slightly. In an effort to hide his hair loss, he has given himself a buzz cut. I can smell the faint smell of cigarette smoke on him.

Slowly I begin to remember. His name is Martin. This is my fourth or fifth time with him. He thinks he is in love with me. The box of roses on the nightstand certainly suggest that is the case.

I try to recall what we did last night. I think our evening involved kissing in the living room, dinner in the dining room, dancing at a local gay club, and passionate love-making in the bedroom. It's hard to remember for sure that is really what happened. In my line of work most evenings blur together.

Martin pushes himself against my body and slowly slides his hand across my ass. Although he appears to want to cuddle with me, I have no doubt what he really has in mind. Sex, of course. That's my job after all.

I wonder if I am encouraging his romantic feelings for me. I don't want to hurt him by promising a relationship that will never be. Still, business comes first and damage control later. He is paying me to play so I'll respond however he'd like.

"Good morning, Martin" I yawn as I snuggle closer to him.

"Good morning, darling," he responds. He smiles as he looks at me, no doubt remembering the night before. He moves his head forward to kiss me. Our lips meet and quickly become passionate.

I roll on my side and slide my arms around him. He cups the side of my face with his hand, slowly tracing his fingers down my chest, over my stomach, and finally between my legs. He discovers my large erection and is delighted at his find.

I allow myself to enjoy his touch for a few moments, but my own plans for the morning do not involve orgasming. Over the past year I have become an experienced escort. I know my sexual energy is a limited commodity. I can have sex with a dozen men in a day, but I will be sexually exhausted if I cum more than once or twice.

With this thought in mind, I slide my hands across his chest. I run them through the dark hair, briefly touching his nipples. I wet my fingers with my tongue and touch his nipples again. He arches his back at the feeling. I softly blow, sending shivers throughout his entire body.

I sit up and spread my legs, allowing him to enjoy the full view of my stiff rod. He is still playing with my throbbing cock, but my hands on his nipples are distracting him.

I continue sliding my hands over his body. I softly caress his face with my left hand while I stroke his rapidly swelling cock with my right. I pull on his dick while running my hand back over his nipples. Their sensitivity is obvious as he arches his back and moans.

I continue stroking to build the sexual feelings within him. I remember he did not actually cum the night before, which explains why he is so horny today. I am more than happy to take care of him now by speeding up the pumping rhythm of my hand.

He moans again and pushes his body upwards with every downward stroke. His cock begins to twitch and

swell. I move my hand on his nipples to his balls. I want to catch the inevitable streams of cum that will gush forth.

I underestimate the speed of his excitement. His first stream of cum launches itself onto the bedspread before my hand can catch it. His remaining streams of cum fly across my hand and arm.

Two spurts, three, four, and five. Cum drips from my fingers. I reach out and touch Martin's chest, smearing the warm fluid across his body. The cum leaves a sticky trail but he does not seem to mind.

His moans slowly lapse into silence as he lowers his body back onto the bed. I remove my hands from him and lay down by his side. His arms encircle me again making me feel safe, warm, and protected. I do not fight them as I close my eyes and relax into his embrace. Moments later I am asleep.

Three hours and $500 later, I am in my car driving home. The smell of smoke still lingers on me. I dislike being around smokers but it's part of the job.

I dial Jeff on my cell phone. "Hello?" he answers in a sleepy voice.

"Wake up!" I cheerily say. "I'm on my way home."

"Home?" he asks foggily. "What about Dean? What time are you seeing him?"

"Dean? Damn, I forgot about that. Go grab my schedule book and look up what time my appointment is with him."

"Okay, hang on," Jeff says. I hear a clunk as the phone is set down.

While Jeff is away, I try to remember who Dean is. I know I have seen him once or twice before, but for the life of me I can't remember the circumstances surrounding our meetings. Oh well, I'll find out soon enough.

A few seconds later Jeff returns. "It's at 1:30. You're meeting him at the Sunset Diner."

I feel a sense of relief. The clock in my car says 11:17. Jeff and I talk for a few more minutes and then say our good-byes.

Half an hour later I pull up next to my apartment. Turning off the motor, I pick my mileage book up off the seat next to me. I record yesterday's date, destination, trip mileage, and tolls.

I silently thank Uncle Sam for tax deductions. Although the feds say what I am doing is illegal and immoral, they still want their share of the money. I've resigned myself to paying them taxes, but I'll be damned if they'll get it all. I'll deduct every cent I can. At thirty-one cents a mile, my drive back and forth to Martin's is another $20 off my taxes.

My visit home is brief. After a quick bite to eat and a bit of cuddling, I am off to my 1:30 appointment. It is not far and I arrive on time. Dean is already there in his Honda CRX waiting for me.

"Shall I follow you over to the motel?" he greets me.

"Sure thing, I'll lead," I reply. "The Ivory Tower Inn is across the highway." The Inn is a dive that rents by the hour, but the staff at the front desk are usually friendly. They should be for the amount of business I bring them.

On the way to the motel, I try to recall what I can about Dean. I don't actually need to know much about his life, but I do want to remember why he is hiring me. Knowing that will allow me to meet his needs more effectively. How I treat straight married men is very different from how I treat my experienced gay clients. Straight clients need a lot more support and understanding, while gay clients mostly want hot and heavy sex.

Unfortunately, I remember little about Dean's life, although I am sure he has told me about himself. I recall he works for a major company in a supervisory capacity. I also know he has a rainbow flag bumper sticker on the back of his car, so he must be openly gay. Other than those two facts, I have forgotten what little I knew about him. I'll have to wing our encounter together.

Luckily, Dean is only minimally interested in conversation. He is extremely aroused, so I begin probing on a very sexual note. "Judging by how hard you are," I say as I put my hand on the bulge in his jeans, "you must not be getting enough at home."

"Tell me about it," he replies. "Stay with the same guy for twelve years and it will happen to you."

"Does he know you'd like more sex?"

"He knows, but he doesn't want to do it. We don't talk as much as we used to. So I like to play on occasion in a way that's safe, but with no strings attached."

I untuck the base of his shirt from his pants. Reaching beneath the fabric, I begin running my hands through his thick chest hair. Although his nipples are not as sensitive as Martin's, he seems to enjoy what I am doing.

We grab each other and begin undressing. Our lips lock together as we eagerly unzip, unbutton, untie, and untuck everything within reach. Within moments our clothes are scattered around the room as we fall onto the bed.

We roll on the bed until I lower my mouth onto his stiff and swollen cock. He moans loudly as he pulls the back of my head closer to him. Although I suck him deeply, I understand instinctively that he will not want to cum from a blowjob. Whether I fuck him or he fucks me remains to be seen. Either is fine with me because I like to be both top and bottom.

I change the rhythm of my blowjob several times as I experiment with different styles and speeds. I memorize his reactions to my touch. Long ago I learned the better the sex, the more likely he is to hire me again.

Moments later Dean pulls back from me. "Whoa, better back off or I'll cum," he warns me. "Go grab a condom and some lube out of your bag." Still not knowing who will play top, I bring my bag back to the bed. My questions are answered as he rips open a condom with his teeth and begins unrolling it onto his own erect shaft.

As he unrolls the condom, I take a close look at him. Dean is an attractive Italian man in his early forties. A nice

layer of carefully trimmed hair covers his chest. The rest of his body has a light tan usually not found this time of year. His endowment is moderate, perhaps five inches in length. I find him very sexy. I suspect my attraction stems from his background. I've always been a sucker for a hot Italian.

He finishes unrolling the condom on his dick. He looks up and pauses, staring at me. After a moment I realize he is waiting for me to prepare myself. I reach into my bag and find my nearly empty bottle. I remind myself to refill it when I get home. I buy lubricant in bulk quantities for just that purpose.

I open the top of the bottle and pour a bit too much lube into my hand. I coat my own ass with it, sliding a finger into the center to lubricate the sphincter. Soon I am primed, lubed, and ready to go. I slide my slippery hand across the condom on Dean's dick and moments later I am sitting on his entire length.

Dean is in better shape than Martin and is considerably more attractive to look at. Even his short brown beard is appealing to me. I remember Dean once telling me he shampoos and conditions it every day to keep it soft.

My interest in his beard is quickly forgotten as I ride up and down on his dick. His pubic hair absorbs the excess lubricant, creating a mild suction between us. The wet smacking sound of my ass against his crotch excites both of us. I find myself becoming harder by the moment.

The fucking continues for a few moments until he accidentally slides out of me. Like many of my clients, Dean finds it difficult to maintain an erection while wearing a condom. Sensing that he is becoming embarrassed with his performance, I try to think of something else that we can do. Distracting him is not as easy as it sounds. I am not going to let him fuck me without a condom, and I am hesitant to go down on him after he has been inside me.

I stuff his cock inside me and continue to slide up and down until it finally shrinks too small to stay inside me. Reaching behind, I grab hold of his dick. "Damn rubbers," I complain, "they take all the sensitivity away." By blaming

the condom, I hope he will not feel any pressure from his own troubled performance.

"Yeah, they're a bitch," he agrees.

"Tell you what," I offer. "The day after there is a vaccine against AIDS, you're welcome to come over and ride me raw." I make the same offer to most of my clients who have difficulties maintaining an erection. It helps relax a tense moment.

"You've got yourself a deal," he says with a grin.

Talking has helped relieve some of the pressure of the moment. We begin kissing and cuddling again. This time our affections are slower and gentler.

Looking him in the eyes, I make him an offer. "Would you like me to fuck you?"

He considers my offer for a moment before he agrees. "It's been a long time. I'm not sure if I'm up to it, but I'll try."

I reach over and grab a second condom out of my bag. I rip the top off with my teeth. As I unroll the rubber on my erect shaft, Dean pours lube on his hand and begins fingering himself. I take the bottle from him and pour a generous slathering of lube on my latex clad sheath. I pull his asscheeks apart and slowly sink my dick into him.

Instantly, lubricant is all over my crotch and his asscheeks. "Sorry," I apologize.

"Don't be," he replies. "I like wet and sticky sex."

I give him a big smile. "Really? How cool! I do too. I remember one client that brought a mattress outside onto his deck. We used up almost an entire bottle of baby oil as we poured it all over each other. We wound up having-- oh, hell with the story!" I lose my self-control and thrust my dick as hard as I can into his ass.

Dean moans loudly to my surprise. I suspect he is far more of a bottom than he realizes. We are fucking in a position I have never seen portrayed in any manual of gay sex. It is like the "spoon" position where one man fucks another while both lie on their sides. Rather than lying evenly behind him, I am reversed with my torso behind his legs. His

ass is extremely vulnerable in this position giving me a great deal of thrusting power. I do not have a lot of experience fucking like this, but the few times I have done so I have enjoyed it immensely. I hump his ass bringing a series of soft moans out of him.

I think about his reasons for hiring me as I fuck his ass. He thinks he is seeing me because he isn't getting enough sex from his lover, but I disagree. I think he is using my services because he wants to be used sexually. Not just used, but totally sexualized for both his and his partner's pleasure. That's not an easy thing to find in a relationship of twelve years.

I switch my thoughts back to the immediate situation as I change positions with Dean. I lay him on his back with his legs in the air. Holding his ankles, I pump him with eight inches of solid dick. As I spread his legs even farther apart, he gives himself completely to the physical sensations overtaking him. Dean's moans increase, signaling he is passing beyond the point of rational thought.

I slow the pace of my fucking to almost a standstill causing Dean to whimper. "Please, Aaron, fuck my ass. It's soooooo good." I withdraw almost entirely and then slam it back in. "Oh, yeah!" he yells. "Fuck me harder. Fuck me! FUCK ME!"

Always happy to comply with a client's request, I begin slamming my cock deep within his ass. I am worried about hurting him but he continues to beg for more. Ironically, his excitement makes me feel uneasy. I am confident in my own sexual skill but I have limited experience being an aggressive top. I slow down out of concern I will injure him.

I hold Dean's legs wide apart and sink into his ass again and again. He begins stroking his own cock so I know he will not last long. After five or six pumps he gives a yell and begins shooting cum over the both of us. Most of it lands on his stomach, but one load hits me square in the chest. I decrease the strength of my thrusts with each suc-

cessive shooting stream. As the orgasm slowly vanishes, I gently pull my dick out of his ass.

Dean lays on the bed in shock and amazement. I can almost hear the sound of his racing heart over his heavy breathing. I study the expression on his face. It is one of pure and utter rapture.

I know from his expression that he is certainly not done with me today. Anyone with that look on his face is going to want a second round. I also know he will want to talk first. I lie down on my stomach and prop a pillow underneath my chin. Adopting a look of boyish innocence, I stare at him until he is ready to speak.

"That was incredible," he begins. "I haven't been fucked like that in years."

I smile and say nothing.

"You are really a good lover. But you know that, don't you, Aaron? I mean you must have heard that before."

I blush guiltily but maintain my silence. He is correct. I have heard those words many times before.

"I wish I could get fucked like that every day," he muses.

This time I speak up. "I'm surprised my curved dick didn't hurt you. Most of the time guys have a tough time taking it. I've always thought of my dick as only being good for fucking around corners," I giggle. "You must be a lot more skilled at bottoming than you told me. Otherwise you wouldn't have been able to take me like that."

My compliments hide my ulterior motive. Whenever I escort, I find something truthful to compliment about my partner. It builds up their esteem and makes them feel more comfortable around me. The habit is a secret of my success.

We continue talking for the next fifteen minutes until I notice his dick returning to life.

"Ready for another session?" I ask him.

"Whenever you are," he answers with a grin.

Remembering his earlier comment about liking wet and sticky sex, I decide to try something different. I reach

for the lube and pour lots of it into my hand. I rub the lube into his chest hair, down his stomach, and onto his crotch and legs. I lie on top of him to let the lubricant and partially dried cum soak into our skin. We kiss and roll across the bed as our bodies slide across each other.

"I call it 'Wet 'n Wild'," I explain. "A sexual game where the object is to get as messy and sticky as possible. The only rule is you are not allowed to clean anything off you until you're done."

Minutes later, Dean's second orgasm echoes throughout the room as I jack his dick. I lay down on top of him and roll around all over his stomach again. The lube begins to dry, leaving a tacky and sticky mess between us. As we lock our lips together, I slide my fingers into his now wide-open ass. I know he loves the feeling of being penetrated.

"Shower time?" he asks with a grin.

Glancing at the clock, I realize we have gone longer than I expected. "Yes, let's."

As we get into the shower, I wonder if he will mention that I have not cum yet. I have intentionally orchestrated our afternoon toward an end where he is sexually exhausted and I am still sexually charged. As a result, I will be able to work again if the opportunity arises.

Ten minutes later I am in my car heading for home.

Arriving at home, Jeff is happy to see me. For the past few days, I have been working a lot and I have not been able to spend any quality time with him. I have earned almost $1,500 in the past six days and hope to make more.

"Just let me check my e-mail, darling," I tell him. "I'll come spend some time with you when I'm done."

Jeff's happy expression vanishes. I have neglected him yet again for my work. Nodding, he turns around and slowly walks into the bedroom. I can tell he's unhappy with me.

I want to follow him and cheer him up, but I have to check my e-mail. I'm expecting several important mes-

sages from potential clients. Like it or not, this is the way my business works. Jeff will have to wait a while.

The e-mail in my box consists of inquiries from potential clients, junk e-mail, news stories from several national wire services, friendly letters from several of my clients, and several letters from my groupies. I find the latter quite annoying. Groupies sap my time by exchanging long but pointless e-mails. I don't mind writing to well-wishers, but I don't have the time to entertain entire masses of bored people.

Before I have an opportunity to complete my e-mail, an instant message appears on the screen. I recognize the handle as that of a former client.

NJFrmGuy: Hi Aaron. How have you been?

"I'm fine," I type back. "How have you been? It's been a while since the last time I saw you."

NJFrmGuy: It's been about four months. Will you be available tonight? Around 7:00?

I'm tempted to say no because I wanted to go to the Townhouse in New York, but my business sense gets the better of me. "Yes, I'm available then. Shall I come by?"

NJFrmGuy: You bet. Come over at 7 for an hour or so. 160, right?

I check my records to find the rate I charge this client. Sure enough, I am charging him a slightly older rate of $160 for the first hour and $100 for every additional hour. "Yup, 160," I confirm. "I'll see you at 7:00."

We say our good-byes and end our conversation. I click the sign off button before anyone else can write me. Although I would like to answer my e-mail, I feel guilty for neglecting Jeff and need to go cheer him up.

I walk into the bedroom and find Jeff staring out the window in silence. I sit down on the bed next to him and put my arms around him. "I wuv you, pookie," I purr in his ear.

He turns and looks at me. "I know, I just wish you'd spend time with me instead of your damn business."

I bow my head guiltily. "I put it aside for at least a little while. Does that count for anything? I'd like to cuddle with you right now if you're willing."

He assents and the two of us lie back on the bed together. Within seconds I can feel Jeff's body responding to me. It is not surprising, especially considering we have not had sex in a week. I know it is my fault he goes so long between sessions, but it is the sacrifice we make for my career. What else could we do that would make me $75,000 per year? I plan for my income to rise even higher than that in the future. This is the only time in my life I will be able to escort like this. Jeff must understand that.

As we begin to kiss, there is a great deal of unspoken communication between us. I will take care of his physical and emotional needs right now. In return, he understands I cannot sexually tire myself. Our sex today, like most other days, will focus around pleasuring him. The nature of our one-sided sexual relationship is a business necessity.

Although I can tell he is still unhappy, he is grateful for the attention I offer him. Rolling over, I slowly climb on top of him. The feel of our clothed bodies rubbing against each other is highly sexual. I reach down and begin unbuttoning Jeff's shirt. He tries to remove mine but I stop him. I want to feel my clothed body against his naked one. It is more sexual to me knowing our entire union is focused on his needs.

I continue unbuttoning his shirt as I slide my tongue in his mouth. He is so excited that he shivers as my hands slide over his nipples. I give each one a tweak then continue sliding my hand down to his pants. His button and zipper hold out for a moment before my skilled hand undoes them.

"Lift yourself up," I command as I roll off him. Grabbing the top of his jeans, I pull his pants and underwear around his knees. I know that Jeff enjoys being constrained by his own clothing. He wants to move his legs apart, but the pants hold them together. I love watching him become

frustrated and aroused as he involuntarily tries to spread his legs.

Lying on my side with an arm around his neck, I reach my right hand toward his cock. It juts a solid six inches up from his body. It isn't huge, but it is nice. I begin pumping it steadily. I kiss him passionately as my hand moves up and down.

Jeff's breathing deepens rapidly. I'll be surprised if he lasts two minutes. I am tempted to slow down and hold him back, but sometimes the best orgasms are the ones that happen naturally. Besides, I can always give him another one later if he needs it.

I slowly increase the speed of my strokes and the tightness of my hand. He begins to moan, softly warning me he cannot last much longer. I kiss him harder, holding his moans inside him. My tongue penetrates his lips again and again while my hand pounds harder against his flesh.

I feel his dick stiffen as he loses control. Pulling us together as tight as I can, his entire body shakes and unloads its first shot of cum. I cannot see where it lands but I feel a second and third shot explode from his shaft. The fourth shot drenches my hand and the fifth pours down my fingers into his pubic hair.

I stare at the cum on his body. It's far more than usual. It must have been a frustrating week. Another twinge of guilt passes through me. I would do it more often, but sex in my personal life is often a chore because I am already sexually satisfied. I enjoy sex even when I'm only half-horny, but when I'm tired it's the last thing I want.

Today's session was a good one for both of us. Jeff is clearly happy at my sexual attention. He leans over and reaches for a towel. "Thank you," he says with a smile on his face.

I understand exactly what he is saying. "I love you too."

A few minutes later I am in my car driving west. This time I am off to Long Valley to see a man named Patrick.

Like my meeting with Dean, I am not exactly sure of the circumstances surrounding our last meeting. And again, I am confident my memory will return to me.

As I follow the directions in my records, the familiar landmarks gradually remind me of my last visit. I remember that Patrick hired me when his lover was out of town. If I recall correctly, Patrick was extremely horny when I last saw him. That's hardly a surprise considering most of my clients are similarly horny.

As I arrive I see Patrick watching me from an upstairs window. He yells down to me, "come on up! I'm in the bedroom."

Once inside, I rediscover Patrick is a man in decent shape for his mid-forties. He has a hippie look about him, mostly from his long gray tail that hangs down his back. Although he is quite proud of his hair, I find it rather unappealing. I will not tell him so, of course. As far as Patrick is concerned, I love long hair.

My host wastes no time in getting started. "Take off your clothes and stand by the bed. I want to look at you." I am happy to comply. I love showing off my body.

Patrick's eyes are riveted to my body as I undress myself. I can hardly blame him. I am pleased at all the weight I have lost. I think I look pretty damn sexy.

As if he can read my thoughts, Patrick tells me so. "You look really good!"

I giggle boyishly at his compliment. He reaches down and touches my rapidly growing erection. He strokes it a few times until a new idea occurs to him. Dropping to his knees, he lowers his mouth onto my almost stiff cock. I enjoy the feeling of him deep throating me. The head of my dick has surprisingly little feeling, but the base of my dick against someone's lips really gets me hot.

He is unable to take my cock entirely, but swallows most of it. Drawing on my days of studying psychology, I fake a loud moan for him. My moans are basic behaviorism. If you positively reinforce a behavior, the chances it

will happen again are increased. By moaning as he sucks my dick, he is more likely to do it again.

It does seem to work. He continues plunging his face as far as he can. I become even harder and he begins to gag. I love the sensation as I pull the back of his head closer to me.

A few moments later we reverse places. I pull his pants off and toss them on the floor. His cock is semi-erect, suggesting that he does not have a full erection very often. That's hardly unusual for my clientele so I scarcely notice it. Sucking him deeply I am pleasured to hear him moan several times in succession.

After several minutes of oral sex, I pause to catch my breath. "Do you get enough sex from your lover?" I inquire. I already have a good idea how he will answer, but I want to hear it from him.

"Well, yes and no," he replies. "We do have a lot of sex, but it's not the type I like."

"You mean you want to fuck him or be fucked?"

"No, we do a lot of that already. He doesn't like giving oral sex. Having someone blow me is one of my favorite things, so it's extremely frustrating. He doesn't like to be fucked either and cums too quickly if he plays top. So our sex life isn't very good. I have the quantity, but not the quality."

I nod in understanding. "Then I'll just have to help you make up for it." I lower my face back into his crotch and begin sucking again.

Patrick stops me before I get into the oral sex. "Let's change positions."

I indicate my willingness to do so. He climbs on the bed and lies down on his side. I climb on as well and gently lower my head into his crotch. I continue sucking while Patrick basks in the sensation. "Oh, this is wonderful!" he moans. "I wish I could have this every day."

"Well, maybe not every day," I tease, "but you can have this anytime you'd like. You know where to find me.

I'm so selfless, aren't I?" We both laugh for a moment before I return to sucking him.

I bob up and down on him until he eventually tells me to stop. He is getting close and wants to feel me inside him. I am happy to comply and reach for my little bag of condoms and lube. Patrick stifles a laugh as he watches me tear open a condom wrapper with my teeth. I unroll the condom on my shaft, and place a slathering of lube on it. For an instant I flashback to Dean, but I force myself to concentrate on my present surroundings.

I spend a moment fingering him to determine how tight he is going to be. To my surprise, I find that he is very relaxed and ready to be fucked. I lay him back on the bed and hold his legs in the air. I part his cheeks and slowly slide myself into him.

At once he tightens up and begins moaning. I am unsure whether he is in pain or pleasure, but guess on the side of pleasure. I know many people hide their initial discomfort, but I trust Patrick's skill and begin sinking my dick deeply into him. Soon my balls are pushed up against his ass.

I hold his legs farther apart. I fuck him in a slow and steady rhythm. He responds by pushing his ass against my crotch. It is a sign of a skilled bottom when he pushes back. Patrick is no novice, and lifts his ass to take every inch.

Patrick's voice becomes louder and louder as I speed the pace of my thrusting. He lets loose a moan revealing the depth of his passion and pleasure with every thrust. I find it thrilling and increase the force of my penetration.

"Oh, Aaron, I want to feel you cum inside me," he pleads.

I am torn. I am nowhere near cumming, but he wants me to blow my load inside him. I don't know if I'll be able to excite myself to cum this way. Suddenly a thought occurs to me.

I change from long and slow strokes to short and fast ones. I deepen my breathing and start moaning more

loudly. Within moments I transform my appearance from someone in control to someone about to orgasm.

"Patrick! Patrick!" I start screaming as I plunge my dick harder and further into his ass. I buck wildly as my fake orgasm echoes around the room.

"Yeah, fuck me. Fuck me!" he yells back. "Give it to me! Slam that dick up my ass." My moaning reaches a crescendo as I appear to deliver a load of spunk. He moans along with me until I collapse in mock exhaustion.

I breathe rapidly as I lay against his chest. The illusion of my orgasm is perfect. "Oh, that was intense," I whisper in pseudo-afterglow. "Give me a minute, I need to get my strength back."

"Take all the time you need," he softly assures me. "I want to try a piece of your ass after you recover. I don't get to do that with Daniel, either."

Listening to him, I am glad I faked my orgasm. Like many men, it is uncomfortable for me to play bottom after I have an orgasm. Had I actually cum I would have great difficulty being fucked by Patrick.

In any case, before he tops me I have one important task to attend to. I reach over and grab a wad of Kleenex from a box on his nightstand. I pull off the condom and wrap it up. Once we're all done, I will make sure I dispose of the condom where he won't find it. I do not expect him to examine it closely but I would rather not allow him any chance of discovering my act.

Once I finish hiding the evidence, he gently lays me sideways across the bed. My ass and legs almost hang off the edge, but are held in the air by his shoulders. Standing on the side of the bed, he places the condom on himself, then slowly slides into me. His dick is hard enough to fuck me with a condom on, although not so hard that it actually hurts.

Like my style of fucking, he starts very slow and deep. He enjoys looking at his dick wrapped in the white condom as it enters me. He grabs my hips and arches his back. His dick grows larger as he fucks me, betraying his

raw excitement at having a young piece of ass. He fucks me harder and faster as he becomes increasingly excited.

Suddenly Patrick pulls out of me. He rips the condom off and blows his load all over my stomach and chest. Stream after stream of cum coat me with his raw heat. When he ceases spewing cum, he reaches out and smears it across my stomach. I love every sticky drop of it. As much as I escort for the money and the excitement, I truly enjoy a satisfied man creaming on me and then playing with it. It's a golden rule of sex - men never play with their own cum unless they enjoyed themselves.

Ten minutes, my fee, and a twenty-dollar tip later, I am on the road again.

Although I had planned to spend my evening hustling at the Townhouse, it's getting late for that. It's nine o'clock and it would take me almost two hours to drive there. I would have time for one client at the most, which defeats my purpose for the entire trip. I've already had a high paying day in any case. I might as well go home and take the night off.

Perhaps I should have expected it, but my return home is short lived. I barely have time to give Jeff a hug and a kiss before the phone rings again. It's a new client, one who has seen my ad in the *Advocate Classifieds*. He would like me to meet him at the Echo Queen Diner in Union before we drive to his apartment in Irvington. I am not thrilled at the prospect of visiting Irvington, an economically depressed suburb of Newark, but decide to take the chance. If things don't seem right I can always leave.

Hanging up the phone, I realize I am hungry. I've been so busy having sex I have barely eaten all day. I make myself a tuna sandwich for the road and depart on my next adventure.

I only have to wait two minutes at our meeting place before he arrives in a blue Buick Skylark. I am somewhat surprised to see he is black. I have several black clients, but not many. My surprise quickly turns to passive acceptance

as I notice he is easily 300 lbs. He is not my ideal client, but I have dealt with much heavier guys.

It doesn't matter anyway. Right now I'm in a moneymaking mood. I would escort for Godzilla if he had the cash.

"I'm Aaron," I introduce myself.

"I'm Ken," he replies nervously. He looks around as if to see if anyone has followed him. "Care to follow me?"

"Sure thing. Lead on," I instruct him. He pulls into the eastbound lane of Route 22. I follow him out of the parking lot and ease myself into the light evening traffic. Over the next few minutes he winds through a number of back roads until we emerge into the town of Irvington. I still do not like visiting here, but at least his neighborhood looks safe enough. We park on the street and quickly walk into an apartment building.

Once inside, I realize Ken is extremely nervous. "I'm sorry about meeting you at the diner," he apologizes, "but I wanted to make sure you were for real. There are a lot of wackos out there. You could have been a cop, too. That would have been very bad."

"I understand, you are not the first to--"

"I would have you over during the day," he cuts me off, "but my brother is here. He's pretty lazy and doesn't like to work. He's out at his evening job right now. So I had to have you over when I knew he would not be home for a while."

"Well," I say resting my hand on his arm, "I'm glad you have the house to your--"

"I'm a teacher," he interrupts again. "I teach music at a high school not too far from here. I really like music a lot, that's why I have so many CDs." He points to several large wall racks of compact discs. "Mostly classical music, but I have a lot of stuff in there."

"That's very interesting. If you don't mind my asking, what made you decide to have me--"

"One of the troubles with being a high school teacher is watching those really hot seniors of mine. Well, maybe

that's not a trouble and maybe that's a fringe benefit, I'm not sure!"

I will be lucky to get a word in edgewise so I decide to stay silent. I rapidly conclude I made the right decision as he continues to talk rapidly on a variety of subjects.

After several minutes I break in to ask, "do you like to role-play? I can pretend I am a student and you are helping me with my homework after school."

"Oh yes, that would be very hot. I fantasize about that a lot. I have this one student I sometimes tutor who..." he goes on and on. I doubt I will be able to role-play anything because I'll never get a chance to speak.

Finally he stops speaking and reaches out to me. One hand rubs my shoulders and chest while the other reaches for my crotch. I arch my back slightly to give him more access to my body. His hands greedily take advantage of me.

Like so many times earlier in the day, I feel my clothes being removed. First my shirt, then my pants, and finally my underwear and socks. Soon I am the naked boy of so many men's fantasies. He is hardly my dream daddy, but he does have a gentle touch. I find myself becoming very erect in spite of his unappealing body. He descends to his knees and slowly swallows my entire dick.

I am surprised. He manages to suck my dick better than Martin, Dean, or even Patrick were able to. It goes to show I shouldn't judge people based on their appearance. I have found that the best oral sex is often from people who are highly overweight.

He continues bobbing his head up and down on my shaft, pausing only occasionally to swallow the entire length. My loud moans are only slightly exaggerated for acting purposes. He really is good at oral sex.

"Shall we go into the bedroom?" he offers.

Once inside, I begin to undress him. It takes a few moments. Removing the clothing of a 300-pound man is not an easy task. Soon my hands are touching his chest the way he so recently touched mine.

My hands gradually descend from his chest to his massive stomach then to his stiff cock. He is uncut, which is another turnoff for me. It's not a major problem though. I'm too professional to be bothered by little setbacks.

Under the guise of foreplay, I pull back his foreskin to make sure it is clean. Fortunately it is. I have no idea what I would do if he were not.

"Oh, Aaron, this is so nice," he tells me. "I haven't been with a man in so long. I only jackoff to men on videos, and that isn't the same."

I feel sorry for him because he is so lonely. I doubt he is out to anyone about his sexuality. Having an escort must be a very personal experience for him. I resolve to make it a memorable occasion for him regardless of what I think of his looks.

I stand up on the bed and brace myself by touching the ceiling. He sits up with his back against the headboard. Standing over him, I slide my cock in and out of his mouth. He swallows the entire shaft causing my knees to shake. For a moment I think I will fall.

Pulling back slightly, I begin fucking his face. I pull myself out to the tip then slide in until my pubic hair grinds against the stubble on his face. I have to move in and out slowly because of my length but he does manage to take it all.

I continue fucking his face until his hands begin to roam. He is gradually moving them toward my ass. He spreads my cheeks apart and starts poking a finger into the center. He is a top, I realize, and I know exactly how to arouse a topman.

I lick the tips of my fingers so they are dripping with saliva. Reaching behind me, I wipe the wetness against my ass. When Ken returns his finger to my ass, he finds the center available for further exploration. He slides his finger an inch inside me. Before he can push any more, I sit down onto his hand and slide the rest of his finger into me. I moan theatrically to let him know I am enjoying his touch.

After a few more minutes of being facefucked and fingering me, he is ready for a change. "Do you have any condoms?" he asks.

"I'm always prepared!" I reply with a grin.

It takes me a moment to grab my bag and return to the bed. I pull out yet another blue-wrapped condom. I have lost count of how many I have used today.

Tearing open the wrapper, I notice his erection has gone down. I can easily solve that problem. I lower my face to his crotch and suck him for a few moments. Familiar odors waft upwards from the nether regions. They remind me of my bad sexual experience six months ago. I repress the memory. I survived that experience so I can survive this. Another half an hour and I'll be on my way.

My oral attentions soon have their desired effect. His dick stiffens and is soon ready to get to work. I unroll the condom on his cock and reach for the lube. I make sure I put an extra-large helping of lubricant on his condom and on my ass. My ass is somewhat sore and I have no idea if Ken cums quickly or not.

"What position do you like best?" I ask him.

"You on your stomach while I lay on top of you."

I am horrified at his answer. Visions of being flattened race through my head. Sensing my worry, Ken reassures me. "It's okay, I won't lay on you completely."

I am still not convinced, but decide to risk death anyway. I bend over and slowly lay down on my stomach. Briefly I wish I had taken out a life insurance policy. I almost burst out laughing at the thought.

He slowly straddles me. True to his word, he does not place the bulk of his weight on me. I guide his dick toward my hole and moments later feel him enter me. He pushes it all the way inside and begins a surprisingly slow and gentle rhythm. Although Ken assures me he has only done this a few times before, he has the skill of a pro. Would that half of my clients were this good at fucking.

"Ken," I begin to say. "I want you to enjoy yourself. Don't worry about my needs. I want you to enjoy yourself

and let all your pent-up frustrations loose on me. I really want you to fuck me good." Ken does not reply, but he does speed up in response. If the truth were known, my offer is not entirely selfless. If he enjoys himself, I may not have to get off again. That's one more day's worth of sexual energy I will have saved.

Ken adjusts himself slightly and begins plowing my ass for all he is worth. Pumping in and out of me, he grabs my butt and lets me have it. His breathing becomes shallow. I feel drops of sweat fall across my back.

My ass eventually betrays me, sore from all the use it has received today. At first it throbs with a mild discomfort, but it rapidly begins hurting me. With every thrust I grimace in pain. "Oh Ken," I encourage him, "I want you to cum in me so badly. I don't want you to wait."

Again, Ken does not respond. He continues to fuck me with the same moderate pace. The pain grows until I am not sure I can take it any longer. "Ken," I begin saying.

Suddenly he lets out a large moan and pushes his dick into me as far as he can. I feel his dick stiffen as it lets out multiple blasts of cum into the rubber. He impales me with his cock, pinning me under his weight before he slides out of me completely. He collapses on top of my back momentarily crushing me.

After a few moments he rolls off and sits down on the bed. "Would you jack off on me?" he asks.

I think for a moment. I would like to save my cum for tomorrow, but I don't recall having anything scheduled. I suddenly decide to go for it. I've had sex with five men today and I deserve a little relief of my own.

He leans back and lifts his knees to create a nice place for me to sit on his crotch. I sit on his lap and begin stroking myself. He reaches down and plays with my balls. His gentle touch is wonderful. I moan repeatedly as he kneads and strokes them.

I slowly increase the speed of my own pumping. Closing my eyes, I fantasize about the sex I have had today.

My irritations and frustrations are wiped away leaving only the fond memories of having sex with so many men.

At last I feel my balls tighten as the tension within me grows. I stroke faster and faster until finally I shoot my load onto his chest. It isn't a big orgasm but it is an intense one. I cry out as small streams of cum pour onto his body. Every part of my body and soul feel sexualized. I am totally content.

I apologize to Ken as my orgasm recedes. "I hope I didn't wake your neighbors." He doesn't realize I am lying. I purposely increased the volume of my noises so he would feel flattered that he helped bring me a great deal of pleasure. It did feel good, just not quite as good as he thinks. The orgasm was missing an emotional component. Emotions I only find from sex with Jeff.

We clean up and I again put on my clothes. We talk for a while, and he shows me his classical music collection. His collection interests me, and he gives me a pair of CDs. I am very grateful to him and tell him I will listen to them as soon as I get home.

With that he pays me and I head on my way.

When I return home, I find a message on my machine from Ken. I left my bottle of lubricant at his apartment. I have no idea when I will be back there, but I am not worried. I earned over a thousand dollars today, and can easily afford to buy myself a new one.

Jeff eagerly counts the day's take while I collapse on the couch. It has been a profitable day. It has been a tiring day. Above all, it has been a busy day.

The Kid

April 21, 1997

The moment I pull into the parking lot, I can see he is young. The thought fills me with excitement.

I exit my car and stand looking at him for the first time. From his voice on the phone, I had guessed him to be in his thirties. Seeing him in person immediately makes me reconsider. He is in his mid-twenties at most, perhaps even younger.

Despite his age, I am more interested in his "look." Standing in front of me is a living, breathing redneck. He is short in height with a weight definitely a bit on the heavy side. Although his flannel shirt and pickup truck both contribute to his redneck image, his accent is what clinches it. "I'm Jim," he introduces himself. His drawl sends images of the South through my head and shivers down my spine.

I am so enthralled with him that I almost fail to respond to his introduction. His blond hair is slightly unkempt, perhaps from sitting under a baseball cap. His piercing blue eyes hold my gaze. His entire appearance has the look of one whose intelligence rests in the practical instead of the theoretical. I imagine him as being able to rebuild an engine, but not being able to name a single law of physics.

I continue to be so taken by his looks that I introduce myself by my real name. I mentally swear at myself. I have never made that mistake before.

"Do you wanna follow me to the motel?" he asks in his sexy accent. "I have a room waiting for us."

"That's fine. You lead. I'll be right behind you." I sit back down in my car and start the engine. Driving to the motel, I feel a wave of giddiness pass through me. I rarely ever get cute guys like this. Last time I was hired by a young man, he was an overweight twenty-five year-old guy looking for his first gay experience. He was a lot of fun, but he wasn't nearly as sexy as this guy.

Jim parks outside a room on the bottom floor. As I step out of my car, I notice several stray cats peering from the shadows of the motel. I have seen the cats many times before. The motel owners put out food by the dumpster for them. To my amusement, I see Jim speaking in baby talk to them.

Slightly embarrassed by the whole situation, Jim walks over to the motel room door. He digs into his pocket before he finds a key connected to a large blue plastic key-ring. He slides it into the keyhole and the door swings open.

I take a few moments to make myself comfortable. I remove my windbreaker and set it on the dresser. I untie my bag from around my waist and set it on the nightstand. Taking off my shoes, I jump onto the bed and lean back.

I look up at Jim. He is almost paralyzed with anxiety. His hands shake visibly as he struggles to light a cigarette. He inhales deeply, pauses for a moment, and then offers me one. "Do you smoke?"

I shake my head, but give him a friendly smile. "No, but you're welcome to." He laughs nervously and begins to relax.

"Why don't you sit down and make yourself more comfortable?" I ask him.

He nods and promptly sits in a chair on the other side of the room. I almost laugh at his inhibitions.

"Would you like to talk for a moment?" I offer. "Maybe it will help put you at ease."

"Yes, please," he says. He takes another puff on his cigarette and looks at me.

"Well, for starters let me say I am not going to attack you. Sexually, that is," I begin. "We can do as little or as much as you would like, and you are welcome to tell me you want to stop at any time. I won't pressure you to do anything you are not ready to do. Do you understand?"

"Yes, thank you. I appreciate that."

"Have you ever been with a guy before?"

He inhales his cigarette again. "No. I've been with several girls. A lot of girls, but never a guy. I've fantasized about it and I have a lot of questions, but have never done it."

"What sort of questions do you have?"

Jim blushes slightly. "Oh, different things. Like does it feel tighter fucking a man or a woman? Would it be more intense to cum with a guy or a girl? Which would excite me more? I want to know what I think of fucking a guy. I want to touch a man's body, too."

I begin to understand Jim's mindset. He wants to explore a man's body in the only way he knows how, by emulating sex with a woman. Gay sex is very fluid. You can do everything in almost any order. In straight sex, the actual intercourse is the centerpiece. Everything else is just foreplay. He wants to fuck a guy because he thinks that is what two guys are supposed to do in bed. Not that I mind. I find Jim very attractive and would enjoy him fucking me. But I do find it curious that his thoughts are so centered on fucking.

Jim diverges momentarily to give me a warning. "One thing I'm definitely not into is kissing. That would be weird with a guy. I don't think I could do it." Again, this says something about his psyche. Kissing removes his mental barriers and admits his own sexuality to himself.

With regret, I accept his limitation. He can fuck a man but he cannot bring himself to kiss one. Patting the bed next to me, I offer him an invitation. "Would you like to come sit next to me? I won't attack you."

"Okay," he accepts. He walks across the room and sits beside me. I put my arm around him and slowly begin

rubbing his back. At first he is wary of my touch, but slowly he warms up to the soft repetitive motion. Soon he is relaxed and my touch is no longer unwelcome.

"Why don't you lie down. It'll make you more comfortable."

This time he does not respond, but instead crushes his cigarette in the ashtray. We move partway across the bed so he can lie on his back. I lie down next to him and slowly touch his chest through his shirt. I slowly unbutton it and reach between the layers of flannel to touch his flesh. He closes his eyes as new sensations and emotions pour through him.

I am surprised to find his chest is totally smooth. Not a strand of hair emerges, making me reconsider how old he really is. The thought is lost as I continue to explore his body. I softly stroke and squeeze his nipples. I lower my tongue to them and lick them several times. He moans softly and runs his hands through my hair.

Jim slowly lowers his hands from my hair and reaches for my crotch. I had expected him to need more coaxing, but his emotions are getting the better of him. He begins rubbing my crotch, trying to find my dick. "Would you like me to remove my jeans?" I ask. He nods once as I slowly undo my pants.

I drop my jeans to the floor and place his hands on my stiffness. He is surprised by its size but quickly begins stroking its length. I realize he is mimicking his own style of masturbation. He strokes me with two fingers and his thumb, a technique commonly used by men with small dicks. Although I have not seen him undressed, I already know he is not as endowed as I am.

Slowly I dip my hands below the rim of his pants. The constrained manhood within is not very big, but is rock hard. Sliding my hand back out, I reach for the button to his pants. Seconds later the zipper is open as well.

He lifts his hips as I slowly pull down his pants and underwear. I leave them around his knees. Sex with partially removed clothes always gives me a feeling of sponta-

neity and rushed sexuality. I hope he is enjoying the same sensation.

Jim's erect cock is about four inches. It is shorter than average, but long enough to stroke and pleasure with ease. Most of my partners believe the perfect sized dick is seven or eight inches like mine. What men forget is that my size makes it impractical to penetrate many of my partners, not to mention being uncomfortable in my pants whenever it is erect. Jim has no such problems. His cock is just big enough for me to wrap my hand around. It's also an ideal size to suck, an act I promptly begin performing.

He enjoys the oral sex immensely. His hands run through my hair as I push my lips into his groin. Grabbing the back of my head, he pulls me even deeper between his legs. I happily allow him to do so because his cock is small enough for me to breathe while sucking him. I take him entirely within my mouth for minutes at a time, letting him feel engulfed in soft and warm wetness.

"Can I go down on you?" he interrupts my fun in a nervous tone.

"Certainly," I respond with a broad grin. We change positions slightly and moments later I feel the beginnings of an amateurish blowjob. He is able to take less than half my length in his mouth. I feel his teeth scratch against my length. He is definitely having more fun at this than I am.

Yet what he lacks in skill is more than made up in enthusiasm. Jim is like many of my inexperienced partners, wanting desperately to pleasure me but not knowing exactly how to do so. I remember them looking at me from between my legs as they ask me if it feels good. I always tell them it feels wonderful and ask them to continue. When Jim pauses to ask me the same question, I answer him with a wide grin and a nod. I gently push his head back down on me, filling him with a new sense of self-confidence.

As he continues his newly discovered pastime, I relax in anticipation of what is to come. I am highly aroused from this encounter with this essentially virginal young

man. Every time he speaks I become increasingly turned on by his hick drawl.

"Can we fuck now?" he asks excitedly.

I am as eager to please him as he is to please me. I reach for my bag to gather my condoms and lube. Out of the corner of my eye, I notice Jim looking slightly anxious. "Relax," I assure him. "I'll take over from here. Just lay back and enjoy yourself."

He nods and appears relieved. "Thanks. I'm not sure how to do this."

"Well to begin with, have you ever fantasized about a specific position?" I inquire.

He nods several times. "On my back with you sitting on me. That would be very hot!" he exclaims excitedly.

I consider his request. His position is great for me because I can jack myself off easily. I'm not sure it will be great for him, because it will be difficult for him to pump while on his back.

In the end, I decide to climb on board. I unroll the condom on his stiff manhood then lubricate myself thoroughly. His shaft, now hard enough to break down a brick wall, has no problem penetrating me. I sit down on him and let out a moan of pleasure.

Jim looks up at me with an odd expression on his face. "Does it feel good to get fucked?" he asks.

I enthusiastically answer him in the affirmative. "Yes. I doubt so many men would do it otherwise."

He nods his head. "That makes sense."

I slowly raise and lower myself over him. His arousal to my actions is obvious. He pushes up his hips every time I lower myself. It is a hot feeling for both of us. His smile lights the room like a beacon.

"Jim, can I tell you something?" I ask him as I completely sit in his lap.

"Sure, what?" he instantly replies.

"I find you very attractive and you are turning me on big time."

My compliment hits him like a lightning bolt. He blushes instantly and becomes unable to speak for several moments. "Thank you," he stammers. "I think you're real cute for a guy. I'm enjoying myself more than I thought I would. I thought you'd be just a body, you know, just fucking around with me. But you're not. I'm glad we met."

I am about to reply when Jim speaks again. "Can we stop talking and get back to the sex?"

The honesty of his request almost makes my laugh. I begin sliding myself up and down on his erect shaft as a way of answering.

Jim is not the only one enjoying himself. Almost all of my clients are over age thirty. They are usually experienced, intelligent, kind, stable, and predictable. Although they all have their own individuality, as a group their behavior is similar. Younger and more sexually inexperienced clients provide an interesting change for me. My lack of experience with them makes everything different and exciting. Put another way, I have more than 200 clients over thirty years old. I have less than ten clients under the same age. Jim is a welcome change from my normal routine.

Thinking of Jim brings me back out of my thoughts. His broad smile is clearly signaling his enjoyment. He reaches up and grabs my hips, pulling me down with every upward stroke. He rams himself into me causing my moans to overwhelm his. I begin rapidly stroking my own dick as he fucks me. I had planned to save my sexual energy for my clients the next day but I am becoming too aroused to stop.

Slowing the pace of his strokes, Jim avoids having his orgasm prematurely. Many young men fall into the trap of cumming as fast as they can. Jim is more patient as he holds himself deep inside me. Although he is inexperienced, I am impressed with his natural skill.

The momentary interlude is too tempting. I look him in the eye. "You can't even begin to understand how much I would enjoy kissing you," I admit.

He is silent for several moments. "I don't feel right about doing that. I'm sorry."

I feel hurt at his answer, although I am not surprised. Even more than feeling hurt, I am angry with myself for pursuing my own agenda. This is his special time, not mine. I'm being paid to make it hot for him.

"It's okay, don't worry about it. Can I ask you one other thing?"

"Okay, what?" he asks.

I am afraid of his answer but cannot resist the question. "How old are you?" I am uncertain how old I want him to be. I want him to be young because it is more exciting for me, but the younger he is, the more trouble I will be in with Jeff. I'm not supposed to have any clients under twenty-five.

Jim's reply surpasses my greatest hopes and worst fears. "I'm nineteen, although I know I do look older," he says. "Then again, ages are misleading. You don't look twenty-four. I'll bet you are a lot younger than that."

I wink at him. He doesn't need to know I'm twenty-six.

The moment ends as Jim returns to his previous pumping motions. This time I know he is not going to stop until he climaxes. His strokes are rapid and deep. He clearly wants to fuck until he loses control. I assist him in his plunges, pushing my ass against his crotch with every stroke. I want him to enjoy himself more than he can possibly imagine. He is grinning like crazy as he fucks me, and I am melting from his expression. I moan louder and louder as he increases the pace of his strokes.

The end is not far. The sexual intensity wipes any semblance of control from his face, contorting his grin into an expression of rapture and ecstasy. At the same moment he loses control, I feel his dick expand to new depths within me. A cry escapes from his lips as the first gush of warmth erupts from the head at the top of his swollen shaft. I can almost feel it blasting my insides.

Load after load fills the condom as he moans himself into a stupor. His grin is totally erased now, washed away by the tides of pleasure which are slowly receding. Replacing it is an expression of peace and relaxation. I hold still as I watch his breathing slowly return to normal.

Minutes pass before Jim opens his eyes. "This was so good," he whispers. "Would you jack off on me? I really want to watch it. Just don't shoot on my face."

"No problem," I assure him as I begin stroking. I am hot from this entire encounter. I touch myself while Jim plays with my balls. I do not remember telling him how sensitive they are, but somehow he knows what to do. He tenderly kneads the sack to encourage their contents to shoot all over his body.

The combination of my stroking, his touch, and the entire encounter brings me to a peak. My orgasm is swift and savage, streams of pearly white cum bursting forth to land on his stomach. Jim is slightly repulsed and quickly wipes most of the cum off him. Yet he is drawn to it and stares at the last drops.

Staring at him, I see the look on his face change. The peaceful expression vanishes as emotions of guilt and anxiety fill his eyes. As he turns his head to look at me, I realize he has erected defensive barriers in his mind. Gone is any look of closeness or affection he may have once had.

He pulls out of me and I stand back down on the floor. I enter the bathroom to clean myself off. When I return two minutes later, he is dressed and smoking another cigarette. He is slightly in shock at what he has done. The magnitude of his actions must be hitting home. I sit on the bed beside him and begin to dress myself.

We talk for a while as I try to break his newly rebuilt shell. I know this is a critical time for him. Whether he leaves feeling guilty or not will determine how he deals with his sexuality in the future. I don't want him to regret this experience. I want him to feel good about himself, to accept his sexuality, and perhaps to call me again. He may feel indifferent about me, but I like him.

"You have a lot to think about," I point out to him as I reach for my shirt. "You may not want to make any decisions about your lifestyle or your sexual orientation until you have a chance to think things over."

"Yeah, this is new to me," he agrees. "Strange, too..." He trails off thoughtfully and inhales his cigarette again.

Pulling on my socks, I continue to speak. "It may be strange to you but you really are good at this. You have what it takes to be a very skilled lover."

"Thanks. You were really fun, too..." he says trailing off into silence again. His defenses are still intact.

Desperately I ask Jim a final question. "Any regrets?"

He thinks for a moment. "Guess not. I just feel weird."

I stare at Jim intently for a moment. He meets my gaze, reflecting the light of the room in his eyes while hiding his thoughts from my view. As I finish tying my shoes, I concede defeat. "As a callboy I really have no right to have any regrets," I tell him. "I just wish I could have kissed you."

As Jim meets my gaze again, I realize he is no longer pushing me away. He puts his hand on the back of my head and pulls me toward him. Our lips touch as his tongue probes my mouth. I return the embrace. For a moment we passionately kiss.

The moment vanishes as fast as it arrives. Jim pulls back from me and looks away. We stand in silence for a moment, marveling at the magnitude of his actions. When he finally looks at me again, his shell has returned. I know it will never again be lowered around me.

We take care of the monetary aspect of our transaction. Before we leave, I give him one last hug. He returns it awkwardly, shying away from my touch.

We walk outside. I tell him I hope he will call me, knowing at the same time I will never hear from him again.

I try to memorize the expression on his face but it is a wasted effort. I am seeing him for the last time.

I watch him as he slowly drives away. I should feel honored and privileged to be his first male lover, but somehow I feel depressed instead. I will never know what difference, if any, I have made in his life. It hurts in its own way, and I don't know if I would have been better off never meeting him.

I doubt I will ever have another meeting like this. Tomorrow will undoubtedly see a return to my regular clients, mature men capable of dealing with their own feelings but lacking the emotional intensity of youth.

I slowly depart from the motel savoring the hurt within.

In the Third Person

May 28, 1997

I think I have stepped onto the set of *The Silence of the Lambs*.

My flashback to the movie is instantaneous. The killer is standing at the rim of the pit. At the bottom is a hysterical woman begging for her life. Ignoring her pleas, the killer commands in the third person, "the girl will do this," or "it will do that."

I have always been horrified at how he dehumanized her through his use of the third person. So when Adam greets me in the third person, I am surprised to say the least.

"The boy will come in," he welcomes me.

Another idea occurs to me. Perhaps he has a daddy-boy fantasy he wants to act out. That could be hot. I've always wanted try something like that.

The thought gives me mixed feelings. I do fantasize about daddy-boy role-playing, but I do not want to be treated like a mindless piece of meat in the process. The way he called me "the boy" instead of "his boy" is creepy rather than erotic.

Although Adam is an average looking man in his forties, something is not right about him. Perhaps my discomfort is from his voice. It is slightly effeminate with a touch of hyperactivity. Something about it gives me a feeling of wrongness.

I shake my head to clear my mind and enter the apartment. Behind me, I hear Adam close the door. Although the door shuts with a small click, it sounds like the clang of a mausoleum.

"Daddy is pleased to see the boy," he begins. "Daddy would like to give a tour to the cute boy, but there is a special rule in this apartment. Does the boy know what rule that is?"

"No, what rule is that?" I ask. I'm not sure I really want to know.

"Oh, I guess the boy wouldn't know," he chuckles to himself. "The rule of this apartment is simple. The person receiving the tour must be in the nude. The boy will take his clothes off so he can begin the tour."

Despite my feelings of uneasiness, I strip off my clothes. Adam touches my body with his hands while I undress.

He must be able to sense my feelings because he tries to put me at ease. "Is the boy nervous?" he asks. "Daddy does not want the boy to be nervous. Daddy wants the boy to feel welcome."

"I'm okay," I half-heartedly reassure him.

Ignoring me, he continues speaking. "The boy has such a lovely cock. Does the boy have a name for it?"

"No, I've never named it."

"Then let daddy name it. Daddy will call it Mickey. Mickey is the name of daddy's dick. Did the boy know that?"

"No," I reply again. "I hadn't known that." Thinking about Mickey makes me wonder just how strange he is.

"Daddy's dick has been called Mickey for twenty years now. Daddy's first lover named it Mickey. So daddy will call the boy's dick Mickey, too."

I am now twice as nervous despite Adam's attempt to put me at ease. I wonder if this is how all psychotics start.

"Now the daddy is going to welcome Mickey to his apartment. Daddy always tries to make his visitors feel welcome." Adam drops to his knees and gently kisses my dick. He reaches up and holds my semi-erect shaft to his lips before he gives it a large lick. He stares at its growing hardness for a moment before he slides it inside his mouth.

The sexual feelings help ease my anxiety. Unfortunately, just as I am beginning to enjoy myself he pulls back and stands up.

"It's time to begin the tour," he announces with a flourish.

Adam takes my hand and leads me several steps into his apartment. For the first time, I look around at my surroundings. I am in a moderate sized two-bedroom apartment with a balcony. The living and dining rooms are filled with overly ornamental furnishings such as statues and a waterfall.

He leads me directly to the waterfall. "Does the boy see this? Daddy is going to put the boy's penis in the water. It will feel very cold but then daddy will warm it up for him. Does the boy understand?"

The boy understands he's a crackpot. "Yes, I understand. Go ahead."

He wraps his hand around the base of my cock and slowly lowers it into the cold water. I involuntarily flinch as cold water touches my skin. My erection vanishes instantly but he does not let go.

"Oh, the water is cold, Adam. Please let me pull it out," I plead.

"Daddy knows the water feels cold on the boy, but daddy does know best," he tells me. I am still uncomfortable around him, but he is right in one aspect. The sexual way he is doing this to me makes it bearable. My erection even slowly begins to return.

Finally he relents. "The boy can stop now." He picks up a nearby towel and dries the cold water from my body. Lowering himself to his knees, he puts his tongue on my balls. The numbness from the cold masks most of the feeling, but as he sucks on my balls, I begin to feel familiar warm and wet sensations.

He sucks on my balls for a few more moments before he switches to my semi-hard cock. He holds it between his fingers for a few seconds then slides it into his mouth. De-

spite the return of feeling into my balls, my cock is still almost completely numb.

After a few moments he stands up. "Daddy will continue the tour now."

I nod politely to cover my thoughts. This sexual encounter is frustrating for me. The way he orders me around is quite arousing, but his constant use of the third person is strange and disturbing. As much as I would love to act out a daddy/boy scene, he is not my image of a daddy.

To me, a hot daddy is a well-built, outgoing, and assertive person. He treats me firmly in bed, but is respectful of my limits. Unlike my fantasy, Adam is skinny and awkward looking, and is freaking me out with his role-play. I am following Adam's orders only because he is paying me, not out of any sexual desire on my part.

Adam continues his tour another six feet into the living room. "The boy will sit down," he instructs, pointing at the couch.

I seat myself and spread my legs for him. He kneels between them, but to my surprise he does not begin sucking me. He grabs my ankles instead and lifts them into the air. Holding them far apart, he lowers his face into my ass and starts rimming me.

After two seconds of rimming he suddenly stops. I wonder if I am unclean down there, but I am sure that is not the case. A more likely reason is that he is living out the fantasy of a wild sex-filled tour of his apartment. The length of time having sex in each room is not important. Once we reach the end of the tour, we will have the actual sex. I am relieved at my insight. It helps me understand what is going on, which in turns means I can better meet his needs and fulfill his fantasies.

Slowly we move into the dining room. "Daddy would love to have a naked dinner with the boy." His reference to dinner makes me think of Hannibal "the Cannibal" Lecter. To my relief, we do not stay long in the dining room as we move onto the balcony.

The balcony overlooks a large parking lot in the process of being repaved. I am surprised at his invitation to stand on the balcony in the nude. Fortunately, there is no one in sight. He kneels in front of me and begins sucking me for a third time. This time my dick is rock hard and ready for his attentions.

As I predicted, he only spends a few moments of time sucking me. The next stop on the tour is an undecorated and shabby kitchen. He lifts me onto the counter and spreads my legs to give him an unrestricted view.

Stepping back to admire my body, Adam speaks again. "The daddy is pleased with the boy. He is much more attractive than the daddy's last boy. The boy is very beautiful."

Adam's reference to his last boy makes me wonder where he is now. Could something awful have happened to him? A shiver runs down my spine. Adam approaches me again and fondles my stiff cock. When he reaches out and touches my balls, I moan to conceal my uneasiness.

"Daddy" becomes more excited as the tour nears its end. He bypasses a guestroom completely and only gestures at a hall bathroom. "That is the boy's bathroom. If the boy needs to pee, he can use this room. Or he can use my bathroom in the main bedroom. Either bathroom is yours to use."

His slip from the third to the first person does not escape me. I think he may be coming out of his bizarre fantasy, but he quickly dashes my hopes.

"Oh yes," he continues. "You can use any bathroom here. I would love to watch the boy pee in the toilet. Or maybe in the fountain in the other room. The boy will have to pee in the fountain next time he is here. If you have to really go to the bathroom, you should use a toilet but daddy will wipe it for you. Just like a little boy, the boy will bend over while daddy wipes his bottom."

I am thoroughly disgusted. He is not the first person to ask me for a watersports fantasy, but his desire to wipe my ass totally repulses me. Now I want to leave and never

return. I remain silent because I do not trust myself to speak. I suspect the expression on my face speaks for itself.

The tour finally ends in the bedroom. Like the rest of the apartment, the room is overly furnished with tacky knick-knacks. In the center of the room is an unmade bed. A small pile of sheets and blankets sit off to the side.

"Daddy's fantasy is for the boy to be my houseboy," he begins in an odd mixture of the first and third persons. "He wants to see the boy put the sheets on my bed while the daddy touches him and molests you."

His speech is bizarre, but at least his request is harmless. I am more than happy to clean house for $150 an hour.

"Before the boy can begin," he continues in the third person, "he needs to remove daddy's clothes."

I begin kissing Adam as I undo his clothes. I remove his shirt, then his pants, underwear, and socks. Finally he wears nothing at all. Dropping to my knees, I take his soft cock entirely into my mouth swallowing it completely. He moans and arches slightly against me.

Suddenly he pulls out of my mouth. "It's time for the boy to begin making the bed."

Although his style of role-playing is odd, I comply as best I can. I step over to the bed and begin unfolding the sheets. I feel his hand rub my butt as I bend over. Making the bed continues in a similar fashion. Every time I pause to tuck or unfold something, I feel a hand or tongue touch my body.

Eventually the bed is made. Grabbing my shoulders, he slowly lowers me onto the bed. Reaching inside a drawer, he pulls out a bottle of lotion. He pumps a wad into his hand and reaches down toward my ass. He slowly penetrates me, sliding his finger deep into the tight center. I feel the lotion spread between my buns by the motions of his hand and fingers.

"How much is the boy enjoying this?" he asks.

"Oh, the boy loves, I mean I like this," I exclaim purposely slipping into the third person. I thought he might appreciate it somehow.

"Is the boy ready to be fucked?"

"I'm always ready, Adam. You can give it to me as much as you'd like."

"It's not Adam," he admonishes me, "it's Daddy. Tell Daddy how much you like it."

"Oh, Daddy," I reply dramatically, "I love the way you are fingering my ass. I want you to fuck me and I want you to make your boy feel really good." Although I can tell from the expression on Adam's face that I am saying the correct words, I feel self-conscious doing so. I find nothing erotic in this daddy/boy scene. I want to get it over with and leave as fast as I can.

Adam is unaware of my true feelings. He grabs his bottle of lotion and pumps several blasts into his hand. He reaches down and to my surprise, he rubs it all over the top of my pubic hair and on my stomach. "Daddy wants to lie on top of you and rub up against his beautiful boy," he explains. "It's his favorite way to cum."

He climbs on me and lowers his body against mine. He begins humping me, sliding his dick against the flesh of my stomach. "Oh, beautiful boy, lie there and don't move. Oh, daddy is so happy with his boy." I briefly wonder if he has a necrophilliac fetish.

He humps me for no more than a minute before he loses control. His moaning and pumping crescendos as spurts of ejaculate cover my stomach. He quickly pulls off and leaves the room. I am glad my work here is done.

He returns a few moments later and hands me a towel. "I wish I could see you more often," he tells me. "You are such a beautiful boy.

"Would you be willing to make a deal? I could pay you less but give you a steady appointment each week?"

He has temporarily abandoned referring to me in the third person. I am not sure why, but I take this as a good sign. "To be honest, I'm not sure I can do that," I explain as I wipe myself off. "I really can't negotiate since this is what I do for a living."

"Well, think it over. I'll call you in a few days and we can discuss it then."

Numerous replies race through my head as I look him in the eyes. I want to tell him to go to hell, or that I wouldn't consider negotiating with anyone that wants to wipe my ass, but I say none of those things. Ever polite to the end, I tell Adam I will think it over.

Adam asks me if I would like to take a shower but I respectfully decline. I've pressed my luck enough for one day and I want to go home. It's safer that way. I still do not completely trust him. One never knows who the truly dangerous clients are.

As I get dressed, I realize my own daddy-boy fantasy will have to wait for another day. His fantasy and mine had nothing in common. Perhaps my fantasy will never be fulfilled through my work. Escorting requires I meet clients' needs rather than my own. I am unsure if the two are ever totally compatible. Then again, I've had enough unusual experiences to know nothing is impossible in my line of work.

We settle the issue of the money in the living room. He kisses me good-bye and lets me out the door. I'm off to home to shower before I depart for New York City for my evening client and yet another adventure. Perhaps the next movie set I walk into will be more like an erotic film rather than *The Silence of the Lambs*. I could get into that.

Both Sides

June 8, 1997

One of the first lessons I learned as an escort is that legitimate clients rarely play games with my time. If someone is serious about hiring me, he is not going to make me jump through hoops before we meet.

Case in point. When I first began escorting, I had several potential clients who wanted to meet me before they decided whether to hire me or not. In each case, they did not hire me. On one occasion, I couldn't even convince the client that I was not involved in some sort of bizarre police sting operation. Others admitted that they were really looking for an S&M slave, a kept boy, or a boyfriend.

So when Richard asked me to meet him by the concierge desk of the Philadelphia Hilton rather than in his room, I was wary. I am much too busy to play games with people who want to check me out at a distance. I know I am on the level. I expect my clients to be as well.

Despite my reservations, something about the person on the phone made me decide to go ahead and meet with him. I wish I could remember what it was. It's 7:38 and Richard is eight minutes late. I know his first name and I know he said he would be "different from anyone else I have met." Outside of that, I know nothing about him at all.

Out of the corner of my eye, I notice someone walking rapidly in my direction. Seconds later, a well-built man with short-cropped graying hair passes in front of me. "Room 834," he mumbles as he continues across the lobby.

Did he do what I think he did. This person, if it is indeed Richard, has startled me. People never walk past me

and say their room number. They walk up to me, greet me in a friendly fashion, and invite me up to their room. I'm a callboy, not a secret agent. I don't play games like this.

The person ahead of me turns around and frowns slightly. He has noticed I am not following him. I start walking toward him wondering what I have stumbled into.

He proceeds across the lobby before he turns down a hall toward the elevators. Several other people wait outside the closed door. After a minute of waiting, the elevator slides open and we all enter. He presses the button for the eighth floor and begins to wait. I wonder again what he is up to.

Moments later the doors slide open again. The stranger and I exit. "This way," he quietly murmurs as he heads off to the left. I follow him in silence.

We reach room 834. Once we are inside, he closes the door behind me. He extends his hand. "I'm Richard. You must be Aaron."

I shake his hand. "That was quite an unusual way of greeting me downstairs. Do you always meet your escorts that way?"

"I wanted to make sure you were on the level," he says.

"On the level?" I ask. "Why wouldn't I be on the level?"

"You never know. Some escorts like to bring along a friend to play dangerous games with their client. I don't like to play games."

"Neither do I. That's why I was irritated waiting for you downstairs. I am accustomed to meeting people in their hotel rooms. I was fairly certain you weren't going to show."

"Well, I'm here," he says. "I'm sorry for keeping you waiting. Would you like to sit down?"

We proceed into the main part of the room where there is a bed, a table, and several chairs. Like most business travelers, Richard's possessions are minimal. I see

only a small suitcase and a leather briefcase beside the nightstand.

Richard walks around the table and sits down on the far side. He motions for me to take a seat across from him, as if I were about to interview for a job. It will be difficult to get close to him with a table between us, but I'm prepared to follow his lead. He is the client, after all.

I take a closer look at him once I sit down. He is in good shape and appears to be in his mid-to-late forties. His short hair gives him a conservative look, but he does not look like a businessman. There is a rough edge to him in addition to the look of intelligence in his eyes. I find myself wondering how hung he is.

"Like I said on the phone," he begins, "I think you'll find me to be quite different than any of your other clients."

"How is that?" I ask.

"For starters, we're not going to have sex."

So much for finding out his dick size. I wonder what else he may want from me. "Oh?" I ask, not trusting myself to say any more.

He reaches in his pocket and pulls out several bills. He places them on the table and slides them toward me. "Here," he offers. "These are for you. Take them if you'd like. You're free to take your money and leave. Or you can stay and see what's my deal."

I recoil from the money as if it is some sort of poisonous snake. I am afraid he may be some sort of cop and the money is being used to entrap me. I decide to be cautious to protect myself. "I may take it later but for now I'll let it sit there," I tell him.

"Why not take it? It's yours," he prompts me.

"I'm not sure about the legality of me taking it. You have to understand," I explain nervously, "you're not acting like my other clients. That throws me off balance."

"I told you I wouldn't be like them. Go ahead, take the money."

I am very confused about why he is pressing the money issue so I decline. "I'll take it later. So tell me, if we're not going to have sex, what are we going to do?"

He is not bothered by my action. "Suit yourself. I don't want to have sex because I want to get to know you instead."

"A lot of my clients want to get to know me," I point out. "That doesn't preclude us going to bed," I point out.

"Yes, but I'm not like--"

"--my other clients," I finish. "I understand. Let me get this straight. You are paying me $300 to talk?"

"Among things. I said we weren't going to have sex. I didn't say we were only going to talk."

"That's true," I admit. I decide to go on the offensive in the conversation. "Have you hired escorts before?"

"Yes," he admits.

"And have you had sex with them?"

"No."

I pause for a moment. "Are you some sort of voyeur? In that you like to watch guys?"

He considers my question. "Let's say I admire the young male physique. But it's not a sexual thing for me."

A thought occurs to me. "Have you ever had sex with a man before?"

"No." Before I have an opportunity to ask another question, he takes control of the conversation. "My turn to ask questions."

I am curious what he will ask. "All right, you're paying the tab. Shoot."

"How long have you been hustling?" he begins.

"Escorting," I correct him. "Just under a year plus another summer after I graduated from college."

"What degree?"

"Two of them. Master's in college and university administration, bachelor's in psychology."

He pauses for a moment surprised at my answer. "Where did you go?"

"Iowa State for my undergrad, Michigan State for my grad."

"Good schools."

"They're all right. Most state universities are similar in nature. Their football teams have more diversity than their academics."

He chuckles slightly. "Why Iowa?"

He's not the first person to ask this question. Most of my clients are curious about this. I usually give a stock answer, but this time I decide to be truthful. "It's the only school which accepted me. My father's family is from Iowa, too. I'm the third generation of my family to go there."

He nods his head in understanding. "I had guessed you grew up in Iowa."

"Nope, New Jersey. Born and raised, spent all of my life there until my college years. Mind if I ask you a question?" I ask.

"If its a good one," he replies with a smile.

Somehow that does not reassure me. I know he is gathering a brief history of my life before he delves into my more personal areas. I suspect he has some training in the area of information gathering. Social work perhaps? He does not seem the type. He is too gruff and direct.

"You said you have not had sex with any of the young men you have hired, and that you are not voyeuristically inclined. At least in a sexual way."

"Yes," he agrees.

"Have you ever touched any of them? More than shaking hands, that is."

He pauses for a second. "Yes, that I have done."

"How? And to what end?"

"I'm surprised you have to ask that. I spanked them. You should have known that. I asked you on the phone if you were into spanking. You said you weren't."

"I only vaguely remember your phone call," I point out. "I get too many phone calls to remember all of them."

"Well, like I said, I asked you if you were into spanking. You said you weren't, so we don't have to do it. It's something I like to do, not something I require."

"Does it sexually excite you?"

"No."

"Then what do you like about it? Is it some sort of domination thing?"

"No," he says. "I can't explain why I do it. Let's say it's interesting to me."

"All right, whatever you say," I concede. This evening is not turning out like I had expected.

The silence in the air indicates it is his turn to interview me. "Why are you an escort?" he asks.

"I graduated from college with a lot of debt. I couldn't find a job, so I began doing this. I discovered that not only did I have a knack for escorting, I enjoyed the work and found it to be rewarding. In other words, I'm a well-adjusted, entrepreneurial, sexual liberal. That's the simple story."

A look of amusement crosses his face. "I don't want the simple story. I want the whole story. You said you did this for a summer before you did it full time. Why did you stop?"

I pause for a moment debating whether to tell him the entire story. I decide to be honest. He will probably pry it out of me anyway.

"I graduated from Michigan State in May, 1995. I began escorting then. I did it for the summer because I couldn't find a job. Jeff, that's my boyfriend, was living in Iowa while I lived in New Jersey with my parents.

"Anyway, my folks saw me getting depressed that I couldn't get a job so they asked Jeff to move in with them. I think they thought he would get me out of my depression and help me find a job. So Jeff moved in that September. I stopped escorting then."

"Did Jeff know you were escorting?"

"Yeah, I told him before he moved in. He was pretty hurt, but didn't break up with me over it."

"What happened after he moved in?"

"I applied for some lousy jobs in retail stores paying like six bucks an hour. I couldn't even get one of them. They kept turning me down. Eventually a social service agency hired me to supervise a group home for retarded adults. It was really awful and I was miserable. I did that for six months before I grew to hate it more than I loved Jeff. So I gave Jeff an ultimatum, let me return to escorting or be prepared for me to do it anyway.

"Jeff wasn't thrilled at what I said, but he knew how much I hated my job. He didn't like his, either. He was working in a bookstore that paid him next to nothing. So we both quit. He went to work for a museum and I started escorting again. The rest is history.

"Now it's my turn. You said you have 'interviewed' hustlers and escorts before like this. What were they like?"

Richard shifts slightly in his chair. "They were very different. None of them were anything like you. Most of them came from broken homes. Alcoholism, abuse, missing fathers, that sort of thing. Now they sell themselves for money. Mostly for drugs or survival. They're a pretty fucked up bunch."

"As you've probably noticed," I point out, "I'm not like that."

"No, you're not," he agrees. "Most of them never had anything to build a life with. You have it all but are throwing it away on purpose."

A wave of irritation passes through me. How dare he judge my life! "I'm making six figures doing this. I hardly call that throwing my life away." The scorn in my voice is obvious.

He leans forward in his chair and looks at me intently. "Did I say I give a shit how much you're making? You could be making millions for all I care. A lot of good it'll do you if you wind up dead. I've seen it happen before. As much as you hate to believe it, it can happen to you."

A flash of insight strikes me. "What do you do for a living?" I ask suspiciously.

"I had thought you would have guessed by now. It's obvious. I'm in law enforcement. If your instincts aren't good enough to pick up on me, they'll never be good enough to pick up on the guys who want to hurt you."

I am not pleased. Cops are nothing new to me. I have five local officers for clients. However, they have always told me what they do for a living after an hour or two of sex, not during a conversation like this. What sort of game does he think he's playing?

I shift uneasily in my chair. "You're not like the other cops who have hired me. Are you a local or a state cop?"

"Federal. My turn," he replies changing the subject. "You really don't like thinking about it, do you? The risks you take. You think you can do this and come out of it no problem."

"Spare me the lecture," I snap back. "I hate to tell you, but you're not the first person who has tried to 'save me' from my work. I've heard it all before."

He leans back in his chair again. "I'm not trying to save you. That's your job, kid. Save yourself. I'll show up at your funeral and think about all the money you made. Maybe they'll bury it with you."

I am becoming quite pissed off now. I want to be blunt and ask him who the hell he thinks he is coming in here with that attitude, but it's not in my nature to be rude. Perhaps even more importantly, I feel him hitting a small seed of doubt deep within myself. I quickly push the thought from my mind.

"Yeah, yeah, whatever. Maybe they'll bury your bulletproof vest with you. You take a lot of risks yourself. Unless you're just a paperpusher with a badge." I hope my insult irritates him.

He smiles slightly in amusement. "Oh, so now you're saying we're alike because we both take risks?"

I nod my head. "That's right."

"No, that's wrong," he corrects me. "The risks I take are very carefully minimized. People in my work have

years of training and experience and have backup available if necessary. Yes, sometimes people die. It's a risk we choose to take because we know we're getting the dregs of society off the street. People who prey on people like you."

"And you're saying I don't do anything to minimize my risks?" I ask. "I admit I don't have years of training but I'm hardly being asked to do the same job. I take steps to minimize my risks, whether medical, safety, social, legal, or whatever."

He almost laughs at my statement. "Legal? I could have arrested you a dozen times over if I wanted to. You'd have walked right into it. And that's presuming I would tell the truth on my report. If I lied then you'd be really fucked."

"I hardly think I'm worth your time in that respect. I'm a small time escort who meets my clients over the 'net and through magazines with dozens of other ads next to mine. Local cops are concerned with street prostitution. Federal cops are concerned with people passing kiddy porn. No one bothers escorts like me. I'm not worth anyone's time or effort."

He suddenly changes the direction of the conversation. "You said that you enjoy escorting and you find it rewarding. What about it do you enjoy and find rewarding?"

I am relieved he has changed the subject, but I have to stop for a moment. My nerves are on edge and it is difficult for me to think clearly. "Several things," I begin slowly. "For one thing, I enjoy the schedule. I love not having to get up in the morning if I don't want to. I also like the attention, money, and sex. It's interesting and never dull. Oh, and I like not having a job I hate."

"The attention…" he trails off thoughtfully. "What was it like growing up for you?"

I don't like where he is going with this line of thought. I understand he is paying me for an interview, but I do not want to delve too deeply into my personal life. "It was fine. Nothing significant about my childhood. I have two parents that are still married to each other. Three

brothers and a sister, all of whom are as well adjusted as can be expected. I'm the only one who lives a life out of the norm."

Before he can react, I throw another question at him. "Are you married? What is your family like?"

"No comment," Richard chuckles. "I'm the one asking the questions."

"I want to understand you," I explain politely. Maybe he will answer my question if I act nice.

"You don't want to get to know me," he disagrees. "You're better off listening to my advice. I could be the best friend you've ever had."

His words echo through my head. The last person to say that phrase was a glorified snake oil peddler who made millions peddling weight-loss pills like some sort of wonder drug. He caused me weeks of stress and I certainly do not wish to repeat the experience.

"I'm not looking for a best friend," I reply curtly.

He ignores me. "What do you want to do with the rest of your life? Or do you plan on escorting until you retire with your millions?"

"I thought about going to law school but decided to postpone it. I'm already making more money than a starting lawyer does. I'll probably go back to school and earn my Ph.D. after I retire."

He leans back in his chair again. "Will you leave part of your resume blank? Or will you lie and make something up?"

I sit up at the opportunity to parry at least one of his attacks. "I'll be up front about it. I would like to get a Ph.D. in sex therapy or sex research. I'll be totally honest with what I have been doing. Some friends have been urging me to write a book about my experiences as an escort. Being a published author will definitely help me get into a good graduate program. But all that is a moot point if I don't keep escorting. I won't have the money to go back to school unless I keep doing this."

"You make this sound pretty noble. All for your education."

"It's more than my education," I point out. "But that is a part of it."

He leans forward and braces himself on the table. "You know, if I had to guess, I'd say you won't be able to quit when the time comes."

The seed of doubt within the back of my mind sends pangs through me again. This is an area of the conversation I definitely do not wish to continue. "Either way," I change the subject in an attempt to distract him. "I guess it's a good thing some of us do this. Or else you wouldn't have anyone to spank."

"I'd be willing to live with that if it meant kids like you don't screw up your lives."

"Speaking of us 'kids', you said you like the male physique. What about it do you like?"

He struggles to answer the question. "I'm not sure how to explain it. I simply like looking at an in-shape young male body."

"But it's not sexual?"

"No, not at all."

"So it's more… artistic?" I suggest.

He ponders this for a moment. "I guess you could call it that."

"But you're not bi or gay?"

"No, I'm straight."

I've heard that many times before from my clients, but this is the first time I've believed it. "Would you like to see my body?" I ask.

He nods his head. "Yes, I was wondering if you would offer."

"I didn't have to offer," I explain. "You could have requested it at any time."

"It's something I'd rather you offer," he says.

"Well, either way…" I trail off. Standing up, I slowly begin unbuttoning my shirt. His eyes are riveted to me al-

though not in a sexual way. I am not sure what to make of his attention.

Moments later my shirt, pants, socks, and shoes are all lying on the floor. "Do you want me to strip down all the way?" I ask while gesturing at my underwear.

"No, that's fine."

I sit down on the edge of the bed positioning myself so he can have a good look at the body. I hope he does not notice I am sucking in my stomach. I am still self-conscious of my small "love handles."

He does not seem to. "You look good," he says. "You're very attractive."

I smile at the unexpected compliment. "Thanks. It's too bad you're not gay. I'd show you more."

"Sorry to disappoint you," he laughs.

Judging from the light mood, my distraction seems to have worked. "Would you like to spank me?" I ask.

I hate being spanked but Richard is frustrating me. He is the first client I have ever met that is not expressing any sort of sexual interest in me. I want Richard to spank me not out of any enjoyment on my part, but because I want to see him enjoying himself.

"Not in the slightest," he responds.

"You don't?" I ask him in a hurt and confused voice. "I thought you said you liked spanking."

"I do but you don't," he reminds me. "I don't want to do it to you if you don't like it."

"I don't like it," I admit. "But I'd be willing to do it for you."

He sits up on his chair with a look of exclamation on his face, as if I have given him the missing piece to a puzzle. "That's it, isn't it?" he asks. "You don't do this for the money. You do this for the affection and the attention. That's why you'd let me spank you."

"Perhaps a little bit," I reply, "but like I said before, I do it because I like the work. I enjoy making great money while seeing interesting guys who--"

"Fuck your ass every time you bend over? Is that what you went to school for?" he asks.

Anger flares in my voice. "No, I went for a degree in college administration. I couldn't find a fucking job doing that so I found one in another field that would take me. It was the shittiest social services job ever offered. I quit to do this and I'm happy. Can't you leave it at that?"

"Oh, pity you," he patronizes. "You had a bad job once so you give up. Now you're going to sell your body until you really screw up your life. Good decision, Aaron."

"It's not like that," I say almost pleadingly. "You don't get it. I also quit for other reasons than because it was an awful job."

He folds his hands together intent on the conversation. "Tell me why you quit."

"It goes back a long time," I try to explain. "I have never fit in. In grad school I was the only student in my program that wasn't offered an assistantship. In my undergrad, I never fit in with the people around me. Even before that I was different. There is something about me, I don't know what it is. I'm opinionated or something. I am not able to succeed in any sort of formal environment."

"Don't give me that! You have a lot going for you. You could easily succeed at whatever you set your mind to."

"That's the point. I can't. I just can't. I've tried, don't you realize that?" There is anguish in my voice as my emotions overwhelm me.

"So what if one job didn't work out for you," Richard replies without a trace of mercy in his voice. "There are a lot of jobs out there. If one didn't work for you go get another one."

I sniffle and wipe the tears from my eyes. "It doesn't matter. I'd only get one that would wind up the same way."

He looks at me in surprise. "Is that what you honestly believe?"

I nod my head. "Yeah."

"Then you're more screwed up than I thought. You know what I think?" he asks.

I don't want to know but he explains anyway.

"I think somewhere along the line, probably in your childhood somewhere, there was something you needed. Maybe attention, maybe affection, I don't know. Something. But you didn't get it and it's screwed you up bad."

His words ring true. My entire childhood is filled with memories of never fitting in. In elementary school I was picked on mercilessly. By fifth grade I was a thief. By seventh grade I was a social outcast. By tenth grade I was considering suicide, and by twelfth grade I was sleeping with every guy I could get my hands on. My parents were always there, but they never wanted to listen, never wanted to understand.

Tears fill my eyes as these and other memories flow through my mind. "Maybe," I softly concede.

"What happened to you?" he asks. For the first time there is genuine concern in his voice. "What was it that you needed?"

It is all I can do to keep from crying. "I don't know. I honestly don't know."

"Look at yourself," he suddenly commands. "You're sitting there almost naked in the hotel room of a total stranger. You're about to cry because he's taking the time to help you look at yourself instead of using you for your body. Why do you do this?"

"Because it's the only damn thing I'm good for," I yell. "I've never fit in anywhere else and because I'm good at this." Tears stream openly down my cheeks and my voice is racked with emotion.

"So that's it. You're gonna keep doing this as long as your body will let you."

I nod my head. There isn't anything else to say.

"I hope for your sake that you get smart and get out before you fuck up your life for good."

The caring in his voice warms my heart. "You know what?" I ask him. "I wish you were my uncle. I've only

met my uncles a few times in my life. I wish I had someone like you to give me advice."

"Oh no you don't," he replies. "If I was your uncle I would make your life more fucking difficult than you can possibly imagine."

I smile a bit. Right now I'll take any caring I can get.

"Not such a well-adjusted, entrepreneurial, sexual liberal, are you?"

"I guess not," I reply with a faint smile. "Right now you're seeing the other side of my life, the maladjusted sex addict who will do anything for attention."

"I'm real sorry your life had to end up this way," he says. "But you really need to get yourself some professional help before you wind up dead." He pauses for a moment debating whether to continue. "I've met a number of kids who hustle. You are the only one I've seen who has a chance to make something of his life. I hope you don't fuck it up. I'd sure hate to see Jeff at your funeral. Unless you take him with you."

His words sting my soul. I have heard them many times before from people trying to save me from myself. The only difference this time is that I'm listening. Yet I already know in my heart this conversation will change nothing. On Monday I will continue my life as usual.

"I think I'd better go," I quietly say. "There isn't much left to say."

"No," he agrees. "There isn't. I just hope someday you'll take my advice and get out while you still can."

"Right after I write my book," I joke with a smile. "I need to get a bit more material for it."

"I think you have plenty enough to write already. I hope I'm the final chapter."

I stand up and begin putting on my clothes. "Somehow I don't think you will be. But you never know. Depends what I do with my life."

"Either way, I hope you live to finish it."

I dress myself and take the money from the table. Shoving it in my pocket, I look in a mirror. I look like hell.

"Maybe I'll call you again," he says. "If you would consider talking to me again."

I nod my head. "I'd like that." To my surprise, I realize it's the truth. I would like to hear from him again.

He walks me to the door and bids me good-bye. Five minutes later, I begin the two-hour drive home. Although it is not late in the evening, I feel as though I have been speaking for hours. I am physically and mentally exhausted and want to go home. For the first time since I began escorting, I regret what I have become.

Driving over the bridge into New Jersey, questions echo through my head. Am I a well-adjusted, entrepreneurial, sexual liberal? Am I a maladjusted sex addict who will do anything for attention? Which side of me is the real one? Neither my brain nor my heart hold answers to these questions.

Tears stream down my cheeks again as I wonder what will become of me.

Drifting Apart

June 10, 1997

The Bridgewater Commons Mall is a good place to meet a client. There are people shopping, walking, talking, and generally having a good time. No one notices a lone person standing across from the movie theater. I look like any other young person waiting for a friend.

I am, of course, about to engage in an act of prostitution. At least I hope I am. My client is ten minutes late and I am having serious doubts about whether he will show up.

Thinking of my experience three days before makes me uneasy. Already the meeting with the weird cop is fading from my memory like a bad dream. I hope I completely forget it. A small voice inside my head points out that an experience like that can never be truly forgotten. I brush the thought aside. Better not to think of such things.

I look at my watch: 7:42. I glance around hoping to see someone looking for me. It is difficult to look for him because I don't know what he looks like. I forgot to write down a description of what he would be wearing.

Suddenly I see cowboy boots. A short plump man with thinning hair is wearing a pair as he paces near the mall entrance. Memory flashes back to me. My client said he would be wearing cowboy boots.

I walk over to him. "Nick?"

"Hi," he responds nervously. "How are you?"

"Doing fine. I was worried you weren't going to show up."

"No, I was here. I was just afraid that wasn't you inside."

"Oh." His answer strikes me as unsatisfactory, but I decide not to press it. "Would you like to walk around the mall?" I ask.

"Okay," he agrees. His voice is filled with uneasiness and something else. I am not certain what it is, but there is definitely something there. Most of my clients are nervous when I meet them for the first time, but he is beyond common anxiety.

"So what made you decide to call me?" I ask.

"Oh, I just thought you sounded interesting," he replies vaguely. "I wanted to meet you and learn more."

"What about me interested you?" I ask, hoping to learn more about what he is looking for.

"Oh, just what you meet people for," he absently replies again.

Warning bells sound in the back of my mind. I have escorted long enough to know that many people are afraid I am involved in some sort of police sting operation. It is likely that he is not answering my questions specifically for that reason. On the other hand, if he were some sort of law enforcement agent, he would want me to commit to a formal agreement in advance. I normally break this stalemate by kissing my client. Unfortunately, the middle of the mall is not a good place to be affectionate with a stranger.

An unpleasant thought occurs to me. "Are you a cop?" I ask him.

He quietly nods his head. "Is that a problem? I'm not on duty," he says.

Not again! I've had enough of cops for one lifetime. I do not want a repeat performance of the previous Friday night. I briefly consider walking out on him, but my trusting nature and greed win out. "No, that's okay. I'm just surprised."

We walk around the mall for some time as we attempt to pry additional information out of the other. He doesn't want to commit himself to anything because he is worried that I am not on the level. I don't want to speak because I am not sure he is either.

In the end, it is our lack of a commitment that brings us to a truce. We agree to go somewhere to do something although we never discuss what and where. We walk out to his car and climb in.

Starting up his car, he becomes more talkative. "So what do you charge?" he asks.

Feeling slightly relieved I am not sitting in an unmarked patrol car, I am willing to open up more. "I'm $150 for the first hour, $75 for additional hours." It isn't nearly as high as I charge new clients, but it is what I quoted him several months ago. He nods his head and pulls out of the lot.

Arriving at the Ivory Tower Inn, he hands me several bills to pay for the room. For a moment I am sure he is going to drive away as soon as I get out of the car. I hold my breath as I walk toward the motel, but he turns off the motor and patiently waits for me to return. Reassured, I walk inside to pay for the room.

The motel attendant is one I am not familiar with. He is about to ask me for my ID until I head him off. "Would you like to see my ID? I'm twenty-six so I'm well over eighteen."

He laughs as he hands me a card to fill out. "Are you really? Okay, I believe you. Don't bother with it."

I laugh with him as I write a fake name on the registry card. I've fooled dozens of motel attendants around the state with my offer. My concern isn't about my age, it's about my name. I'd rather they not have my real name on record.

The room total comes to $31.80 for four hours. I give him a pair of twenties and he hands me the change. I walk back outside to find Nick still waiting for me. We drive around to the back of the motel.

Inside our room, I am embarrassed to find we have been given one of the trashier rooms. There is graffiti carved into the wall panels, a damaged television bolted to the dresser, and the sound of dripping water from a leaky

faucet echoes from the bathroom. A twenty year-old bed-spread damaged by cigarette burns covers the bed.

The room is warm and smells funny so I turn on the air conditioner. "I apologize for the room. I hadn't known it would be like this."

"That's all right," he answers. "We're not here for the ambiance."

"Are you ready to talk now?" I smile. "Or are we going to play our little game for a while longer?"

He laughs at my directness. "I guess we can talk."

He sits down on the edge of the bed. I seat myself behind him and begin massaging his shoulders. "Why don't you tell me about yourself," I suggest.

"To begin with," he answers me, "I'm actually a federal agent, not a cop. Nothing big, I work for the Treasury Department. Nothing interesting like you'd see on television."

"Got it. You wanted to make sure I was on the level because you were worried about your job."

"Well, not as much about my job," he explains, "but about my family. I took my ring off. I'm married."

"You don't have to take your ring off around me," I point out. "Half of my clients are married. It really isn't an issue to me."

"I'm sorry. I didn't know that."

I laugh slightly. "And you don't have to apologize either. You should be comfortable with who you are." I hope speaking like this will put him at ease. I want him to understand I am not judgmental about the way he lives his life.

"Well, I am. Except this gay thing. It's pretty new to me."

I've heard the story many times before, so I know he needs to get it out of his system. "Tell me about it."

"I met a guy at a seminar two years ago. He was the instructor, actually."

I laugh again. "Screwing our way to the top?"

He chuckles with me. "No, nothing like that. I had to go to San Diego on business again a year later and I saw him then. But I broke it off with him. I was worried I'd become too involved and mess up my marriage.

"So for the past year I've wanted to go to bed with a man. You're the first opportunity I've had since the other guy."

"Hiring an escort can be a convenient solution," I agree. "No messy strings other than a set of fond memories. And no x-rated pictures or e-mails for the wife to find."

I can see in the mirror an embarrassed look on his face. "Yeah, I have those too. But I keep them where my wife won't see them." He lapses into silence.

It's time to begin the second part of the evening, so I begin touching him. I stroke his arms and legs until I eventually lean over to kiss him. He is extremely excited and equally nervous. Touching him is like going to bed with a young male virgin. He wants to do all of the sexual things he has imagined, but he is too nervous to initiate any of them.

Luckily, Nick has my experience to guide him. He unbuttons his shirt and lays it on the bed next to us. I remove my own shirt and throw it onto the floor. He laughs as I do so, turned on by my carefree attitude. I further enhance the mood by kissing him while sitting on his lap. Even through our pants, I can feel his stiff dick pushing up against me.

He continues to relax while becoming more excited. I kiss him hard as we lean back and forth. His arms encircle me and rub my back. The feeling of his chest against mine drives us both wild.

I lean down and lick his nipples. I am surprised when he moans loudly. They are very sensitive so I give them a great deal of attention. My hands move slowly down his body into his pants. I adjust the erect manhood and give it a few gentle squeezes. He closes his eyes as he experiences his fantasies coming true.

I undo his pants and remove them. I take off his socks and underwear, leaving him nude on the bed. I begin stripping off my own clothes as his eyes follow my every move. I am aware that I am not as toned as I would like to be, but I revel in the attention of his gaze.

His attention doubles as I drop my pants. Although I am only semi-erect, my cock juts out a good six or seven inches.

"Wow, you're hung!" he marvels.

I grin. "Thanks. If you like it, why don't you play with it?" I invite suggestively.

He reaches out and begins stroking me. When he accidentally brushes his hand against my balls, I let out a loud moan. He is a quick learner and moments later he is rubbing my balls with both hands. The sensations he gives me are incredible. I moan softly at his electric touch.

His attention eventually wanes and I realize this encounter is going to be predominantly me servicing him. I'm used to that in my work, so I know exactly what to do.

Like hundreds of cocks before Nick's, I lean toward him and take it in my mouth. It is a comfortable act, one I have done many times before and will do many times again. I love the feeling of having a new cock in my mouth. It is one of my favorite things in life.

I bob up and down, pausing only to lick his hairy balls. He is obviously enjoying the attention. After a few minutes of oral sex, I take a slight break. "Ever get a blowjob like this at home?"

"No," he admits in an embarrassed tone. After a moment of silence he adds, "My wife has never done this before."

I realize I have touched a nerve so I begin playing with his dick and balls. I want him feeling very relaxed and sexual as we discuss the more intimate parts of his life. "What is your sex life with your wife like?"

"We don't really have one. I spend over half the year on the road. I don't see a lot of her. Or my children for that

matter. Sometimes they are like strangers to me..." he trails off.

Shaking his head, he continues speaking. "I should have never taken this job. Whenever I'm home, my wife and I are very distant. It takes months at home to cross the distance between us, but I never have that long. I always have to travel again. Now I'm too old to change jobs."

I feel sorry for him but know there is nothing I can do. His career decisions are his own, along with the rewards and consequences therein.

"When was the last time you told your wife you loved her?" I ask instead.

He thinks for a second. "Well, last night on the phone."

"No, no," I admonish. "I don't mean just saying you love her. When is the last time you really expressed it to her? By telling her that you really, honestly, truly love her. It doesn't have to be in words. Maybe you did something intimate or unexpected."

A sad look appears on his face. "It's been years," he admits.

"Then why don't you do something for her?" I suggest. "Next time you're home, go into your bedroom a bit early with her. Light a dozen candles around the bed and slip into something comfortable. Sit down on the bed beside her and tell her how much you love her and how you wish you could be there more.

"Reach out, Nick. Touch her hair, touch the lines of her face, and touch the curve of her body. Be romantic," I continue almost poetically. "Tell her how beautiful she is. Tell her how happy you are that you married her, and that you are glad she helped bring your two wonderful children into the world. Look her in the eye, give her a smile, and ask her if she would like to join you for a candlelight bubble bath. You never know, it might work."

Nick looks at me oddly. "I'm quite serious, Nick. One of the reasons people drift apart is because they forget their passionate youth. Romance isn't only about bringing

home flowers on your wedding anniversary. You need to do more than that. If you try all this, I guarantee it'll get through to her."

He stares at me thoughtfully. "It even works on male lovers," I add jokingly.

"Do you ever do anything like this for your boyfriend?" he inquires.

This time it is my turn to fall silent. "Not enough," I admit quietly. I think about the many times Jeff went to sleep alone because I was up late working on my e-mail. "Gay couples sometimes drift apart, too."

The silence becomes awkward and uncomfortable for both of us. I climb on him again and begin licking his nipples until he starts licking mine. The awkward mood vanishes and is replaced with a sexual one.

I return my face between his legs, this time in a sixty-nine position. Both of us lie on our sides and begin sucking each other. My cock is hard again, although I find little pleasure in his sucking.

I discover Nick is enjoying his blowjob far more than I realize as he shoots a wad of cream all over my face. It spatters all over me as I half-suck, half-jack him off. I love the feeling of his warm fluid pouring all over me. I slide my mouth onto his cock again and rub his cum from my face into his crotch.

Standing up a minute later, I search for a towel to wipe off my face. I can barely see where I am going but manage to find my way to the sink. I wash off the worst of the cum and return to the bedroom. Nick is already putting on his clothes as he prepares to leave.

"Wait for me," I jokingly remind him as I grab my underwear. "You're my ride."

A few minutes later we are silently driving back to the mall. A wad of bills sits uncounted in my pants pocket. Nick is either feeling guilty or uncomfortable at what we have done, and I am not in the mood to talk about it.

I decide to speak as he pulls up next to my car. "I had a really good time."

"Thanks. So did I," he curtly replies.

"I hope you'll take my advice. Do something romantic for your wife. Go home and tell her..." I trail off. Nick isn't even hearing me. He just wants me to leave. "Well, remember what I said. Anyway, good luck and take care."

He begins driving away almost before I can close the car door. I am surprised he wants to leave so quickly but I do not take it personally. He opened up to me quite a bit during the evening. I was probably out of line when I gave him so much advice. Not to mention a bit hypocritical.

Getting into my car, I understand he touched a nerve in my own relationship. In the past month, I have visited thirty-six clients and had sex well over fifty times. I can also count the number of times on one hand that Jeff and I had sex. My sex life with Jeff is one of the many sacrifices I've made for my career. I would do well to bring a bit of romance back into my own life. I'm just so busy with work. I promise myself I will spend a day with him soon.

I wonder what the future is for my own life with Jeff. Will I retire from escorting in time to rebuild the intimacy we miss? Or will he eventually make me decide between him and my career? Deep inside, I already know what I would choose.

Wet Jock

June 20, 1997

Two years ago, I jacked off to a Bel Ami porno movie for the first time. The young men were absolutely gorgeous, the directing was excellent, and the scenery was stunning. It was an almost flawless video. I hated it immediately and have despised their company ever since.

Bel Ami boys like Lukas Ridgeston and Johan Paulik are everything I will never be. Ranging from toned to moderately muscular with perfect tans and beautiful eyes, it is no wonder their looks have taken them to heights of fame and pornographic stardom. While most gay men become aroused at the sight of a Bel Ami boy, I become jealous and upset with my own appearance. I hate them for their success and my failure.

Whenever I experience petty jealousies toward Johan and Lukas, I try to remind myself I have surpassed them in many ways. My education is almost certainly superior to theirs. My escorting is also a skill that can earn me a living for ten years or longer, while their porn careers will last half that time at the most. I am also sure that I make far more money from my escorting than they do from their stardom. These days, my income is about six figures per year.

All of this is why I enjoy Cats so much. Cats is one of New York's sleaziest gay strip bars. Their dancers rarely dance, instead they spend their time nuzzling up to the customers. I think I look better than most of the dancers, and I know I make far more money. As for fame, there isn't

much to be had working at such a hole in the wall. I enjoy myself at Cats because I do not feel threatened.

When I visit Cats, I often find myself enjoying the attentions of both the customers and the dancers. One young man, a beautiful dancer by the name of Juan Carlos, always takes a moment to slide his hand down my pants. He says it's because he finds me attractive and not because I tip so well. Whether he is telling me the truth or not, I enjoy his company and respect the work of a fellow professional. I always like to repay him with kisses, compliments, and a twenty-dollar bill or two. These kisses are the highlight of my evenings at Cats.

Sadly, I will not be receiving any attention from Juan Carlos this evening. According to one of the other dancers, Juan is away on an extended trip back to Mexico City. No one is certain if and when he will return.

"Cheer up," my friend and client for the evening tells me. "He'll be back someday. Or we'll find you another stud."

In truth, I don't think I will be able to replace Juan Carlos easily. He is the only dancer I have any interest in seeing. Most of the other dancers are either not my type, too muscular, or losers who dance because they lack the intelligence and skills to hold down a regular job.

Although I want to explain this to Stephen, it is easier to let him think he is cheering me up. "You're right," I lie. "It's just he was so sexy. I love the way his body has been looking since he started working out."

"Oh, isn't it hot?" he agrees. "Though I prefer Eddie. He's got such a nice butt. I could play with it for hours."

I begin laughing. We both know Stephen can also talk about Eddie's butt for hours. To my surprise, I am not jealous of Stephen's attraction to Eddie. I usually become jealous if my clients pay too much attention to other working boys, but somehow Stephen is different. We have developed a friendship closer than any of my other clients. I prefer being his friend more than his escort. I doubt I have ever opened up as much to another client.

The fact that I like Stephen so much is one of the reasons I agreed to see him this evening. It is the night before New York City's Gay Pride Day, and tomorrow we will watch the parade together. Although I had planned on spending the day with Jeff, I was willing to make that sacrifice for Stephen.

"Oh, look!" Stephen says, pointing at a hand-lettered poster behind the bar. "What's that?"

It is difficult to see the poster with half of the bar crowded nearby. I nudge myself forward and eventually am able to read it.

Cats' First Annual Gay Pride Wet Jock Contest
Time: Midnight
Location: Here
Wear your jockstrap and be prepared to get wet!
Prizes (and free drinks!) for the winners

Stephen reads the sign over my shoulder. "Interesting!" he says. "That ought to be fun to watch."

"Yes, it is interesting…" I trail off thoughtfully.

Stephen notices the expression on my face. "Are you thinking about entering it?"

"Might be! It sounds like it could be a lot of fun to enter."

The idea of entering both terrifies and thrills me. I would be scared to death in front of that many people, but I would be turned on as well. I'd love to parade myself in front of a throng of cheering guys. I can almost picture myself standing in front of them, slowly stripping down, and getting them all horny at the sight of the raging erection inside my underwear. Stepping back down from the stage, I'd feel guys reach out to shake my hand, slap my ass, and touch more intimate parts of my body.

"…hearing me at all?" I suddenly hear Stephen ask.

"Sorry," I apologize. "I was thinking about the contest. What did you say?"

ou were serious. I think you'd be really

s encouragement is all that I need. "Yeah," I
. "I'm serious. I'm nervous but I'm serious."
hen's smile lights up the room. "I'll be here for

"It's not that I'm worried about. I'm worried I won't
ble to get it up!"

Stephen laughs. "I think I'm about to have my wildest dreams fulfilled. I get to play fluffer to a hot stud like you."

"I might just need it. I'm going to find out how to enter."

A few minutes later I am talking to a friendly dancer. I have spoken to him several times before, usually when he is asking me if I would be interested in a "private show."

"What's the deal with the contest tonight?" I inquire.

"Oh, you're going to enter it?" he asks with surprise.

"I'm considering it," I reply vaguely. I hope he doesn't laugh in my face.

"Cool, I think it's like a $200 prize."

"Two hundred dollars? Not bad money. That would add quite a bit to what my client is paying me."

"Your client?" he asks.

"Yeah, you know. I've told you before. I'm always here with my clients. I escort, you know."

"Oh, that's right. How much are you getting for tonight?"

"He's paying me $500 for an overnight, plus another $200 to stay with him till late afternoon tomorrow for the parade. Add another $200 from the contest and I'd be raking in the dough." I realize it is bad form to be bragging, but I am feeling insecure about the contest. Boasting about my business makes me feel less threatened.

As intended, he seems impressed. "Five hundred dollars for overnight?" he asks with surprise in his voice.

"Yeah. I charge most of my clients $600, but I like this one so I'm nice to him."

"Oh, wow. That's good money."

"How much do you charge?" I ask him.

"Oh, I, umm, I usually charge $500 for an overnight." The fact he is lying is obvious to both of us.

"It's a pretty standard rate where I'm from," I politely say. There is no need to start a fight.

"Yeah, well, about the contest," he changes the subject. "You basically strip down, get it up, and sit down in a big tub of water to get your jock all wet. Then you get up and show off your jock. Whoever is the hottest and has the biggest bulge wins."

The premise seems simple enough. "What sort of guys enter the contest? Would someone like me have a chance?"

He looks me up and down for a moment. "Sure, you never know. You should enter it."

"Are you gonna give it a try?" I ask. It doesn't hurt to scope out the possible competition.

He laughs. "No, last time I entered one of these the tub was filled with cold water. I'm not taking that chance again."

"That would make it a bitch to get it up, wouldn't it?"

We both laugh as I walk back to Stephen.

"I'm going to do it," I announce confidently. "I'm going to get up on that stage."

"Great!" he cheers me on. "We're gonna make you a winner yet."

"Perhaps," I consider. "But first we need to figure out what I'm going to wear. I don't have a jock strap in New York with me, and I'm wearing my old red underwear. Hardly appropriate for dipping in a tub of water."

"You could always go back to the room and pick out a pair of the Speedos I brought. There are plenty to choose from." He's not kidding, either. Stephen has a fetish for young men in Speedos. He always brings anywhere from ten to twenty pairs to model for him.

"Hmmm. Oh, I know. I could always go put on my rainbow g-string. If I had a hardon in that thing, it would stand out like a tent and barely cover me."

"That would work. I've seen you wearing it. You can really see it all."

Having settled the matter of what to wear, I need to go get it. I tell Stephen I will return in a few minutes and quietly exit the bar. We are staying in the Days Hotel around the corner. Five minutes later, I am in the room trying on the g-string.

Looking in the mirror, I study the image of my body. I definitely have the boyish look. I wonder if it will be enough to win tonight. Even thinking about the contest makes me nervous, but the prospect of winning is too much for me to pass by. As shallow as it may be, I have always longed for the sexual adoration of other men. This is my chance to do it. Maybe I'll have what it takes, maybe not. There is only one way to find out.

Returning to the bar, I find that Stephen has not missed me. He is in the arms of a tall Ukrainian dancer named Mikael. I dislike Mikael because of his irritatingly aggressive approach to the customers at Cats. I am not jealous of Stephen with the dancers, but I do want him to get rid of Mikael.

Leaning over toward Stephen, I take his face in my hands and turn it my way. I gently touch my lips to his and begin kissing him passionately. At first he is surprised, but rapidly becomes excited as I slide my tongue between his lips. He even begins to forget about Mikael, which is exactly what I planned.

Eventually Mikael realizes I have Stephen's full attention and there will be no more dollars coming. Mikael walks off seconds later. I lean into Stephen's arms and embrace him. We stop kissing, but he continues to hold me. It feels wonderful. He is a sweet guy and will make someone a wonderful lover someday. If I were single, he might be interesting to… but no sense in following that line of thought. Having Jeff in my life makes me a "married" man.

"Do you honestly think I have a chance of winning?" I eventually ask Stephen.

He pauses for a moment. "I don't know. I don't know who you're up against."

I nod my head. I need to stop worrying about this. Right now, I'm stressing over nothing. The only way to find out is to wait until the contest begins.

At about half past eleven, Stephen and I walk into the back of the bar. The back is a large room with chairs lining the walls. Customers and dancers mingle throughout the crowded room. We find a pair of empty chairs near the stage and seat ourselves. All we can do now is wait.

A few minutes later, a dancer approaches us. "I'm Dennis," he introduces himself. "Would either of you like a lap dance? Or would you prefer a massage after my shift tonight?"

I am surprised he is so blatant in publicly offering to prostitute himself, but am even more surprised he might have any takers. His decently formed body is marred by several ugly tattoos. He has a badly shaved head and a mouth with several missing teeth. The only thing I feel toward him is disgust. I suspect he is dancing at Cats because it's the only place that will have him.

"We're not looking for either," I reply, "but what can you tell me about the contest tonight?"

"Oh, I'm entering it," he announces confidently. "I've got a big dick and I have a pretty hot looking jock. So I figure I have a good chance of winning it."

"Oh really?" I inquire. "Good luck to you then. I was thinking of entering it myself." I am curious how he will react.

He looks me up and down. "Oh, you're cute 'n all, but you need to be more defined for this. You'll never win," he pronounces arrogantly. "But good luck to you. There's a list floating around here somewhere. Find it and sign yourself up if you want to enter." He turns around and walks off.

"That fucking bitch," I complain to Stephen. "What a

jerk. I would never say something like that to someone."

"Yeah, its okay," he reassures me. "He's not very friendly or bright, otherwise he'd be working at a nicer place."

An idea occurs to me. "I'm definitely entering. My purpose tonight is to beat Dennis in the contest. I don't care if I come in second-to-last, I just want to beat him."

Stephen assumes I am joking and laughs at my comment. I decide not to point out I am totally serious.

I search the bar to find the sign-up list Dennis mentioned. I find it in the front. There are six names ahead of me on the list. As I write my name on the paper, I am filled with anxiety and feel like I am signing my own execution.

A good-looking Latino bumps into me as I walk back upstairs. As I continue walking, I overhear him saying to a friend, "...contest. I really need the money so I'm going to..." Another opponent revealed.

I sit down next to Stephen. "Do you see him over there?" I point at the Latino.

"Sure, what about him?"

"I overheard him saying he was going to enter the contest," I explain. "Think I can take him?"

"I dunno. Depends on what he has in his pants."

We both laugh, but I realize Stephen is correct. I am confident I have a chance. If I manage to get myself fully hard, I may do well.

My anxiety increases as the minutes tick by. By the time the staff readies the tub, I am almost ready to pass out from my nerves. When no one is looking I sneak forward and touch the water. It's warm. One more worry out of the way.

Sitting back down next to Stephen, I hear the emcee announce the start of the contest. He introduces three judges that have been selected from the audience to rate the dancers. Precisely what they are rating is unspecified but is obvious to all. They're being rated on the size of their dick.

The emcee continues talking, explaining how each contestant is to strip to his underwear and soak himself in

the tub. They will then stand and model themselves for the judges and the audience. From there they step down and are free to dry off and get dressed.

Listening to the emcee, I suddenly realize I am totally unaroused. My dick isn't the least bit hard. I am the sixth contestant on the list so I'm not panicking, but I do become concerned.

"Would you do me a favor?" I ask Stephen as the emcee invites the young Latino to the stage.

"Sure, what?"

"Slide your hand up my shorts and play with my cock and balls. Help me get my dick hard."

He is happy to comply. As the young Latino begins stripping, I feel Stephen's hand slide into my pants. He wraps his hand around my balls and slowly begins stroking and kneading them. It is a pleasurable feeling, allowing me to relax slightly.

As the second contestant is announced, I find myself becoming more worried. My dick isn't responding at all. I'm not the least bit hard despite the hand in my pants. Panic floods my system as I see visions of being seen without an erection.

"Play with me with both hands," I instruct. I open my legs slightly to give him full access. Although we are sitting in the front of the room, no one notices. All eyes are on the stage. I vaguely hear the emcee calling for the third person.

Now with two hands down my pants, Stephen is trying to calm me. "Relax, Aaron, its okay. Just relax and let me play with you." He repeats himself over and over in a vain effort to put me at ease.

Nothing helps. If anything, my dick is becoming smaller. I can't believe this! I am about to strip in front of a hundred men and I can't even manage the smallest of erections. What's wrong with me?

I bitterly understand I am not hard because there is nothing erotic about this situation. I'm nervous about stripping in front of everyone and I'm self-conscious about my

looks. One or the other may be manageable, but not both together. Certainly not with such time pressure.

"Oh, Stephen, what am I going to do? I'm going to make such an ass out of myself."

"You'll be fine," he assures me. Pointing at the contestant stepping out of the pool he says, "look at him. He doesn't have an erection either."

"You're right," I concede, trying not to notice the contestant's extremely defined pecs.

"And the fifth contestant is Aaron!" the emcee suddenly announces. "Aaron, where are you? Come up here on stage."

A wave of panic grabs me. I'm supposed to be sixth! I have the urge to run, to hide, or to do anything to avoid going up on stage, but it's time to meet my doom. I stand up and prepare for the inevitable. Stephen gives my hand a quick squeeze as I walk toward the stage. The idea of not entering the contest at this point never occurs to me.

My dick feels half an inch long. I doubt an hour in a locker room with a male gymnastics team could make it budge right now. I step up to the stage and begin stripping. I vainly wish I could find this erotic enough to produce even the smallest of erections.

Moments later I am wearing nothing but the most revealing of g-strings. It normally covers my cock and balls, but in my super-flaccid state the g-string is extra large. The emcee helps me into the tub where lukewarm water covers me instantly.

As fast as I entered the tub, I am climbing back out. Water drips from my body all over the stage. I know the audience is seeing a scrawny, out-of-shape kid who looks like he has no dick. As near as I can tell, I've earned a well-deserved last place.

At the emcee's prompting, the audience gives me a polite smattering of applause. Enough applause to thank me for making an ass out of myself. I feel totally humiliated. I wanted to be idolized and adored like the Bel Ami boys. I wanted people tell me how beautiful I am. All I did was

prove I will never be like them.

I almost begin crying as I reach my seat. It is painful to feel ugly and undesired again. I feel like I am back in high school where the kids teased me because of my bad acne. Closing my eyes to hold back the tears only makes it worse. I am a crybaby who isn't mature enough to play with the big boys.

I towel myself off in silence and begin putting on my clothes. Stephen senses my mood and says nothing, giving my shoulder a squeeze instead. I'm glad he is being quiet. Discussing this is the last thing I want to do right now.

"Let's go."

"All right," he agrees. The two of us walk across the room toward the stairs. As we leave the bar, I hear the young Latino being pronounced the winner of the contest.

We walk back to the hotel in silence. As we round the corner onto 8th Avenue, Stephen reaches out and takes my hand. "If it's any consolation, I thought you were the best looking guy up there," he says sweetly. "And I'm not just saying that. I really mean it."

If it's a lie, it's a well timed one. I desperately want to believe him. I look him in the eye. "Do you really mean that?"

"Of course!" he says. "Tell me. What type of guys do I like?"

"Well, boyish ones," I answer.

"Exactly. And were any of the other contestants boyish and cute?"

"No," I reply thinking back to the contest. "Some were pretty built and some had a nice ethnic look to them. But none were boyish and cute."

"Then why are you getting all upset comparing yourself to them? You're not like them and they're not like you. The only thing this proved is that you can't get an erection on demand in an uncomfortable situation."

My urge to cry vanishes as I listen to Stephen. He is so sweet to me. I give him a big hug and hold him close. Holding hands, we walk back to the hotel together.

"Besides," he continues. "You have one other thing going for you. You've got a brain. That's why you're getting $700 out of me for the night, while the winner of that contest is only getting two. I wouldn't hire you if you weren't intelligent and didn't have a good heart."

I give Stephen's hand a squeeze as we continue walking back to the hotel. He is such a sweet person. I hope someday that we will progress from a client-escort relationship to a traditional friendship.

I'm lucky to have him. I may not look like Johan or Lucas, but it's nice to know that at least one person will always think as highly of me.

Pity Fuck

August 7, 1997

It's a warm summer afternoon and I'm driving northbound toward the New York Thruway. The speedometer needle points toward the number 86 while the CD player reads VOLUME: 35. Unfortunately, neither the thrill of high speed nor the upbeat music blaring through the speakers are able to penetrate my gloom. I am on my way to a "pity fuck," one of the worst possible types of clients.

A "pity fuck" is when I have sex with someone because I feel sorry for his looks, personality, career, lifestyle, or whatever. I always have a miserable time because I feel too sorry for the person to enjoy myself. Even our mutual orgasms are solely to give him a small highlight in his miserable life.

Pulling onto the thruway, I think back to how today came about. When I left my social services job to return to escorting, I was unsure if I would make enough money to survive. I set my rates low to attract business and took on clients requiring considerable travel time. One such person was Bill. He lived three hours away from me in Albany. I knew he was older when I set up the meeting, but was dismayed to find he was sixty-seven going on ninety.

Fifteen minutes into our first meeting he removed his pants revealing a hernia the size of a bowling ball. It was so large his dick and balls were actually lost within it. I remember almost becoming ill at the sight.

In that instant I realized I had a decision to make. I could leave with nothing to show for my day and crush the

ego of a man who had not had sex in fifteen years. Or I could stay and pity fuck the idiot who was too scared to have a simple operation.

I chose to stay and suffer. I couldn't bring myself to hurt him, despite the fact that I would only earn $325 for five hours of sex and six hours of driving time. Sleeping with him was a horrible experience. I promised myself I would never see him again.

I became very creative over the next few months about why I couldn't see him again. I told him I would not see him again until he had the operation "because I feel terrible watching you feel self-conscious about your body." That worked until he had the surgery. Then I informed him I no longer traveled to Albany. He countered by offering to meet me halfway. He rapidly wore me out of excuses.

In desperation I tried one last ploy. I argued the old rate I had charged him was not sufficient to merit driving all that distance. He responded by playing off my conscience. He sent me numerous e-mails saying, "I really want to show you how I look now that I've had my operation," and "you don't realize how important you are to me." I finally broke down and gave in. I could not bring myself to tell him that he disgusted me.

As if things couldn't get any worse, two days ago Bill called to ask me a favor. He wanted to know if I would be able to meet him in Kingston instead of Newburg. I agreed, but was irritated that I would have to drive another thirty minutes each way.

So today I find myself driving to Kingston, New York. I know it's going to be an awful day and I know I'm going to have a miserable time. Some small part inside me hopes the day will improve, but I know that isn't going to happen.

The only consolation for my suffering is a small one. I am here today because I am extremely kind and sensitive to the needs of my clients. Those characteristics are what make them so loyal to me. My business would not be so successful if I were a different person.

I exit at Kingston and find the motel within moments. My clock reads seven minutes after eleven, meaning I am seven minutes late. As I pull into the lot, I notice Bill is standing in front of the motel waiting for me. He is more gruesome looking than I remembered.

I cannot help but to stare at my fate. Bill's ugliness goes beyond simple age. That doesn't bother me in the slightest. The problem is that Bill's face consists of unattractive features surrounded by a mass of wrinkles, lines, bumps, moles, and other skin conditions I can't name. What little hair he has left has faded into a pasty grayness. As an escort, I often have sex with very unattractive men, but this one is well above and beyond the call of duty. Forcing myself to exit the car and walk toward him, I give him a friendly wave.

"Hello," Bill greets me with a squeeze of my arm. "It's been a long time."

"It has been a while. You're looking good," I lie.

He takes my hand and leads me inside the motel. I feel embarrassed holding his hand, but I don't pull away. Embarrassment is the least of my problems.

He keys open the lock to a nondescript hotel room. I barely have time to enter before he turns around and grabs me. He pushes himself against my body and moves his face toward mine. I recoil from the disgusting taste of his tongue.

A few moments later we walk into the bedroom and slowly begin to undress. I watch in horror as he exposes his body to me. The wrinkles, bumps, and lines extend across his entire form. Although he once claimed to have lost weight after the operation, he has gained it all back and more.

I utter a quick prayer of thanks when I see the hernia is gone. Unfortunately, in its place is one of the biggest sets of balls I have ever seen. They are so huge they are actually repulsive to behold. My day is rapidly becoming more disgusting than I had feared.

The next several hours are spent lying in bed together.

We talk about a lot of things. I find myself opening up more than I normally would. He enjoys learning about my life and asks me increasingly deeper and more thoughtful questions. Although I am uncomfortable talking about myself in such detail, I answer the questions for him. The more we talk, the less I have to touch his body.

Eventually the time for sex arrives. He begins deep kissing me. I respond warmly to convince him I am enjoying myself. For all my noxious feelings, I am a skilled escort. A professional escort always remains in control of his emotions when he is with a client.

"Ohhh, Bill," I lie romantically between kisses. "You're better than I remember."

He caresses me all over, placing special attention on the curves and lines of my body. Eventually he slides his tongue down my chest, over my stomach, and across the top of my pubic hair. He lifts himself up and slides his face onto my cock. I moan loudly as I pretend to enjoy myself.

I continue giving Bill the performance of a lifetime. I want him to believe I am incredibly aroused although I feel nothing of the sort. It is only through sheer willpower that I am able to maintain an erection.

He reaches down and grabs my ankles. Lifting them into the air, he begins playing with my ass with his tongue and fingers. I normally enjoy having this done to me, but this encounter removes any pleasure I might have otherwise felt. Instead of a hot, wet, and sensual experience, his tongue and fingers feel cold, clammy, and uncomfortable.

The encounter slowly shifts to me servicing him. The sight of his mammoth balls make me want to heave violently, but instead I continue with my awful course of action. Trying to avoid touching his balls with my hands, I stroke his cock up and down.

"Suck on it," he suddenly commands.

I feel every muscle on my face tighten as I begin sucking. It tastes awful. I repeat to myself over and over that I am a professional escort and must behave like one. I must not allow him to sense my true feelings.

Somehow it seems to work. Although I am not a fan of uncut dicks, I manage to suck him while maintaining a positive outward expression. It is difficult, especially once I notice the faint smell of sweat and urine emanating from his body.

A few moments later I sit up. If I have to suck on him for another moment longer I am going to throw up. I begin stroking him furiously with my hand. Perhaps if I make him cum he'll fall asleep on me.

For the first time today something goes right. He gives a small yell and suddenly shoots a load of cum across his stomach. I almost cheer out loud. I'm safe for another hour while he recharges.

Bill snuggles up against me as he basks in the afterglow. "May I tell you something?"

"Sure," I reply. "Anything." He is welcome to talk as much as he would like.

"I didn't tell you the truth about something last time I spoke to you."

I honestly don't care what he may have said. "Oh? About what?"

"I don't work in a bookstore. I said that because I didn't feel comfortable telling you what I really do for a living."

"Mmmm… That means you're a priest or a cop. Or you work with kids." I am actually surprised at his revelation. I consider Bill somewhat dim, and at least a moderate amount of intelligence is needed for those careers.

"Pretty much," he smiles. "I'm a priest."

My jaw almost hits the floor. "Catholic?"

"Actually, no. I'm Orthodox."

I don't know whether to laugh or cry. I have never given any thought to the ethics of being hired by a priest. I do know, however, that if he is bashing gays from his pulpit I am going to tell him off and leave. The money is not remotely worth selling out my principles.

He understands my concerns and assures me he has never said or done anything to cause harm to the gay com-

munity. I am unconvinced, but can only take him at his word. Sensing my unasked question, he also assures me he is not bound by any oath of chastity.

Eventually the conversation switches back to sex. "Would you mind fucking me?" he asks.

I vaguely remember him trying to fuck me during our last meeting. It was awkward because he was mostly impotent and what little erection he could muster was buried in his hernia. In the end, I had to fake an orgasm while fucking him.

I shake my head slightly to erase these visions from my mind. "I'll give it a try," I agree.

Looking at his ass, I cannot imagine what would be less arousing than fucking him. His ass is flabby, splotchy, smelly, and is attached to someone I dislike immensely. I console myself knowing he didn't ask me to rim him. That would be too much even for me.

Ripping open a condom, I pull out the rubber sheath. I gently set it on the tip of my semi-hard dick and begin unrolling it. I know I am about to lose my erection completely so I open my mind to my darkest and most forbidden fantasies. It works. My erection not only remains, but also actually grows. I finish unrolling the condom onto my nice stiff cock.

I open the bottle of lube and pour lubricant into the center of his ass. Leaning forward, I rub the lubricant into the valley with the head of my dick. He moans and spreads his legs in pleasure. I am glad he likes the feeling, because I am using my dick to spread the lube to avoid touching the center of his ass with my hands.

I pull his legs higher into the air as I push myself into his ass. It feels like I am sinking in quicksand. Pausing only to adjust his ponderous balls, I begin rapidly pumping his ass.

I find it difficult to fuck him because of his bulk and inexperience as a bottom. He leaves it entirely to me to support his weight. I frequently have to stop fucking and stroke my own dick to get it hard enough to continue.

Just as I am beginning to slightly enjoy the fucking, something awful happens. I notice in horror that the condom is covered with shit. Not just traces of it, either. Lots of it getting all over everything.

I stop fucking in absolute disgust. Grabbing a towel, I clean everything off as best I can. Sticking my dick back in, I immediately moan like crazy. I want this encounter over now! I moan, writhe, and tell him how much I love fucking him. Seconds later I fake an orgasm with him.

I collapse in mock exhaustion until I realize the condom is again filthy. I rush into the bathroom and throw it into the toilet. I flush the toilet and reach for a bar of soap and a washcloth. I feel unclean and have a tremendous urge to bathe.

Pausing for a moment, I study my reflection in the mirror. I look like hell. I am having one of the worst experiences of my life for a measly few hundred bucks. All because I cannot bring myself to destroy the self-esteem of the person in the next room.

Setting the now stained wash cloth down on the counter, I return to the other room with a clean towel. Bill is staring at the newly formed brown stains on the sheets. "I guess I made a mess. I'm sorry about that," he apologizes.

I cannot bring myself to feel anything but disgust and pity for him. One of the cardinal rules for a bottom is to make sure they are anally clean before they have sex. "Don't worry about it," I reassure him as I toss him the towel. "It happens to us all."

I walk back into the bathroom and close the door. I sit down to compose myself. The day is far worse than I could have imagined. I can deal with anything that has gone wrong today individually, but the total combination is too much for me to handle. Bill's ugly looks, his guilt trips, the revelation he is a priest, the scar from his hernia, his huge balls, the smell of his ass, and a dozen other things are too horrible to contemplate in one package.

I stand up and walk back into the bedroom. As I return to the bed, I notice he has politely lifted a new sheet

across the bed. Thankfully he even had the common sense to remove the dirty towels.

"What time is it?" I ask.

"Dunno," he says. "Look at my watch."

I walk across the room and look at his watch. "It's twenty after three," I tell him. "I think our time is till four."

"You were seven minutes late," he replies after a moment of thought. "So you can stay until seven minutes after four."

Expressions of shock and anger cross my face. For him to demand I stay the extra seven minutes is unbelievable. I have gone out of my way to accommodate him at every step. For the sake of his guilt trips alone, I have taken on the most disgusting client ever for less than I would charge the hottest of young studs. Even with the extra hour of driving time, he is still demanding I stay for seven minutes. How dare he!

Bill fails to notice my sudden change in mood. "Suck on my cock," he thoughtlessly commands.

I am tempted to tell him to go to hell, but even in my state of righteous anger I cannot violate my sense of professionalism. I do, however, give him a sarcastic "yes, sir!" before I give him the world's worst thirty second blowjob. I'll be damned if I do any more than this for him.

If Bill notices my attitude, he doesn't care. I jack him off until he cums several minutes later.

We spend the rest of the time talking until it is clear our meeting is over. As our time winds down, we take a shower and talk for a few minutes more. We both dress, he pays me the money, and we leave. It's 4:20. I have not only stayed the extra seven minutes, I have remained longer with him on my own time.

Back in my car, I pause for a few minutes before I begin my drive home. I am enraged at the way he treated me. There is no reason anyone should be subject to such an experience. I swear to myself I will never give another pity fuck or suffer these indignities at the hands of a client again.

Yet at the same time, I find myself considering my own behavior. Was it his fault I was subjected to this awful experience? Or did I bring this upon myself by accepting the pity fuck? What should I ethically have done to avoid this?

After considering these questions, I realize I don't care about the answers. I went way above and beyond the call of duty today. I am too angry and too upset to endure this ever again. As far as I am concerned, today is entirely his fault.

And if it's not? I'll let the world judge me. I've done my best and I'll be damned if I go through this again.

Void

August 14, 1997

I am irritated. It is ten minutes past the time of my appointment and I am caught in urban traffic. I am driving past 26th Street in Hoboken and my appointment is almost sixty blocks away. The directions my client gave me said nothing about traveling for miles in busy city traffic. Of course, his directions also sent me on a twenty-minute detour in the wrong direction.

Weaving through the midday traffic, I begin swearing at the idiot I am about to meet. I dislike being this late for my clients. It makes me look unprofessional and irresponsible, even when the poor directions are their fault. I hate appearing unprofessional.

Ten minutes later I arrive at my destination. It is a run-down two-family house with boards over several gaps on the front porch. Not a good sign. I prefer clients who are a bit more financially secure.

Next to the door are two doorbells side-by-side. Another wave of irritation crosses me. His directions said to press the top button. I press a button at random and wait.

Footsteps enter the front hall. A moment later the door opens revealing an Italian man in his mid-forties with a short-cropped beard and a cigarette dangling from his mouth. His hair is graying and his face is beginning to wrinkle with age. He is quite overweight, which does not go well with his spandex shorts and unbuttoned shirt.

"Follow me," he says with a slight frown. He walks inside leaving me alone on the porch.

I follow him inside and close the door behind me. He is already halfway up the flight of stairs leading to the upstairs apartment. I realize he has not bothered to introduce himself. I hope it doesn't lead to any odd moments, because he never gave me his name on the phone.

Walking into his apartment, I stop in shock and amazement. Calling his home a mess would be the understatement of the century. Dishes, books, papers, and piles of refuse are strewn everywhere. With the exception of a small path leading to each doorway, the entire room is covered with trash and junk.

He notices me staring. "Sorry about the mess," he offhandedly apologizes. "It's been hard to keep up with the cleaning ever since I kicked my slave out."

"Your slave?" I ask in surprise.

"Yeah. I caught him fucking around so I got rid of him." He walks through a doorway leaving me alone once again. I follow him into the bedroom wondering what unpleasant surprise awaits me this time.

He walks amid the piles of clutter until he reaches the bed. He lies down on it and begins looking at me. I glance at the chairs but they are covered with junk. Not sure where to sit, I seat myself on the edge of the bed. There is a moment of awkward silence as we stare at each other.

"Are you going to bother to take off your clothes?" he suddenly asks.

A sharp retort instantly comes to mind, but I refrain from being rude to him. Passive as always, I stand and slowly undress myself. Normally, someone watching me remove my clothes excites me, but in front of this client I feel oddly vulnerable. His eyes bore into me without the slightest hint of interest. He stares at me as if I am some sort of inanimate object.

Standing naked, I wait for him to say something. He glances at me for another moment then turns away. He crushes his cigarette in an ashtray, reaches for his pack, and lights another. He turns back to me and resumes the same expressionless gaze.

I sit next to him on the bed and begin unbuttoning his shirt. For the first time in months I am nervous in front of one of my clients. His lack of any communication is extremely disturbing to me. I have never met a client who was so inhumanly nonexpressive.

"What do you do for a living?" I ask, hoping he opens up through small talk.

He replies in a bored tone. "I own several hair salons and do the hair for a daytime drama on television."

"Oh, how interesting," I lie. "Do you like what you do?"

"It's okay," he replies neutrally.

My attempt at conversation lapses into silence. So much for small talk.

His shirt is now unbuttoned so I begin rubbing his chest and nipples. I slowly work my hands down over his stomach. Grasping the edge of his spandex shorts, I gently pull them down. A short but erect cock springs into the air. I am relieved he is not completely inhuman.

Grasping his shaft, I begin stroking him slightly. I vainly search for some indication of pleasure in his eyes, but I find nothing. He lies there like a living corpse, smoking as he dissects me with his stare. My discomfort begins to turn into frustration and confusion. Why won't he show a reaction?

I lean over and begin sucking on him. Despite his erection, the rest of his body shows no response to my touch. Throughout all of the more than 400 men I have slept with, I have never seen someone show so little interest in sex.

I continue sucking him for about ten minutes. I desperately want to stop and get to know him, but he doesn't show the slightest interest in doing so. He doesn't show interest in anything!

I finally decide not to let this upset me. If he isn't going to let me know what he wants, then he will have to deal with not getting much in return. Having made that decision, I begin to feel better about the whole situation.

A few moments later I think he is about to come to life. He sits up and begins moving. My hopes are quickly dashed as he crushes his cigarette in an ashtray and lights up another one. I find it strange that he chain-smokes during sex. I suspect it is a symptom of a much deeper psychological problem.

He pulls my head off his dick and looks at me. "So wait, let me get this straight," he asks in a tone of incredulous disgust. "I'm paying $150 an hour for a blowjob?"

I am filled with a sudden urge to tell him to fuck off. People have treated me badly before, but no one has ever shown so little interest in my feelings. Even the hockey player who attacked me believed I was enjoying myself. This asshole doesn't care how I feel.

Of course my kinder and gentler side steps in. "I'm sorry," I find myself apologizing. "I didn't realize you wanted anything else. You didn't say you did. But I can do a lot more. I can give and receive oral sex, I like both fucking and being fucked. I love being affectionate. I can cuddle and kiss--"

"Let me give you a piece of advice," he interrupts. "Your clients don't want to kiss an escort. No one wants to bother getting that close to you."

My jaw drops open in amazement. "I'm surprised you say that," I stammer. "If anything, most of my clients are all over me to kiss."

"You must have a strange type of client," he responds crushing out his cigarette. "Take it from me, no one wants to kiss an escort."

Looking at him, I realize I have made a grave error in judgment. In this man's world, hustlers are worthless and are meant to be treated with contempt. Even common courtesy is not necessary when dealing with one. That attitude pisses me off immensely.

"I think I had better leave," I tell him. I bend down to reach for my underwear and start to stand up.

Suddenly he grabs me. He spins me around and pulls me down on the bed. Before I can react, his lips are locked

against mine. I feel his tongue slide into my mouth. He wraps his arms around me tightly and pulls me close.

I am more confused than bothered by his actions. I wonder if he is he into some sort of dominance scene. I dislike scenes like that, but at least he would be doing something other than lying there.

I roll over on top of him. Reaching behind me I grab his hands, pull them over his head, and pin them down. For an instant I see a spark of life in his eyes.

Then he pulls back. "Are you trying to hold me down?" he asks in a voice filled with scorn and contempt.

Any hope of salvaging this encounter dies within me. I have never met anyone as empty as this client. Even the most abusive and dominant clients express some emotion. At some point they can be pleased, their desires and lusts satisfied. There is nothing I can do to meet the needs of this client. As near as I can tell, he has none.

I wonder if I should try to leave again. I cannot begin to comprehend why he hired me.

"Would you like to be in a porno movie?" he suddenly asks.

It is something I have considered recently. "How much does it pay?" I ask, knowing I would never consider having anything to do with him and his porno project.

"Ten thousand dollars," he replies.

I stare at him in surprise. "I may not know the porno industry well," I reply slowly, "but I do know five hundred to a thousand dollars a day is standard for a newcomer. Only stars like Jeff Stryker ever make ten grand in a movie. What's the catch?"

He pauses for a moment as if deciding what to say. Reaching some sort of decision, he opens his mouth to speak. "You have to fuck a twelve year-old."

"You're kidding," I say stupidly, although I suspect he is not.

"No, I'm not. I don't kid. The boy is really hot. He's good in bed, too."

I am appalled. "Have you ever seen him?"

"Not in person, just in his movies. But you'd look good next to him. We'd have to shave the hair off your body to make you look younger, but you could do it. The movie would only be released overseas, so no one would find it here."

"Well, I'm not interested either way," I decline. Even if I was, I would not work with someone as evil as this man.

I go back to sucking on his dick so he won't talk to me again. He lays back and lights another cigarette.

He puffs away for another five minutes. Eventually he grows bored, or begins to experience some other emotion beyond my comprehension. "Why don't you have an erection?" he asks in a belittling tone. "You haven't had one the entire time you've been here. Every other escort I have hired has gotten one. Why can't you?"

He does not seem angry. Indeed, I cannot detect any emotion at all. I stammer for a moment. "Because you haven't done anything to excite me."

"What do I need to do to get you hard?" he asks.

I choose my words carefully. "You can't. You aren't able to. I can't get hard because there is nothing within you to excite me."

"What's that supposed to mean?" he asks in his usual uncaring manner.

This time I do not even bother to reply. He cannot understand me because he isn't human. He has no passion, no emotion, and no sign of life. I cannot have an erection with him because he is dead on the inside. He is empty. Soulless. A complete void.

"I'd better leave." I stand and begin dressing myself. This time he does not try to kiss me. I decide not to bother asking for the money he owes me. I cannot comprehend what he wanted out of this meeting.

As I walk toward the kitchen, he puts his hand on my arm. "I'm surprised with you. You're very nonassertive. I don't understand how you can be an escort and still act the way you do."

I shrug my shoulders. I no longer have any interest in

what he thinks or understands. I walk out of the apartment and away from this freak of nature.

Driving away, I think about what the evil client said. He was right when he accused me of not being assertive. If I even remotely asserted myself, I would have told him off long before. I would also have asked for the money up front when I saw the inside of his apartment. I console myself knowing I at least walked out. That was a big step for me. I know this is the start of a new phase in my work – one where I stand up for myself.

I think about what I should have said when he asked if he was paying for just a blowjob. I should have explained he was paying for my time. I would be glad to make love, suck his dick, or even sit and watch him smoke. What he chose to do with our time was up to him.

Sometimes people cheat me because I am overly trusting, friendly, and do not often stand up for myself. Yet these same characteristics are what make me a high quality escort. The vast majority of my clients treat me with respect, and are treated well in return. Only on occasion do people like this slip through.

I remember a quote I once read. It went something like, "sometimes the shadows that cloud one's soul mask the absence of any soul at all." I have met such a man today.

I shiver at the memory of his stare. Even miles away I can feel the void in his soul.

Group Session

August 22, 1997

It is ten o'clock on a Friday night, and I have nothing to do. I should be happy that I'm not doing anything. I have entertained twenty-six clients in the past twenty-one days. I'm quite exhausted from the experience, but somehow I'm not content. I'm bored and in the mood to work.

Having nothing scheduled is uncommon for a Friday night. Usually I have one or two clients, sometimes even three. I suppose even the most successful escorts have off days. This is one of mine.

To combat my boredom I am sitting at my computer playing around with America Online. Sitting behind me is Jeff, his arms wrapped around me as I type.

A small chime breaks the silence of the moment. An instant message has appeared on the screen. I click a button and read the new message.

Kevin17432: Are you available tonight?

I respond quickly. "Hi. Yes, I am."

Kevin17432: There are 3 of us. Would you be up to working for a group?

I am surprised and skeptical. I have been approached several times by people claiming to speak for a group. In well over a year of escorting, none of them have ever panned out. They are probably fantasies of a very bored and lonely person somewhere in cyberspace.

Knowing all of this, I decide to give the person the benefit of the doubt anyway. I type my reply. "Sure, I'm not doing anything tonight. Let me send you my picture so you can decide if you have any interest in hiring me." I

click a few buttons and instantly e-mail my picture to their computer.

A moment later a reply appears on the screen.

Kevin17432: We like what we see. You are quite cute. And REALLY young looking, too!

I tap a few keys on my keyboard. "Thanks! What else can I tell you?"

Kevin17432: How much would you charge for two hours?

I think for a moment before I respond. Normally I would charge $300 for two hours for a single client. I think I should be paid more for three clients. I respond, "$450 for two hours."

Kevin17432: We think that is too much, $300 for two hours seems fair.

"Are you going to do it?" Jeff asks.

"I'm thinking about it. They should be paying me more, but if I insist on $450, I may lose them and earn nothing tonight. Three hundred is better than nothing."

In the back of my mind, I am aware of another thought. A fourway would be quite erotic and exciting. I'd rather not point this out to Jeff, although I am sure the thought has occurred to him.

My excitement eventually gets the better of me. "Okay, you're on," I type. "I just ask you keep in mind I'm working for less than I normally would charge for a group. So go easy on me. Would you like to call me?"

A few moments later my phone rings. Although I am somewhat wary of three clients at once, the conversation puts me at ease. They seem very much on the level.

As the conversation continues, I am glad Jeff doesn't notice the erection inside my pants. Although he knows talking on the phone always gets me hard for some reason, I am sure the subject matter of tonight's meeting would make him misunderstand. Or perhaps he would understand all too well why I am excited. Tonight has the potential to be one of the hottest nights ever.

I finish writing down the directions and hang up.

"So you're going to do it," Jeff says in a disapproving tone.

"Sure, its good money. A bit more work than usual, but I'll survive. Is it a problem that I'm going to do this?"

Jeff shakes his head. "No, it's all right. I'm just worried about this call."

I hold him close. "It's ok, Jeff. I know you worry I enjoy my work a bit too much at times. But this one is really just work. I'm doing it for the money, not for the adventure. But if you want me to stay, I will." I'm know I'm making a safe bet. Jeff chooses his stances very carefully, and this won't be one of them. We'll go back and forth over this issue until I promise to spend time with him the following day.

Ten minutes later, I am on my way.

I force myself to drive slowly to my destination. Besides not needing a speeding ticket, I don't want to appear too eager once I arrive. I do have to admit that I am excited. My mouth is watering as I think of all the cocksucking ahead of me.

I pull up in front of a townhouse in a friendly neighborhood. I have difficulty finding the entrance until a figure emerges and guides me to the outside patio.

"I'm Kevin," he introduces himself. "This is my house. You must be Aaron."

I offer my hand. Kevin is an attractive man in his early thirties. Short and dark, his Italian background is obvious. His smile brightens the entire patio. My evening is off to a good start.

He shakes my hand and leads me inside. "This is Jack," he introduces as he points to a person in the corner of the kitchen. Like most men in their late forties, Jack is losing his hair, but I suspect he was very attractive in his prime.

"Oh! Hi, Aaron," he bounces up to me. "You're cute! You look so young. How old are you?"

His bubbly personality makes me laugh. "I'm twenty-four," I lie with a smile.

"No! Are you serious? You look way too young for that."

His personality is cheerful, although something about him seems uneasy in Kevin's presence. I make a mental note to learn what is making him uncomfortable.

Jack leans over and begins kissing me, sliding his tongue in and out of my mouth. I respond by pushing my body into his. I want everyone to know they are welcome to be as sexual with me as they would like.

I hear the third person enter the room behind me. Instantly he starts laughing. "Can't you keep your hands off him? If you wear him out before we get a chance to do him, you're paying the entire bill."

Jack pulls back and begins laughing. The three are obviously friends who enjoy teasing each other. He takes my hand and leads me into the living room. Kevin and Tony join us a moment later with several glasses of ice water. Jack seats himself and immediately puts his arm around me. If experience is any indicator, the three will spend the next several minutes getting to know me before things become interesting.

"So how did you begin escorting?" Kevin inquires.

I answer his question with my stock reply. "I began after I graduated college. No job offers, but I had a pile of student loans. I'd done it before for spare money, so I began doing it for a living. I decided I liked it, and the rest is history." My answer is not totally accurate, but is easier than explaining my whole life story.

They quickly field other questions. Do I have another job? Where did I go to college? When did I graduate? Does my family know? Do I have a boyfriend? What do I do when I show up and find the client is ugly? How often do I work?

After answering their questions, a silence fills the room. It is time for the fun to begin. I lean back against Jack. He begins kissing my neck and running his hands

across my chest. The others watch until Jack begins unbuttoning my shirt. As soon as my chest is exposed, the others join in.

Tony begins unzipping my pants while Kevin kisses me. Jack continues licking my neck and unbuttoning my shirt. Soon Tony is removing my pants while the others pull off various articles of clothing. Within moments I am nude between them, my erect cock sticking straight into the air.

Tony begins sucking on me while Kevin removes his clothes. Jack turns me around slightly and touches his lips to mine again. "Kissing is my favorite sexual thing to do," he whispers.

"Fine with me," I whisper back as I slide my tongue into the depths of his mouth.

Now entirely nude, Kevin shoves his crotch into my face. I pull back from Jack and begin sucking Kevin. Jack stands up and removes his shirt. He is too shy to remove any more than that. I try to put him at ease, but it is difficult while I'm being sexually used at both ends.

"Shall we go upstairs?" Kevin suggests to the tangle on the couch.

I pull back from his cock. "Good idea. As long as you promise to be naked up there."

I begin removing Tony's pants before we move upstairs. The bulge is obvious to everyone in the room. "You look like you're ready to cum already!" Jack jokes.

Once Tony's pants are removed, I turn toward Jack. Unlike Tony, Jack is not remotely hard. "I may be ready to cum but you can't get it up," Tony teases. Everyone laughs, but I noticed an expression of hurt on Jack's face. This is no laughing matter to him.

Although Jack should be able to take a joke if he is going to dish them out, my compassion kicks in. "Cheer up," I reassure Jack. "It doesn't matter how hard you are. I can kiss you all night long either way." He perks up with a smile.

Kevin leads everyone upstairs into the master bedroom. There is a large bed in the center of the room. On the nightstand rests a tube of KY and a small pile of condoms. Kevin has definitely prepared for this meeting. The three lay me on my back in the center of the bed as they circle around me.

Jack moves toward my head and begins kissing me. Tony slides down to my crotch and begins sucking. Kevin surprises me by sitting on the bed and not touching me at all.

"I'm a voyeur. I want to watch for a while," he explains.

It does not take long before Tony moves toward my head. With all the finesse of a third rate porn star he orders me to suck on him.

I comply immediately. Sucking on his cock is extremely fun. He is well hung, probably seven or eight inches. I usually prefer small and medium dicks, but right now I feel like cocksucking. I am in the mood for a big dick like the one Tony has been kind enough to provide.

I hear someone move behind me and begin to finger my ass. I continue sucking dick while pubic hair rubs my face. I am in heaven.

Tony pulls away from my face and moves behind me. Now without pants, Jack takes his place. I am amazed at how big he is. His cock is even bigger than Tony's. At least it would be if it were erect. Jack is still having difficulties getting there.

"I'm sorry. I usually do better than this. I'm a bit nervous," he apologizes in an embarrassed tone.

"Stop that," I gently scold him. "It doesn't matter." To my surprise, neither of his friends tease him. I suspect they remain quiet because Jack is hung so large. If Jack was fully erect, he would be bigger than the other two put together.

The hand playing with my ass vanishes for a moment before it returns to rub lubricant all over my hole. This is one of my favorite moments as a bottom. Moments later I

feel the brush of a condom-clad dick touch my ass. It slides toward the hole and slowly begins to enter me. Tony's moans are audible as he pushes forward.

Out of the corner of my eye, I notice Kevin rapidly stroking himself. I can't see him well because I am still sucking on Jack, so I pull my head back to give myself a better view of Kevin. He smiles at me making my erection instantly swell. I find him very attractive.

Jack takes advantage of my pause to stop putting his cock in my face. He moves down and begins kissing me again. "I enjoy kissing more," he explains.

Tony continues to fuck me. Although he is a skilled top, the size of his rod makes me squirm a bit. I slowly grow used to his strokes as he penetrates me deeply. I appreciate his efforts and tell him so by moaning loudly. He responds by increasing the speed of his fucking.

Just as I begin to become excited, he stops and pulls out. He removes the condom and looks at me. "Stop kissing him and suck on it," he commands in his porno voice again. I open wide as his cock slides into my mouth once more.

I suck Tony as best I can. I slide my mouth back and forth on his dick while rubbing his balls with my hand. He moans in pleasure at my touch. Jack and Kevin watch him as he finally reaches his peak. Streams of cum emerge and fill my mouth. It tastes strong but good. I suck him deeply in search of every drop.

He pulls out and collapses helplessly on the bed. Kevin and Jack look at each other in surprise but are too excited to stop for long. Jack returns to kissing me while Kevin continues to jack off.

When Tony sits up again, he realizes Jack is uncomfortable with their presence. "Why don't we go downstairs for a few minutes. We'll give them a few minutes alone," he suggests in a moment of insight and compassion.

"Thank you," Jack quietly says as his two friends walk back down the stairs. He apologizes the moment the two of us are alone. "I'm sorry. I've never had sex with

either of them before. I never wanted to. This whole thing is making me uncomfortable."

"It's okay," I reply. "You don't have to apologize for anything."

"Yes I do. This is all my fault. Or my doing, I guess. I've seen you online before, but have always been too scared to meet you alone. So when Tony and I were playing with Kevin's America Online account this evening, I got him turned on by the idea of hiring you. We convinced Kevin to have you over. I started all this because I wanted to meet you. Now I can't get it up," he wails miserably.

"Well, now that you've met me are you still scared to meet me alone?"

"Of course not!" he replies in shock at my suggestion. "You're so cute. I could kiss you for hours."

"Then you can hire me any time you'd like. I'll give you my number before I leave."

"Wow, can I? That would be great. I definitely want to see you without the two of them around."

We stop talking and resume kissing. This time Jack responds to my touch. I feel his dick growing as I wrap my hand around it. Although it never becomes rock hard, it does become large enough to make most men jealous.

"I really like your touch," he moans leaning back to enjoy more.

I continue kissing him while I slide my hand up and down. He is circumcised. Like me, he has enough skin so I can masturbate him while holding the outside layer tight. The longer I stroke him the harder he becomes.

He surprises me with a pair of loud moans. I vaguely wonder if he is approaching his orgasm when I feel cum spurt all over my hand. Load after load streams down my fingers. I continue stroking until every drop emerges from the tip.

The sound of footsteps approaches the room. Kevin and Tony have returned from downstairs. They are surprised to see Jack's cum-soaked body, but he just smiles proudly. "He was wonderful," he explains happily. Both

Kevin and Tony laugh.

As the two join me on the bed, Jack walks off in search of a towel.

Kevin looks at me intently. "Would you like to jack off for me? I would enjoy watching you."

"He can jack off later," Tony unexpectedly answers. "I want to fuck him again." He puts his now familiar dick back into my mouth. It does not take long before he becomes hard again.

After a few minutes of sucking, Tony makes an announcement. "I've changed my mind. I want to see you fuck Kevin."

Kevin is surprised, but willing to comply. Always eager to please my fans, I reach for the KY and a condom. Kevin lifts his legs in the air while I kneel in front of him and unroll a condom down my shaft. I place a generous slathering of KY on his ass and quickly move toward his opening. After an hour of sex, I am not feeling particularly subtle. I want to shove my dick in his ass and fuck him as hard as I can.

As I slide into the eagerly awaiting Kevin, I see Tony unrolling a condom on himself. Understanding flashes through me. He wants to play "Lucky Pierre," meaning he will fuck me while I am inside Kevin.

"This time I'm going to cum inside you," Tony whispers as he slides himself back into me. He begins fucking a deep and steady rhythm. It isn't quite as comfortable the second time around. I'm feeling slightly used from his previous fucking.

In an effort to keep my ass from hurting too much, I try to encourage Tony to cum quickly. "Fuck me hard!" I call out. "Keep fucking me and bang your balls against my ass." I feel his hand slap my butt, stinging it until my buns turn red. With every thrust I plunge deeper into Kevin. I am not able to pump very well in this position, but the look on Kevin's face tells me he is feeling enough pleasure for both of us.

"Come on Tony, fuck me!" I shout out. "You know

you want to. Give it to me. Pump that dick in my ass." I sound like I'm the bad porn actor now, but it really is how I feel. I want his dick inside me bad. The hurt has completely turned into pleasure.

Behind me, I feel Tony beginning to lose control. His pumps become faster and deeper giving him the extra bit of stimulation he needs to achieve release. He begins moaning as he dumps load after load inside me. I barely have a chance to react before he pulls out and collapses on the bed again.

I pull out of Kevin and remove my own condom. I am extremely aroused and need to jack off. In a different situation I might save my orgasm for another client, but I know Kevin wants me to cum. I might as well enjoy it now while I can, rather than be forced to cum later on demand.

I stroke my own dick and push it up against Kevin's balls. He pumps himself with his hand repeatedly.

"Let me sit up," Kevin requests. "I like jacking off while sitting up."

I move away from Kevin and sit on Jack's lap. I straddle his dick so I can feel it touching my ass. It makes me even hotter as I jack off.

"Pump that dick. Let me see how hard it is," Kevin urges me. "Make that dick hard until it's ready to cum. I want to watch it shoot!"

I am enjoying everyone watching me masturbate, but I want more excitement. "Come over here and help me out," I half request and half order.

Tony moves toward me but Kevin remains in place. I feel a wave of irritation until Tony pushes his chest up against my back. His arms circle around me and begin playing with my balls. As he touches them, my sack tightens and barely holds back from cumming.

Tony continues to touch, pull, and knead my balls while I stroke myself. Soon I pass the point of no return. I shout wildly as my orgasm erupts from the head of my dick. Streams of cum land all over Jack. All three stare at my swollen organ as my hand pumps every drop of cum out of

it. The orgasm finally recedes and I am spent. I can barely sit up.

Kevin begins to climax as well. His orgasm sounds less intense than mine, although I am too exhausted to tell for sure. Either way, he recovers before I do and walks downstairs. I stumble toward the shower and begin the process of cleaning up.

I depart ten minutes later with money in hand. I am leaving with my $300 fee plus a $40 tip from Jack. I know Tony and Kevin only wanted a quick fuck, but Jack will call me again. He wanted something far more personal.

The evening has been a success. I had great sex while making another $340 toward my weekly goal of $2000. I've even found another client who is a good tipper. Not to mention this entire encounter relieved my Friday night boredom.

Not bad for a day's work. I'll have to do this more often.

Daddy's Boy

September 8, 1997

Two minutes after my arrival at Anthony's house, I am naked with his tongue down my throat. This isn't a record in my work, but it does make him one of my faster clients.

His speed is only one of the ways he is different from my usual clientele. Most clients typically kiss me tenderly, slowly, and nervously. Very few people grab me the way Anthony does, their tongues sliding into me in a burst of raw sexuality and power.

"Yeah, boy. You really love it," he whispers to me.

The words ring a note of familiarity within me. The hockey player that attacked me said much the same thing. I hope this encounter is not like that one. I resolve to leave long before it gets to that point.

His clothed body holds my naked one. Coarse hands slide across my soft skin. My already evident erection stiffens even farther as it pushes against him. I feel a similar response from inside his pants.

I reach my hands down and start kneading the crotch of his jeans. Although his dick is not overly large, it is extremely hard and virile.

"Go ahead and open it, boy," he invites me quietly.

I slide my hands inside the top of his jeans. Undoing the button, I reach my hands across the denim. I pull his zipper down slowly and sexually, increasing the eroticism of the moment. Behind the top of his pants, I find a set of white cotton briefs. Briefs that contain the luscious source of the bulge I detected a moment before.

I run my hands over the waistband and reach inside Anthony's underwear. I carefully avoid touching anything sensitive as I pull his pants down to mid-thigh. A thick six-inch cock springs forward and stands at attention. I clasp his balls in one hand while the other wraps around his stiff cock. He involuntarily twitches.

"I can feel it pulsating," I tell him. "I can even see a drop of precum."

"You'll be able to feel a lot more than that, boy. Get down on your knees and start sucking."

I immediately drop to my knees and swallow him whole. Although I prefer requests to orders, he is exciting me with his forceful style. I love playing the part of his boy as he plays the hot daddy.

Sucking on his cock, I take a moment to look up at him. Anthony is an attractive man in his mid-late thirties. He is in good shape and has a developed chest full of nicely trimmed hair. On his face he wears a beard. Although I do not normally care for beards, it looks good on him. He is my hot daddy fantasy brought to life.

Wanting very much to please him, I suck his cock the best I can. I lick my way from base to tip while ravishing everything in between. He throws his head back and thrusts his hips forward as he moans from the pleasure I deliver.

"Oh, yeah, boy! Suck me. Suck that cock!" he bellows.

I need no encouragement to deep throat him. The engorged tip swells, giving me the sensation of being filled with cock. I gag, but I push forward anyway. The sensation of being stuffed is wonderful. I want more. Saliva drools out of my mouth and down the side of his shaft.

Abruptly he grabs my hair and pulls my head back. "Not so fast, boy. You have a lot more ahead of you."

I give him a big grin. I hope my look betrays the raw sensual urges I feel. I want him to know I am in a sexual mood and need him bad. The more he thinks I want him, the more he'll make me play the part of his boytoy. That is exactly what I want to be tonight.

He pulls me to my feet. "Let's go upstairs. I have something I want to show you."

As he leads me up the stairs, I take another good look at him. He is strong and fit with a confident expression in his movements. Although his hair is graying, he is aging gracefully. The lines on his face accent his masculine appeal. He really is quite sexy.

Reaching the top of the stairs, he leads me into a bedroom. The walls are covered with posters of rock groups and bikini-clad women. "It's my girlfriend's son's room," he explains in response to my questioning look. "This is her house actually. She's on vacation."

"Oh, really?" I ask in erotic surprise. "We're going to have sex on his bed?"

He blushes for a moment but nods his head. "Yeah. I jack off there all the time."

I keep the conversation going as he leads me to the bed. He has my curiosity peaked and I definitely want to learn more. "How old is he?"

"He's sixteen and really sexy. Oh, I haven't touched him," he reassures me. "I'm smart enough not to play in the family."

"But you fantasize."

"Yes. All the time. Now lie down and put your ass in the air."

I kneel on the bed with my head buried in the pillow. My vulnerable ass is exposed to the air while my semi-erect cock dangles between my legs. I patiently await Anthony's attentions as he removes his clothes behind me.

Moments later footsteps approach the bed. "Oh, yeah, son. That's the way I love it." Hands gently touch the sides of my buns pulling them apart. Feelings of warmth radiate through me as a tongue slides up the center.

I moan loudly as sensations overload my body. "Oh daddy, that feels good." My cock rapidly returns to its formally erect state.

"Then take it, son," he tells me from between my cheeks. "Take it like the boy you are."

I do want to take it. I push the muscles to open myself up to him. Hot and wet sensations fill my backside until I feel him start to move lower. I feel my legs being spread. A hand reaches up and angles my cock behind me. The familiar tonguing sensation slides up and down my cock and balls.

Now it is my turn to change positions. I roll over onto my back. Holding my legs in the air, I spread them wide to offer Anthony complete access. He lowers his head onto my cock and begins sucking.

"Oh, daddy," I groan in pleasure as be continues to suck me. "I love your cocksucking." It's true. I am enjoying myself immensely. The feeling of his lips descending all the way to my base is incredible.

After a few minutes of deep throating, he pulls back gagging. "I need a break from sucking you."

I sit up on my knees and turn around. "You've earned it. Let me suck you for a while."

I lower my head into his lap and lick the swollen head. The initial taste is wild from all his oozing precum. I lap up as much as I can, then I begin sucking the tip. As I swish my tongue around the sensitive surface, I am rewarded with another small blast of fluid. I savor it for a moment until I lower my face into his pubic hair.

I try to suck Anthony gently, but he has other ideas. His hands grab my hair. "Suck it hard, son," he commands as he thrusts my head down. "Take that whole dick in your mouth." Using his hands on my head as guidance, he speeds up my strokes. Small moans and words of praise encourage me to continue my faster blowjob.

After several minutes of heavy sucking it's my turn to collapse in exhaustion. "Whoa, daddy," I gasp. "Now I need a moment to catch my breath."

"That's why we need your brother here with you. To keep sucking on me when you need a break."

"That would be hot," I reply. "Real hot." In fact, it would be exciting to me. In the past year, I have slept with perhaps five men under the age of twenty-five, compared

with a hundred or so men over the age of forty-five. Although I sexually appreciate older men, I often long to be with younger ones. I find it natural that these desires are growing stronger, because my fantasies of older men are met almost daily.

In the past year, my sexual desires for young men have expanded to include boys much younger than I am used to looking at. I find myself looking at boys in their mid to late teens. Their smooth bodies, youthful faces, and high sex drives all excite me. It's just as well I never meet anyone below the age of consent in my work, but the fantasies are still there.

All of this makes Anthony's idea of a threeway with his girlfriend's son a highly erotic idea. Just lying on the son's bed is making me hard as a rock.

It does not take long for Anthony to notice. "Looks like you won't be needing that break. Turn over on your stomach."

I roll over and raise my ass back into the air. Behind me, I hear the sound of a drawer opening and the gentle snap of a bottle of lubricant being opened. Anthony's hand slides down over my ass covering it with the wet gel.

I worry he will attempt to slide into me unsafely until I hear the faint tearing of a condom wrapper. Moments later I feel Anthony begin to mount me. He is thicker than most men, but my ass opens wide to admit him.

"Oh, yeah," he moans plunging into my ass. "That's hot, boy!"

I push my muscles open to admit him inside me. I am rewarded as he takes advantage of my offer, thrusting himself into my awaiting depths. For the second time this evening, I feel like I am stuffed with cock.

"Get fucked, boy!" he cries as his hands slap down against my ass. It stings but the feeling is exquisite. My bare ass turns red as he slaps me.

His hands descend again and again as he rides me like a wild animal. Every time I raise my head to howl in pleas-

ure he slams me back down. "Keep your ass up in the air, son," he commands me. It does not take me long to obey.

Just as my ass begins to hurt from his mild beating, he stops to change positions. He turns me over and lifts my legs into the air. Holding them apart at the ankles, he leans forward to enter me.

His cock feels much larger from this angle. "Oh, daddy, slow down," I beg. "It feels so big inside me."

"That's right, son," he replies tenderly and sexually. "That's a big cock up your ass. But I'm not going to slow down. You're just going to have to take it." He pushes deeply into me sending pain lancing through my body.

Only it isn't pain. It's exquisite pleasure. I gasp loudly as he fills me with his manhood. The feeling is wonderful. It is everything Brett could have been when he attacked me what seems like a million years ago. Their styles of sex are similar, yet Brett cared nothing for my well-being, while Anthony wants nothing more than to see me surrender myself to my own pleasure.

Anthony resumes pumping me with a series of deep strokes. Grabbing my thighs, he plows my ass with the lust that only a sexually deprived man can muster. He wants my ass bad and I am more than willing to give it to him. Any traces of hesitation about our role-play have completely vanished.

Suddenly he pulls out of my ass. "You're too hot for me, boy," he pants. "I don't want to blow my load yet."

We laugh together. "What can I say, daddy? When you're good, you're good."

He reaches out and touches my face. "And you're great, boy. I just wish your older brother was here to share you with me."

Older brother? I wonder how young a boy is he fantasizes I am. The thought sends a thrill through me. In recent months, my sexual fantasies about younger men have taken an odd turn. Instead of fantasizing about being with a young person, I fantasize about being him. Sometimes I

even dream about being twelve or thirteen years old while an adult has sex with me.

I am not sure how or why I have these fantasies, or even if they are psychologically healthy. I console myself by knowing that fantasies are harmless as long as I do not act on them. It also helps that my fantasy is to be that young boy, not to have sex with him. In either case, I am smart enough not to experiment in that direction. My career is much too important to me to risk for a few moments of forbidden pleasure.

Of course, Anthony knows none of this. His fantasy of me being illegally young is pure coincidence. "That would have been really hot," I tell him. "I wish I could be younger for you. How young would you want me to be?" I am curious what his answer will be.

He pauses for a moment looking at me. "Thirteen or fourteen," he finally admits.

Another question occurs to me. "How young a boy have you been with?" I ask.

He pauses for another moment. "Do you really want to know?" he asks.

Confronted with this question, my curiosity wavers. The younger he answers, the more disturbed I will be. Even my policy of not judging my clients has its limits. After a moment of internal debate, my curiosity wins out. "Yes, tell me."

"Twelve."

"Twelve?" The shock in my voice is obvious. I am suddenly very unsure of myself.

He nods his head. "I didn't intend to. It just kind of happened," he begins. "I was in Denmark on vacation house-sitting for a friend. The hot tub stopped up so I went to the neighbor's house to borrow some tools. Their fifteen year-old son came over to help me. Once the tub was fixed he stripped off his clothes and jumped right in."

"Are you serious?" I ask.

"Totally. Anyway, I climbed in right next to him. He slid over to me and started feeling me up. There was never

His orgasm slips away as quickly as it arrives. He slides off me and collapses on the bed. "That was incredible, boy," he whispers.

Taking me in his arms, he holds me close. My face pushes up against his chest hair, mingling the sticky cum between us. Semen is beginning to dry on my face but I don't care. All of my cares, worries, fears, and insecurities have totally vanished. For a brief moment in time, I know I am daddy's boy. The feeling is beyond anything I have ever experienced.

An hour later I am sitting by my computer describing the experience to Jeff. He has a look of faint disapproval on his face. I prudently gloss over the more controversial details of my evening experience.

The phone rings. "Is Aaron there?" a familiar voice inquires.

"Daddy?" I ask, ignoring the look on Jeff's face.

"Hi, son," he greets me in a somewhat embarrassed tone. "I'm still horny and I was wondering if you would consider coming back down..."

Five minutes later I am back in my car. Daddy's boy is on the way.

The High Life

September 19, 1997

The warm air of the last days of summer rushes through my hair as I drive a sexy red convertible along the Pacific Coast Highway. Seated beside me is Roger, a handsome millionaire and senior banking executive. We have been enjoying the California experience since our arrival two days ago. I can hardly believe I am here.

Roger and I were dining in an upscale New York restaurant scarcely a week ago when he popped the question. Would I like to go to California with him? He would pay me $4,000 in addition to my expenses. The four day trip would be taken in the most luxurious manner possible.

I was shocked. My trips in the past have been very middle-class affairs involving weeks of planning. Even the destinations were typical middle-class America, such as Chapel Hill, North Carolina and Brainerd, Minnesota. Never before has someone invited me on an adventure in such high style.

The flight to Los Angeles alone was an experience I will never forget. A limousine picked me up at my door to drive me to JFK Airport. I waited for Roger at the American Airlines Admiral's Lounge where a Special Services representative had left instructions that I was to be admitted. The instructions stated I was to be treated like a VIP because I would be flying with a Platinum Card member, an executive who brings the airline millions of dollars in business each year.

Naturally, our seats on the plane were in Premier Class, the highest level of service. Champagne was served

before we even left the gate. "Why hold back when this is an experience you have never had before?" Roger asked. I couldn't argue with his logic, so I gleefully ordered both caviar and salmon while comparing the tastes of several white wines. I was quite stuffed by the time the lobster course arrived.

Part of what made the experience so special was having someone to share it with. As a person accustomed to the finer things in life, Roger helped teach me to appreciate a world of luxury beyond anything I had ever experienced. Even basic lessons about how to hold a glass of wine took on a whole new meaning as I watched the reflection of my excitement in Roger's eyes. For all my love and loyalty to Jeff, these were experiences that he could never offer me.

I rouse myself from my thoughts as we catch up with the traffic ahead of us. Signaling left, I pull around several slow moving cars. I control my urge to accelerate and leave everyone behind. I feel as if I am on top of the world.

Looking in the mirror, I see my smiling face behind a pair of new sunglasses. These are courtesy of Roger and yesterday's shopping trip. I never saw the receipt, but I did see him hand the cashier several hundred dollars. The sunglasses store was only the first stop on our shopping spree.

The new clothes Roger bought me came in handy at Spago's last night. According to my host, Spago's is perhaps the best restaurant in Los Angeles. It certainly seemed to be a place to rub elbows with the stars. Over the course of the meal, I observed Carol Channing and Tony Curtis among the clientele.

I found it uncomfortable that I was the only person in the restaurant under thirty without his parents, but Roger assured me I fit in perfectly. "The fact you are here at all makes you look famous. Everyone is trying to figure out which movie you were in." I was unsure if it was true or not, but I did notice several people glancing in my direction.

The food at Spago's was ordered and eaten without consideration of the price. Roger was concerned only with what would provide me the finest culinary experience in my

life. I was grateful when he ordered for me. His judgment was impeccable and he assured me an excellent meal. Neither the staff nor my host disappointed me. The Dover sole was the best fish I had ever tasted.

Even more than the food, the wines were the evening highlight. Both at dinner and on the town later that evening, Roger ordered numerous glasses for me to taste. My palate exploded with flavors I had not thought possible. I will never forget tasting Dolce. I knew I was in love after a single sip of the sweet dessert wine.

Back in traffic, I look at Roger and gaze into his eyes. Nothing needs to be said because we both understand the affection in each other's thoughts. He reaches out and gives my hand a squeeze.

I smile at him as I continue driving. I know the effect my innocent look has on him. I wonder how much of an impact he is having on me. I am certainly confused about my feelings. Am I falling for him? Or am I falling for his lifestyle?

For a man in his early fifties, Roger is very attractive. His bright eyes are the centerpieces of an always-thoughtful face. His mind is one of the sharpest I have ever met, and his past is filled with one business success after another. A man like him could teach me a great deal.

Or it could be his wealthy lifestyle I like so much. On this trip alone, we are enjoying shopping, theater, fine dining, and numerous other luxurious activities. When he talks about taking me to London and Paris, I know that these are real possibilities. My mind staggers at the thought.

I reach out and touch his hand. Regardless of what I may feel, he is a person who can open doors for me.

"What are you thinking?" he asks me with a twinkle in his eyes.

I blush. I don't want him to know I was thinking about his money. "You. Or rather why you would choose to share all this with me." I gesture toward the car and the mountains around us.

"Because you make me feel young. You know that," he reminds me.

I do know it. More specifically, I know that in all of his travels he has never met anyone like me. My ability to be openly gay and totally free about my sexuality intrigues him. In that way, we complement each other. Roger has a successful career and a brilliant mind. I have my carefree lifestyle and warm heart.

"It's a nice feeling. You appreciate feeling young again when you get to be my age." He pauses for a moment, then adds hesitantly, "It's a feeling I'd like to have all of the time."

"You can feel that way all of the time," I reply, misunderstanding the intent of his statement. "It has to do with your attitude on life."

"Well, yes, it does have to do with that," he admits. "But that wasn't quite what I meant."

"Then what did you mean?"

He pauses for another moment to choose his words carefully. "I meant it would be nice if we were romantically involved over the long-term. I know that isn't possible because you have Jeff. But if for some reason you were single, I would divorce my wife for you in a heartbeat."

I am shocked. "I would think dating an escort would be very difficult for you," I stammer.

He looks at me in surprise. "You wouldn't be an escort. You wouldn't have any need. I'd take care of you."

The conversation lapses into silence as the full impact of the conversation settles in. "I don't know what to say," I finally answer.

"You don't have to say anything. Just think about it." He reaches out and gives my hand another squeeze as if to say I love you.

Maybe he is in love with me. Perhaps my emotional seduction worked too well. I never expected an offer like this.

And what an offer it is! With his backing there is nothing I cannot do. Do I want to go back to school for my

Ph.D.? He sits on the Board of Trustees of one of the top universities in the country. Do I want to start my own business? He can bankroll any endeavor I wish to undertake. Or would I rather play trophy boy and travel the world? He can take me anywhere I wanted to go.

My mind is caught up in the fantasy. Every meal can be served to us on silver platters. Every vacation can be taken first class, new adventures awaiting us with every landing. Sports cars, shopping, theater, fine wines, and socializing with the faces from the society pages. All of these can be my new life if I choose.

All I have to do is leave Jeff, the person who cried over and later blessed my career as an escort. He has been faithful to me without question for the five years of our relationship. He has never given me any reason to question his fidelity or his love, even when I did not offer him the same in return.

And leave my career. The one job in which I truly excel. From a suburban hustler to a hi-tech callboy, I have come to love the sense of accomplishment escorting brings me. I know now that I will gross well over $100,000 this year, and I will have earned every penny of it. In future years I aim to earn even more. No one but myself is responsible for my success.

In an instant I realize that my decision is made. Roger can offer me everything in life but the two things I truly want: my life with Jeff, and my own sense of accomplishment. No amount of money can replace them.

Having made my decision, another thought occurs to me. Roger is used to getting what he wants. He isn't going to like being turned down for a struggling illustrator and a career as a prostitute. Perhaps I had better wait until after we see RENT before I decline. I would hate for him to put me on the next plane to New York.

The thought makes me smile. I may not be visiting high society for long, but I will be back in my own time and on my own terms.

Of that you can be sure. The high life awaits me.

Afterword

Now you know how the chubby suburban hustler became a successful hi-tech callboy.

In the year since I wrote the final chapter, my business has continued to evolve. My online presence has become stronger, my clientele has increased in both numbers and quality, and my rates have gone up considerably. The Aaron you met in the first few chapters would never have foreseen the Aaron of today. I'm still not quite the high class callboy envisioned in the story "Reality", but I am headed in that direction.

In addition to my escorting, I have expanded my business into the world of pornography. I have appeared in my first major adult video, posed for several websites along with *Freshmen* and *Inches* magazines, and have produced four amateur videos. By the time you read this, my presence in the adult entertainment industry will be even stronger through a major adult movie called *The Dream Team*. I'd tell you even more I have in store, but I need to save something for a future book on suburban pornography.

Changing the subject, I feel I would be remiss if I ended the book without a word of caution. Those considering entering the prostitution industry should understand two points of view. The first is the one I espouse in this book, that the sex industry is a perfectly valid career option for those who have a brain as well as a body. The second viewpoint would be argued by Richard ("Both Sides"), that anyone who thinks like I do is deluding himself and in dire need of psychological help. The truth is probably somewhere between the two. Consider both perspectives very

carefully before you follow in my footsteps. There is certainly no dishonor in selecting a more traditional vocation.

Regardless of your interest in becoming an escort, I am curious to hear your opinions about the book. Drop me a line at the address on the copyright page, or better yet, visit my website at www.aaronlawrence.com. I think you will find it as daring and unusual as my career.

Aaron Lawrence
January 31, 1998